SCOT FREE

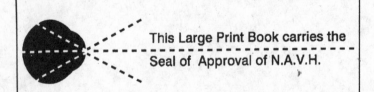

This Large Print Book carries the
Seal of Approval of N.A.V.H.

I would like to thank Terri Bischoff, Nicole Nugent, Dana Kaye, Kevin Brown, Bill Krause, and all at Midnight Ink; Lisa Moylett and all at CMM Literary Agency; my wonderful family and friends; the people of California who welcomed me so warmly and who will not confuse Lexy's views with mine, right?; and most of all, Neil McRoberts, for all the adventures we've had since he first looked up and said, "Hey, there's a job at UC Davis. What d'you think?"

A LAST DITCH MYSTERY

Scot Free

THE LIGHTER SIDE OF THE DARK
UNDERBELLY OF THE CALIFORNIA DREAM

Catriona McPherson

THORNDIKE PRESS
A part of Gale, a Cengage Company

GALE
A Cengage Company

Farmington Hills, Mich • San Francisco • New York • Waterville, Maine
Meriden, Conn • Mason, Ohio • Chicago

Thorndike Press® Large Print Mystery.
The text of this Large Print edition is unabridged.
Other aspects of the book may vary from the original edition.
Set in 16 pt. Plantin.

LIBRARY OF CONGRESS CIP DATA ON FILE.
CATALOGUING IN PUBLICATION FOR THIS BOOK
IS AVAILABLE FROM THE LIBRARY OF CONGRESS
ISBN-13: 978-1-4328-5170-5 (hardcover)

Published in 2018 by arrangement with Midnight Ink, an imprint of Llewellyn Publications, Woodbury, MN 55125-2989 USA

Printed in Mexico
1 2 3 4 5 6 7 22 21 20 19 18

To the baristas of Mishka's coffeeshop in Davis, CA, and their stand-ins at Starbuckses from Oregon to Edinburgh. Truly, I could not have done this without you.

ONE

Outside my window, mortars fired rockets into the darkness and the night was rent by the crack of gunpowder and the screams of children. I flinched at every report and hugged myself, rocking back and forward, trying not to cry. One more hour, one short meeting in this blank little room, then I would be on my way to the airport, on a flight back to Edinburgh. Up and away, a continent and an ocean behind me.

There was a sudden lull in the shelling and I was sure I could hear footsteps on the stairs, thought I could smell a blast of acrid smoke from someone opening the street door. Then, after two of the loudest bangs yet, a pounding came at the flimsy door to the room where I was hiding, each blow making the cheap lock rattle. Why were they trying to break it down? I was expecting them. They were the reason I was sitting here.

I crept forward and whispered, "Is that you? What's wrong?"

Another bout of hammering began and I heard something split at the hinge side. Then a voice bellowed, "Po-lice! Open up!"

I scrabbled with the latch and threw the door open.

"Police?" I said. "Has something happened?"

"Are you . . . ?" said one of the cops, frowning at a note in his hand.

"Yes," I said. "That's me. Officer, is something wrong?"

"You skipping town?" said the other one, pointing to my suitcase and roller bag.

"As it happens," I said. "Look, why are you here? I was expecting Mrs. Bombaro."

"She's in jail."

"And Mr. Bombaro," I added. "Wait, *what*?"

"He's in the morgue."

"What? What did you just —" Then, as a bang like a nuclear bomb went off so close that the ground shook under my feet, I shrieked and threw myself into the arms of the bigger of the two cops, feeling some nameless object attached to his belt hit my hip with a clang.

"Ma'am?" said his partner, slowly. "What do you know? What's got you so nervy?"

"I'm sorry," I told him. I knew my voice was shaking. "I just really hate fireworks. I'm not trying to spoil it for you. Happy Fourth of July!"

TWO

California architects never hew *much* granite, but the police station was a lot more
solidly built than the little suite of offices
that rented out rooms by the day. Once
inside it, the cracks and fizzes were no more
than an irritation, like a guy in the next train
seat listening to Motörhead, but with his
earbuds in deep. Anyway, they left me waiting for so long, with nothing but a paper
cup of tea or coffee (hard to tell), that the
fireworks were over by the time they came
to interview me. I scraped up what was left
of my dignity and interviewed them right
back.

"Full name?" said the big soft cop with
the hard things on his belt.

"Lexy Campbell. Can I see Mrs. Bombaro? I'm her therapist."

"Yeah, she said. But that's not the name
she gave."

I sighed but tried to do it quietly and

12

rolled my eyes but tried to make it look like ordinary blinking. "Yes, it is," I said. "Lexy, spelled L-E-A-G-S-A-I-D-H. It's Gaelic."

"Pff," said the one I hadn't grabbed, whose consistency I couldn't pronounce on.

"I know," I said. "If we hadn't been so busy learning to spell we could have had a stock market and a film industry." But I had lost him.

"And you had a meeting set up with the both of them?" said his partner.

"A counselling session," I said. "You know Mrs. Bombaro is eighty-six years old, don't you? Have you got her in a . . . tank? With . . . meth — crack — Where is she?"

"Because it looked like you were leaving town."

"Yes, afterwards. We all were."

"You were planning to leave town with the Bombaros?"

"What? No! He was leaving and so was she and so was I, but not together. I was going to wrap up our therapy programme and witness their signatures, then I was go-ing to the airport to go back to Edinburgh."

"Edinburgh, Scotland?" said the slow cop. He'd caught up.

"That's the one. Mr. Bombaro was going to Seven Mile Beach with his — Oh my God, the poor girl must be still be sitting in

13

San Francisco airport!"

"Seven Mile Beach, Grand Cayman?" the slow cop asked.

"Yep, Grand Cayman." It stuck in my head because I had always thought John Grisham made it up. Turns out it's a real place. "And Mrs. Bombaro was headed up to her sister in Bend, O —"

"Bend, O — ?" he tried to ask.

But I was moving too fast. "— regon. How did he die?"

"What time was the appointment?" asked Soft Cop.

"Seven."

"And yet you were still there waiting at nine."

"I was. It was a big night for the Bombaros, and it was closure for me too."

Soft Cop's lip curled at the word *closure*. "So," he said, staring at me, "were you alone there between seven and nine p.m. this evening, Ms. Campbell?"

"As it happens."

"No one saw you?"

"Wait a minute," I said. "Why are you asking that?"

"Because Mrs. Bombaro was pretty insistent that you would vouch for her."

"Oh," I said. "Right. Well, I can confirm that she's a sweet little old lady who would

14

never murder her husband, if that's what you mean."

"Exactly," he said, giving me his first smile. "We don't believe she could do it alone either."

"Wait a *minute*!" I said. "You think I was involved in this? How did he die?"

"Signatures?" said the slow cop I was starting to think of as the Mills of God.

"On their divorce papers," I told him.

"What kind of therapist are you, exactly?" Soft Cop chipped in.

"I'm a marriage guidance counsellor," I said. His lip curled again. "Happy endings," I added, drawing myself up, "come in all shapes and . . . Oh, what's the use?" I was a recently divorced and a squeak less recently *married* marriage guidance counsellor whose only client had been arrested for murdering her soon-to-be-ex-husband. It was high time I kissed my pride goodbye.

"So she wouldn't kill him, but she would dump his ass after all these years?"

"They wanted to wait until the children were retired," I said. "That was a joke. They don't have children. But they *were* trying to protect the family business. You know what his business is, I suppose? Was, I mean."

"Fireworks," said Mills of God. "Yeah, he's a local celebrity."

"Nothing goes *Boom* like Bombaro!" I said. "Mrs. B. used to say it was ironic because when it came to their marriage, he needed a rocket up his . . ."

"Did she?" said Soft Cop. "*Did* she now? She actually said in your hearing that he needed a rocket up his . . ."

My eyes widened. "How did he die?" I said. They didn't answer. "Oh God."

"Yep," said Mills of God. "Mr. Bombaro went boom."

THREE

How did it come to this? Where did it all go wrong? How did I, Lexy Campbell, strong modern Scottish woman, end up homeless, jobless, and broke, thousands of miles from everyone and everything I knew, all my belongings locked in a room with a now-expired keycard, my plane ticket useless because I'd missed my flight, my brilliant attempt at being a witness turning me into a bigger suspect every time I re-opened my mouth, and no one I could call for help except . . . No! No one I could call for help. No exceptions.

Because that — the lack of exceptions, the non-helper, the no one — was where it had all gone wrong.

Bran.

Bran Lancer, to give him his favoured name.

Branston Frederick Lancer the Second, to give him his full name.

17

Branston Fucking Lancer the Scumbag, to give him the name he'd earned.

I had looked across a crowded room, seen his face, and taken the first step towards the California cop shop where I sat right now.

In my defence, I *had* just boiled my head. I was at Turnberry for the spa. He was at Turnberry for the golf. And he was so . . . American. So very . . . un-Scottish. He was tall, brawny, sun-kissed, and *clean*! He came off the eighteenth green cleaner than I came out of a sauna. His teeth were like a double row of little oblong paint samples (if a DIY outlet would ever have two rows of fourteen samples of the same paint shade: American Teeth). His hair was by Abercrombie, his nails by Fitch, his clothes . . . His clothes were god-awful, actually. Elvis wouldn't have worn them to brunch in his Vegas days, but that's golf for you. And he was soon out of them anyway.

I took a sip from my plastic cup of tea-possibly-coffee, which had base notes of cocoa as it cooled, and remembered the taste of our first kisses: room-service Champagne and spearmint floss.

I listened to some over-refreshed patriots being brought into the cop shop somewhere a long way from this interview room and remembered the sound of his honey-dipped voice saying, "The crazy is what makes it so sane!"

I looked down at the graffiti scratched into the plastic tabletop — *You'll take my gum when you chip it out of my cold dead jaws,* which I thought was pretty funny, and *Gil is a douche-nozzle,* possibly less so — and I remembered seeing the diamond, sitting in its velvet box, big as an ice cube, glinting with the same fire as his eyes.

It took four months in total from "who's that" to "I do." A week at Turnberry, a week in Dundee after he followed me back there, while I saw clients and supervised trainees and he sat in the waiting room flirting with the receptionist and nipping out for nine holes at Carnoustie whenever it stopped raining. Then he gave me the ice cube, mounted his "so crazy it's sane" argument, and returned to California. Two weeks of Skype sex later, I followed him. My visa waiver allowed me ninety days before I had to get out or go rogue. Day eighty-nine saw us standing in line at city hall. It was so romantic.

Seriously. American brides might want dyed doves at the Four Seasons, but I was from Dundee and standing in line at city hall had all the exotic allure of gas station coffee, drive-thru burgers (with a *U*!), and

19

right on red.

My heart wasn't listening to my head, and my guts weren't listening to my heart. My loins were running the show. When my guts finally told my loins to pipe down and my head told my heart to wise up, there I was, drinking gas station coffee that tasted like fried shoes and eating heinous drive-thru burgers flipped by people who could neither cook nor spell. And I was married to a dentist called Branston with colour-coordinated golfing outfits. Right on red is a wonderful thing, but it's not enough to base a life on.

"A *dentist*?" my best friend Alison said, hiccupping from trying not to laugh. "You couldn't find a traffic warden?"

"You went out with that road-worker that time," I reminded her.

"That saved us both a fortune in taxis," she said. I remembered: Dead Cat Cabs. Every Saturday night, Jordie the road-worker would call his pals on the backshift and tell them there was a dead cat on the road outside the club. Dogs have to be investigated. Urban foxes can stay where they drop. But, if someone reports them, the local authority always picks up dead cats. Or, as the case may be, Jordie and his friends. "Anyway," Alison said, "a road-worker is, in essence, an urban lumberjack. I've always been fascinated by the intersection of landscape and masculinities." She's a sociologist.

What I wouldn't give for Jordie, his high-viz jacket, his intersected masculinities, and his Dead Cat Cab to swoop down on this cop shop right now and take me away, squashed on the bench seat with Alison and the backshift. That was a life I understood. *This* was Bizarro-world, lit only by the sun shining into the rabbit-hole high above me.

Bran's house should have told me. Should have told me *something.* He hadn't reacted to my flat in Dundee, beyond asking where the hall bath was.

"Hall bath?" I echoed.

"Half bath?"

"Wouldn't the water run out?"

It transpired that he couldn't shit in the same room he showered in. He went for a walk and hit a caff. But listen! I didn't know that back then. I mean, if I had heard *that,* my loins would have washed their hands of him.

Back to his house, though. The Beige Barn. I was never great with houses at the best of times. I lack the nesting instinct. Either that or I just never found the right nest. I couldn't have cared less when my mum turned my old bedroom into a study. And I left my rented flat in Tay Street without blinking.

The thing about Bran's Beige Barn was it didn't have any walls. Oh, it had walls separating it from the outside, but inside it had furniture called rooms. He led me, that first night, into a kind of hangar and started pointing. "Kitchen," he said, nodding at where some units and appliances were lined up and a sink was set in a big block of dark wood like a sarcophagus just sitting in the middle of the floor, right where you'd bump into it when you were drunk. "Breakfast room," he said, showing me an oval table on the far side of the sarcophagus. I looked at the door on the table's other side.

"Through there?" I said.

"A closet," he answered. Then he pointed to a bigger table with a candlestick on it. "Dining room," he said. He showed me a telly on the back wall with a couch in front of it. "Family room," he told me. Finally two couches facing each other, "and formal parlour."

I turned round, looking at all four corners of the one single solitary room. "Right," I said. And just like that I understood American divorce rates. There are no bloody walls! If your beloved is bugging the shit out of you, there's no escape. Don't get me wrong, British couples can't stand each other either — thankfully, or I'd be out of a job — but they never see one another unless they pass in the kitchen when they both want a cup of tea.

Bran picked up my suitcase and roller bag and led me through an arch (so close to being a door, but no banana) and along a corridor into . . .

"Master bedroom," he said. He nodded at two armchairs and a magazine rack. "And reading room."

No walls, but there was a bed. There was a huge, high bed with banks of white pillows and a snow-scape of a duvet and I was knackered. I stripped to my t-shirt, wriggled out of my bra, Crocodile Dundee–style, and dropped.

I woke up from the jet lag at half past five. Bran was on his back with his golden arms thrown over his head and the faintest wink of new stubble just beginning to show on his golden chin. I slipped out from beside him and crept away to explore.

There was a two-person shower in the nearest bathroom and a door leading out to a pool! An honest-to-God swimming pool. It was bright blue and shaped like a bean with a little baby bean of hotter water in its inner corner. It sat between the patio, full of very shiny plants in brushed-steel planters, and a lawn of Kermit-green velvet grass stretching to where a grey-painted fence almost hid the neighbour's velvet grass, blue pool, and beige barn. I shrugged off my t-shirt and dived in.

I hadn't swum in the scuddy since student days, and never alone, floating on my back in warm water like silk, staring up at a pale pink sky as it slowly turned gold and then the gold turned lilac, promising blue. I smiled, rolled over like a seal, and caught just a glimpse of a pair of wide-open eyes, and an even wider open mouth, before I went under and came up coughing.

There was a young man in jeans, boots, and a white t-shirt standing on the tiles at the edge of the pool trying (now at least) not to look at me.

"Pool," he said.

"Um," I said. "Can you get me a towel?" He shook his head. "Can you turn round maybe?" I said, twirling a hand to give him the idea.

He turned his back and that was when I saw *Cuento Crystal Clear Pool Service* written on his back. I thrashed my way to the edge and slithered out, grabbing my t-shirt and scampering for the bathroom door.

When I had added a towel skirt to my wet t-shirt, I went back out to say a proper hello.

"Sorry about that," I said, walking up to where he was crouched at the business end of the pool fiddling with a filter. "Thanks for not laughing or puking. Lexy Campbell." I stuck my hand out.

He shook it, saying six or seven syllables I took to be his name.

"Pleased to meet you," I said. "Do you come at the same time every day?"

"I don't speak English," he said.

"And *yo no hablo Español,*" I said. "That looks like that then. *Adios* and . . ." The only other thing I knew that wasn't about food or bullfights was *via con Dios,* which might come over a bit threatening, so I waggled my eyebrows and went back inside just as two more guys in jeans, boots, and white t-shirts let themselves in through the gate from the drive, carrying what looked suspiciously like plant-shining gear.

"*Buenos dias,*" I said.

"*Que pasa!*" said one, to which I had no answer.

In the kitchen a short, round woman with a long black ponytail was going over the wall above the cooker with a feather duster.

"*Yo no hablo Español,*" I said.

25

"Me either," she told me. "I'm from Toronto."

"Jesus, I'm sorry," I said.

"I'm kidding," she answered with a wink. "I'm Lupe," she added, when I had finished laughing. "From Merry Maids."

"D'you want some coffee, Lupe?"

She frowned. "You gonna drive like that? No shoes? They won't serve you."

That was how I found out Branston didn't possess a coffeemaker, and there was no way to get any caffeine inside me without driving through a Starbucks. Luckily, Lupe had started her day with a vente and was willing to share. There was God knows what assorted crap in it that wasn't coffee (definitely cinnamon, vanilla, and big cold blobs of cream), but there was a seam of black stuff somewhere underneath and I could feel it flooding my blood at the first sip.

I padded along the passageway and entered the master bedroom on tiptoe. The bed was empty but, following the sound of rhythmic pounding and clanking, I found Bran in a second bedroom going at a treadmill like a crazed hamster, curling dumbbells up and down in each hand and watching a huge television screen high on the opposite wall where two more golden people were discussing the Nikkei index. They could have been twins. I looked from their faces to Bran's. They could have been triplets.

"Hiya," I said.

"Hey!" He jumped off the treadmill, put the dumbbells in their rack, and wrapped his arms round me. "Where were you?"

"Meeting your household," I said. "Lupe and them. I didn't catch the pool guy's name, though."

Bran shrugged. "Who's Lupe?" he said. And a bell rang. I wish I could say it was an alarm and I heeded it, but actually it was his phone. He snatched it up, shouted with joy at whoever it was on the other end, and then spent five minutes telling them he couldn't, he was busy, he couldn't say, he was tied up all weekend, he wouldn't free up half an hour even if he could, all the while twinkling at me. When he hung up and threw his phone down again, I snuggled up shamelessly.

"Completely tied up all weekend sounds nice," I said. "But it's Tuesday."

"Right," he said. "I'm going in late and I'll leave early. If you give me a ride you can have the car. Knock yourself out. Meet me for lunch. Show me round my own town by moonlight. You'll find great stuff I've missed for ten years. I just know you will. So let go of me and let me finish my workout. Sooner I'm done, sooner I can get you your coffee. What do you get in the morning?"

Back in the here and now, I took another sip of the cop shop's nameless brew, noticing for the first time that tomato soup definitely came down the same spout as the cocoa, coffee, and tea.

I'm not the first person to fall in love and make a poor decision. I might be the first person trained in relationship psychology to fall in love with a town and marry a dentist, though.

FOUR

And it was definitely the town of Cuento I fell for. I never warmed to the Beige Barn — who could? — but Cuento was a different story. The wide downtown sidewalks with benches and dog bowls and hippies playing the street-corner pianos. The street-corner pianos! The quiet streets in the old residential neighbourhoods with the shade trees and the basketball hoops and kids on skateboards waiting their turn at the stop signs. I liked the way the pizza joint would start selling hot slices at closing time, and I liked the taco wagon with the outsize burritos. I liked the way people put free stuff out on the sidewalk with cardboard signs saying FREE STUFF and the way it took ten minutes to buy a newspaper. "Hey, how are you today?" "I'm good. How are you?" "I'm great, thanks for asking. What can I do for you this morning?"

Bran was the one who brought me to it all

and shared it with me, and he was so pretty and horny and he laughed all the time. And any time he puzzled me, I assumed I was picking him up wrong. Oh, how I chuckled at the way we didn't understand each other. Oh, how blithely I assumed it would all make sense in time. Oh, how much more attention I should have paid.

When we went out for dinner with his partner and his partner's new husband, I thought I was missing something. Or they were joking. Americans, I told myself, are known for their irony. The partner, Brandeee (with three *e*s), had got married just before Bran set off for Turnberry and his own whirlwind romance, and they were still at the nauseating stage: feeding each other forkfuls of pasta, dropping hints about their sex life, trying out various pet names. I asked them about living in Cuento just to stop the *pookies* and *punkins,* since we were trying to eat.

It sounded, to the untrained ear, as if all three of them agreed: the benches in the downtown attracted vagrants, the dog bowls harboured mosquito larvae, the pianos were scruffy. The roots of the shade trees in the residential streets wrecked the suspension of their Infinitis, the basketball hoops took up parking spots, and the kids on the skateboards were breaking the law. None of them had ever eaten a hot slice and when I waxed on about the burritos from the taco wagon, Brandeee and Mr. Brandeee wrinkled their noses and Bran stared at me. I didn't tell them I'd got my Converse from a pile of free stuff.

They couldn't object to the extreme friendliness of the guy in the newspaper shop, but that was because all three of *them* got their news on a screen during their morning treadmill session.

I told myself I would learn their ways. They couldn't all be complete tossers. Bran couldn't, because I was falling for him and he was nuts about me. He had to be a good guy because he had proposed and I was sorely tempted. He must have hidden depths. If I said yes, I would dive in and find them.

Reader, I married him, as Jane Eyre said. And he was a tosser, wrapped in a blanket of wanker, dipped in asshole batter, and deep-fried in dickhead oil. As she probably didn't.

I married him, I started working toward counselling accreditation in the California system, I called myself a life coach in the meantime, I hung my shingle (and started learning America-speak like *hung my shin-*

gle). And to help my case, as soon as I was a legal resident, I applied to become a notary. Who could witness legal documents. Like divorce papers.

I took another sip of my cream of tomato mocha chai latte, now with a hint of lemonade concentrate, gagged, and searched my bag bottom for stray Tic-Tacs.

How soon did I know I'd made a mistake? Well, the honeymoon was great. We went to Saratoga, another real place, as it turned out. Cold drinks, hot sex. Low stress, high hopes. Then we came back.

I had been a marriage guidance therapist for nine years by this time. I had seen dozens, scores, legions of marriages contracted between well-matched couples who knew each other inside out and shared common goals. I had sat there trying not to roll my eyes while most of them descended into pits of lye.

Also, I assumed good intentions. Bran had wooed me, pursued me, and swept me off my Uggs like something from a Regency romance. With Uggs. He wouldn't have done that for no reason, I told myself. I was right.

The first crack formed on the outer layers at an Easter potluck at Brandeee's house. And that's another thing. The bloody potlucks! Dear American people: Have a party or don't have a party, but don't have half a party that's more trouble than it's worth for everyone. Personally, if I've made a big bowl of guacamole, I'd rather stay in my own house on my own couch with Benedict Cumberbatch and eat it, than go and stand around in someone's back garden with a paper plate and enter it into the guacamole-off with a crowd of passive-aggressive housewives who bought the seasoning mix from Trader Joe's. And while I'm talking about the paper plates, what's with the paper plates? And plastic forks? And polystyrene cups? American people! Parties mean dishes. Suck it up. Because nothing says "B-list" like being made to eat Trader Joe's guacamole off a paper plate with a plastic fork at the house of someone with a dishwasher and a housecleaner.

Not all of which is technically Bran's fault. So back to the Easter Potluck at Brandeee's.

"What were you thinking of taking?" I asked him. I was sitting on the beanbag I had bought in Target and dragged into his "gym" so I could hang out and chat while he was on his treadmill in the morning.

"I thought you might want to take care of it," he said. "You know, bring something . . . appropriate . . . that they might not have had before. Make your mark."

I thought he meant something British. I think if you asked a hundred people in a studio audience, they'd have thought the same.

So I made spotted dick.

And I put a sign on it, because the name's half the fun.

And there it was on a long trestle table (with a paper cloth) in Brandeee's back garden, beside the primavera salad and the electric slow-cooker full of lamb meatballs and the bunny-shaped chocolate mousses sitting in a tray of ice. And fourteen plates of recombined product from Trader Joe's and Costco, let me say.

"What is *wrong* with you?" Bran muttered with his teeth clenched hard enough to split his veneers. I had found out they were veneers during a night of unusual positions. It endeared him to me at the time.

"Communication breakdown," I said. "Soz."

"Was it supposed to be funny?"

"No 'supposed to be' about it," I said. "It is funny. Spotted *dick,* Bran. Come on."

"No one is laughing," he said, looking around like the wrath of God while everyone pretended they didn't know we were fighting but at the same time spoke very quietly so they could hear us. Paper and plastic are great for that, at least. No clashing and clinking to cover the sweet sound of someone else having a public domestic.

"Blaike laughed like a drain," I pointed out. Brandeee's son, Blaike, had just about swallowed his tongue.

"Blaike is fifteen years old," Bran said. "He'd laugh at a . . ."

"Fart gun?" I suggested. It didn't help.

"I even *said* 'appropriate,' " Bran hissed. "I clearly said 'make something appropriate.' I meant for *Easter.*"

"Fine!" I said, quite loud. "Nail it to a fucking cross then."

And that's how I found out that, even in California, about as far from the Bible Belt as your bobble hat, in a town with a mosque to its name, there's still a line.

I talked him down later in the day. Cultural norms, learning process, the long tail of Puritanism informing American — But he started frowning, so I dialled back.

"You remember what it was like in Scotland?" I said. "Even in a golf resort. Remember when you tried to get a bucket of ice and that waiter asked if you had sprained your ankle? It's just that we've got different expectations, Bran. To me, Easter is more about . . . daffodils and chocolate and . . .

it's not as if you go to church. Does Bran-deee go to church? Only, you said Burk was her third husband and I just —"

"Burt."

"Blurt?"

"BURT!"

"Burt. You said Burt was her third hus-band and I just assumed she was pretty secular, you know."

"She attends the Unitarian Universalist congregation, as a matter of fact," Bran said, and I had never heard him sound so . . . prissy. Also, I didn't know what Yooyoos were then and so I missed the chance to deliver a snort.

"My mistake," I said.

"I forgive you," said Bran.

I chewed that over for a good long time before answering. Long enough to go from sarcasm (*you are a benevolent master*) and nit-picking (*I didn't apologise*) all the way to what I finally said which was:

"Well good then."

It fills me with a kind of nostalgia now: my very first *well good then*. Like tasting something that, years before, gave you volcanic food poisoning.

These were the memories I was lost in when the door of the interview room opened and a woman put her head round it.

"You're free to leave, Ms. Campbell," she said.

"Oh?" I said. "Says who?"

She came a little further in and I saw the empty shoulder holster she wore. Plainclothes.

"We ran the tape from the building entrance," she said. "In at six and still there when the officers arrived. You are good to go."

"Great," I said. "Thanks."

"Sorry about the coffee," she said, nodding at the half-empty cup.

"You're a detective then," I said. She quirked her head. "I couldn't get beyond 'hot beverage' and that was after drinking it." She smiled, understanding, and then turned away and set off along the corridor. I kind of wanted to run after her. No one else within a ten-mile cordon would have understood me, I was sure.

I restrained myself and was rewarded when she turned back.

"Like I said, you are absolutely free to walk out. But if you felt like coming back in the morning . . . Mizz Visalia is going to be arraigned and if I had money on it, I'd guess bailed, so she could use someone around."

"Have you got any recommendations for where I could spend the rest of the night?"

I said. It might have come out weird, because she blushed and cleared her throat before she answered.

"Nearest motel's just down the block," she said. "But can't you just go home? You're Branston Lancer's wife, aren't you?"

"Ex," I said. "So no."

She grunted. "Shuffled the pack again, huh?"

I grunted back. It was a bit too horribly accurate.

About a month after the Easter Potluck came the fateful day. I was supposed to be going to a book club after work, but work had been great. The first actually good day. I had picked up a client — two clients, technically. Clovis and Visalia Bombaro, both in their eighties, needed some guidance on ending their marriage amicably — and I wanted to share the news with Bran. I wanted to tell him that they had met at the age of twelve at a family picnic. They were cousins. In fact, Mrs. Bombaro, sixty-seven years into the marriage, still called him Cousin Clovis, which was weird but hardly worth the effort to change now. After all, he would still be her cousin when the papers were signed and the property divided. Whatever. I looked forward to regaling Bran with the failure of a marriage between people of exactly the same background, the same ethnicity, from the same village in Italy, from the same *family,* who worked together in the family business Bombaro Pyrotechnics (Nothing goes *Boom* like Bombaro!), and yet were giving up. It made me hopeful about the two of us, in comparison.

And the book club was reading *The Goldfinch.*

So I went back to the Barn. I let myself in softly and closed the door behind me with a gentle click. Mrs. Bombaro's words were still ringing in my ear.

"*Boom?* Boom is right! Boom, he's gone. Boom, he's back. Boom, the toilet seat is up. Boom, the toilet seat is down. He puts a water glass down on a cork coaster and it wakes the dog!"

"Sixty-seven years I work hard all day and come home to this!"

"Minor irritat—" I said, before I gave up. But it made me conscious of the way I usually slammed in and yelled his name, crashed my keys into the bowl, and clomped over to the fridge.

It was Lupe's day and the house was gleaming. I took my shoes off at the front door so as not to put Converse rubber on the perfect polish of the floor and shushed along the bedroom corridor in my socks.

It was a complicated set of sounds. At first I thought a small animal had got caught in some moving part of the air conditioner. There was a rhythmic squeaking and a wet sort of slapping noise and there were little snuffling sounds. Then I came around the bedroom doorway and saw, on the bed, Branston's bottom, pure snowy white where the sun had never penetrated his golf shorts. It was bobbing and swishing, looking as if it was chewing on something bouncy. Waggling on either side of it were Brandeee's regularly pedicured feet and, clutching his shoulder blades, were Brandeee's regularly manicured hands. Her engagement ring winked away in time.

My first thought was that not many therapists get to take part in such a classic scene. It would be no end of help professionally. Next up, I knew this was my chance to be either very cool or very lame. I would be telling this story for years and this was the moment to make sure I came out of it the winner. Third, I couldn't help noticing that I didn't feel shocked or hurt. I felt the kind of profound relief I had only ever felt once before in my life: when I thought I'd lost my wallet and then found it behind the couch. Last, admittedly, I wondered how bad *The Goldfinch* could actually be.

I leaned against the doorjamb, checked Facebook, did half a BuzzFeed quiz, took a couple of pictures of Branston's bum — one clenched, one flexed — and waited. Finally, with a moan from him and a few unconvincing gasps from her, he fell flat. Their sweaty chests made a wet fart sound as he landed. Neither one of them laughed, although I had to bite my cheeks. Branston, after a few deep breaths, rolled off.

"Cheers, love," I said, catching Brandeee's eye. "I don't suppose you'd do my ironing as well, would you?"

And out it all came. She *had* had three husbands. Blaike's dad was the first. Poor Burt was the third, and the second was *guess who*. He was so mightily pissed off with her for marrying Burt that he flounced off to Scotland to show her he didn't care. And while he was there, he thought of something even better.

"I didn't expect it to get this far," Bran said. He was sitting up in bed, right at the edge, as far as he could get from Brandeee, who was sitting up right at the other edge, holding the sheet up like a bulletproof vest. "I thought she'd come round before the wedding."

"Ours or hers?"

"Well, first hers and then ours," he said. "I'm sorry, Lexy."

"No hard feelings," I told him. Then at his look, I added, "That was sarcasm, Branston, you total fucking creep. Do you think maybe you could have hooked up with someone who lived in Cuento anyway? Someone who wouldn't have given up a job and moved thousands of miles for your little game of chicken?"

"I see that now," he said, squirming. He was physically squirming.

"Are you trying to wriggle out of a condom?"

"No," he said.

"Wrong answer," I said. "Now I'll need to go and get checked for skankitis."

"There's no need to be crude," said Brandeee. Her first contribution.

"Really?" I said. "Seriously? I've fallen short of your standards of gracious behaviour, have I? Wow." Then I went into the walk-in wardrobe and took a suitcase down from the high shelf. I dumped it on the bed between them.

"I can't leave tonight!" Bran squeaked.

"But I can," I said. "I'm going to Reno to divorce you and I'm taking your car because I'll still have to come back to Cuento to see clients. Some of us" — I flicked my best

42

disgusted glare at Brandeee — "honour our commitments."

I thought I had played it so well, but if I'd chucked *him* out on *Goldfinch* night and stayed put, I'd have a clue where to go now. If I'd sent him to Nevada for the nine weeks it took our divorce to go through (Americans can certainly hustle), I'd have friends and neighbours and Lupe to turn to now. Unfortunately, I'd spent those weeks on the couch of a hotel room and didn't even get the same housekeeping three days in a row.

Apart from that, it was a delight. America is a wonderful place to be bathed in self-pity: Netflix serves up such endless comfort and the twenty-four-hour supermarkets serve up junk food of such great diversity and in such gargantuan units. I watched an entire season of *The Good Wife* (irony absolutely intended) in one breaded boneless barbecued choc-chip sitting.

"Nearest motel's just down the block," I repeated as I left the cop shop. The car park was brightly lit, but when I got back to the street it was dark and deserted in both directions. Which way was down, in a town like a billiard table? The locals probably knew — *2nd and B; catty corners; make a right* — but it was all Greek to me.

I looked left, towards where the street

43

dipped under the railway line and came up in total blackness. Then I looked right to where it crossed the downtown and headed for the suburbs. Somewhere that way was Bran's house. That way were green lawns, blue pools, and beige tiles tended by elves at dawn.

I was headed where the elves came from. If there was a motel I could walk into after midnight on the Fourth of July, it was that-a-way. I followed the road towards the railway line, literally crossed to the wrong side of the tracks, and somewhere in the close damp dark of the underpass, finally left my old life behind me.

"You are kidding!" I said, as I caught sight of it. LAST DITCH MOTEL, the sign said in pink and yellow neon tubes like balloon animals. *Clean and comfortable,* the small print added as I trudged closer, *free continental breakfast, fast WiFi, bug nets.*

The office (OPEN!) was at the end of one horseshoe arm. The other end was a launderette called Skweeky Kleen. In between were an empty pool and maybe twenty rooms, double-decker. Some were in darkness. Some shone like pumpkin lanterns, lamps glowing behind orange curtains, but most flickered television blue.

I pushed open the office door braced for

pimps and roaches. Inside, a room perhaps ten feet square contained two wrought-iron patio tables and four chairs and on a counter beside them sat a microwave and a bagel cutter. There was a red plastic basket with bags of oatmeal arranged in it and a pair of coffee jugs. It was hours till breakfast but already the shoes were frying.

On the other side of the room, behind a reception desk of Formica mended with leopard-print duct tape, sat a woman of perhaps sixty years, slumped in a Barcalounger with the footrest extended, deeply asleep. Her chin was on her chest and her glasses had slipped down her nose.

I cleared my throat.

"Plate?" she said, coming awake without so much as a flicker. She sat up, kicking her footrest back and launching herself out of the chair, coming to rest perfectly centred behind her reception desk, with one hand on the mouse of her computer and one hand on her phone.

"Plate?" I said.

"The license plate of your Prius, hon," she said. "Hybrids have ruined my system after fifteen happy years. I used to wake up whenever a car pulled in, but it's all over now."

"I don't have a Prius," I said. "I don't

actually have a car."

"Where's your luggage?"

"I don't have any luggage either," I said. "I just need a room."

"For?" she said. She narrowed her eyes. With a close look and now that she wasn't nestled into her chins, I wondered if she was *even* sixty. Her skin was dewy and her eyes bright. It was just that her hair was silver and cut in a no-nonsense Grandma style and she wore a t-shirt that read *I don't like morning people.*

"Well, the night," I said. "And maybe tomorrow night. What else would I want it for?"

"An hour," she said, bone dry. She turned away and looked at her keyboard. An honest-to-god board with hooks on it and keys hanging from them. The back of her t-shirt read *Or mornings. Or people.*

"Two queens or a king," she said, turning back.

I thought she was giving me more information about how prostitutes order motel rooms. "Definitely not," I said. "Absolutely nothing of the kind." I took my credit card out and slid it over the Formica towards her. It was my and Bran's joint account, platinum of course. I was using it all the way up to the gate at SFO international departures, then I'd snip it and send it back to him.

She glanced at it and then regarded me for another silent minute or two, until at last her face cleared like Alka-Seltzer. "Lancer," she said. "Tooth-fairy Lancer?"

"I left him," I said.

"I like you," she said, her voice as dry as ever and not so much as a twitch at her lips. "Sonofabitch whistled show tunes clear through my root canal."

I had a mental image of some sort of trumpet (I was so tired by that time I was getting spacey) but mystifying as most of her utterance was, there was no mistaking *sonofabitch,* and any enemy of Bran's was a friend of mine.

When she had swiped my card, she shoved a key at me. "Room 213," she said. "The fan rattles like a mother but I can give you earplugs."

"Not a problem," I said. "See you in the morning. If you're still on shift."

"Ain't no lottery drawing 'tween now and then," she said. "I'll be here. No lean."

"Sorry?" I said. "To get the door open?"

"My name is Noleen," she said, then looked at the card as she handed it back. "Lego . . . *what*?"

"Lexy," I said. "Campbell. Lexy Lancer

was . . ."

"One of Stan Lee's off-days."

I laughed. I had decided somewhere around half-past nine that I might never laugh again, but Noleen got a chuckle out of me. It was as short as a snapped biscotto, but it was unmistakably mirth.

As she settled herself back into the Barca-lounger and strained the foot and headrests apart, I let myself out and closed the door softly.

By the time I opened the door to room 213 I would have curled up in a dumpster full of soup cans, so it was no miracle that it looked welcoming. No roaches, no mould in the bathroom, sheets pulled tight enough to bounce pennies off the bed. I drank two plastic cups of tap water, brushed my teeth with the corner of a towel, and slotted myself into the tight sheets like a library ticket.

The fan was indeed symphonic. I just had time to say to myself, *What a bloody racket. I'll neve*— and the next thing I knew the sun was shining in the open curtains and my cheek was attached to the pillow beneath it by a patch of drool.

FIVE

I squinted at my watch and started fully awake when I saw it was eight forty-five. I staggered to the bathroom, stared helplessly at my hair, which looked on one side like my hamster's bedding when he'd just been let back into a clean cage and gone wild, and on the other side like a patch of flattened bracken where deer have been sleeping. I wet my hands to dab at it and then shrieked as a knock came — *bam, bam, bam* — on the door. It sounded exactly the same as the knock last night. No doubt, I thought scurrying to answer, it was the cops again.

I opened up and got as far as "How did you know where" when a young man in Hello Kitty shorty pyjamas shoved past me, leapt across the floor, and dived into my bed.

"Emm," I said.

"Can I stay here?" he said. He had the covers clutched to his chin, a chiseled chin with perfect stubble and a dimple you could have filled with melted chocolate and dipped marshmallows in.

"Emm," I said.

"I saw the bed was slept in so I knew someone was here," he said. "Can I use your phone?"

"Are you in some kind of trouble?" I said.

"I'm Todd," he said. "I live next door. In 214. But I just got up and went into the bathroom and there is a s-p-i-d-e-r the size of Godzilla's grandpa in the shower. So if I could just stay here and use your phone to call Roger — my hubs; he's at work — to come and kill it, that would be a really big help to me."

"Or," I said, "I could go and kill the sp— *it* for you."

He had pulled the covers up to his eyes when I started to say the word, but he let it drop again. "For reals?" he said. "It is bigger than my first apartment."

"I'll take care of it for you," I said.

"Okay," he said, getting up and springing over to the window. He looked out, peering towards his own room, as if the spider might be following him. "You have to kill it dead. Don't save it and lie to me. And you have to take the body away. Don't put it in my trashcan. And you have to clear up any . . .

residue."

"Got it," I said, and took a step out onto the walkway.

"And don't bring it back in here, whatever you do!" Todd shouted after me. "And don't drop it over the railing. And if you can't find it, don't tell me you've killed it because it might still be in there."

"I've got it!" I shouted back.

"Can I still use your phone to call Roger?" he was saying as the door of 214 closed behind me.

It was the same room as mine: same size, same shape, same doors, but the furniture was carved with birds and fruit and painted in peacock colours. An enormous oil portrait of . . . could have been Deborah Kerr . . . hung above the bed and there was a gif of a waterfall looping on the eight-foot telly. Frog-shaped foot mats led in a winding path from an impressive cross-trainer near the front window towards the bathroom. I followed them to the bathroom door and peeked round it.

The Last Ditch towels had been banished. There was a hanging holder, every one of its ten cubbyholes stuffed with one of the plushest, thickest, blackest bath sheets I had ever seen. Two matching robes with satin lapels hung from the door-back hooks, and enough cosmetics to fill the ground floor of any Macy's were crowded around the basin.

I pulled back the shower curtain — also not Last Ditch standard-issue; more like the roof of a Bedouin tent — and peered in, poised to run if Godzilla's grandpa was hauling itself up the near edge and heading my way. There was nothing there.

I stepped closer and looked into the plug-hole. Still nothing. I checked the tiles and the inside of the shower curtain and eventually, on the high windowsill, apparently about to leave of its own accord, I saw a little pale brown spider with thin, thready legs. The whole thing was smaller than a lentil.

Shaking my head, I ran through the options my promises to Todd had left me, then I put one finger on it and squished it. I held my finger under the tap, turned it on and washed away the remains, not wanting to waste a whole sheet of loo roll.

" 'Tis gone," I said, coming back into my own room. Todd was under the covers again.

"I heard the faucet," he said. "Did you just wash it down the sink? Because they come back."

"I didn't just wash it away," I told him. "It's dead."

"What did you — No! Don't tell me! But

what did — No!"

"It's not out the window. It's not in your bin. It's not over the rail. It's not back here with me. It's gone."

"Where? Don't tell me!"

"Okay," I said. "Now, if you'll excuse me, I've got to go. I need to bail a friend out of jail this morning and I'm running late."

"Would you like to borrow a hat?" Todd said.

"It's too hot to wear a hat," I said.

"Hot?" he echoed. "It's not going to be hot today. I'll get a hat for you," he added, standing. "The judge is never going to let your friend walk free with your hair like that."

For the second time since I'd arrived at the Last Ditch, I laughed.

I passed on the hat, gave my key to Todd so he could "straighten up in gratitude" (I hadn't left anything there anyway), and headed back across the tracks. A warm wind blew through the underpass like the blast of a hairdryer and already the day felt flattened out by the heat; not recovered from yesterday's and not nearly ready for today's. I fanned my sundress and snapped my knicker elastic to get a quick draft up there, then I was out of the shadows again.

I arrived at the cop shop just as Plain-

53

clothes from last night was leaving.

"Oh good," she said, stopping with the front door open, balancing a coffee cup, three fat cardboard folders, and a teddy bear origamied out of folded nappies. "Mizz Visalia is outta here any minute. She's gonna need you."

"She's getting bail?"

"She's going up to Madding for arraignment." Madding was the county town, where the courthouse was. Arraignment was . . . an American thing, like escrow and credenzas. I nodded with my eyes narrowed to look shrewd. "The judge is a Cuento kid, like me," the cop said. "Mizz Vi taught him piano and probably Sunday School too. She'll be out before they stop serving pancakes at the Red Raccoon."

"He's going to let a murderer walk free because she taught him piano?" I said.

"Uh, no. He's going to let an old lady out on steep bail because three firefighters were helping her change a tire on the freeway at the same time the Bombaro neighbors heard the explosion. Look, are you coming or aren't you?" She was straining towards her coffee cup, looking a bit like a gorilla pursing up to strip a branch of its leaves.

"Can I help?" I said.

She snapped her chin into her neck and

54

frowned at me. "I can't let you carry evidence files," she said. Neither one of us mentioned the teddy bear.

"I better get a wiggle on then," I said. "I'm going to have to bus it up there."

The cop sighed, managed to squint at her watch despite the armload of stuff, and then contorted herself in a way I didn't understand until I heard a chirp behind me.

"Get in and I'll give you a ride," she said, nodding at a dusty car sitting in the twenty-minute spot near the door. "Just need to ditch some of this first."

"Great," I said. "Can we swing back by the Swiss Sisters?" It was the drive-through coffee shop where she'd obviously already been. She shook her head and rolled her eyes, which I took to be a yes.

I stopped with the car door open and one foot in and called to her. "Ma'am?"

Two uniformed cops coming out of the door gave me a smirk and said, "Her name is Mike."

"Thank you," I said. I raised my voice: "Mike? Can I just ask — *explosion*? Did the old boy literally . . . ?"

"Literally," Mike said.

"Shit."

"That too." We both shuddered and went our separate ways.

"This is my first ever hurl in a panda," I said, minutes later. "Ride in a cop car," I translated as she frowned. "What are the chances of you putting your mee-maw on? Siren, I mean. Not Grandma. Oy."

"How do you counsel people if they can't understand a word you say?" she asked me. "Nil, by the way. No lights, no music."

"It's a good metaphor for the challenges of miscommun—Yeah, you're right," I said. "Can I ask you something?"

"I can't comment on the case," Mike said. She had twisted round in her seat to check the freeway as she hurtled up the on-ramp, closer and closer to the car in front, which was dawdling.

"Careful," I said. I couldn't help it.

"Really?" she asked me, indicating, pulling out past the dawdler, joining the traffic stream, and taking a sip of her coffee all at the same time. "You gonna help me drive? How about solving the case as well while I bark up the wrong tree, Mrs. Fletcher?"

"I wouldn't dream of it," I said. "Here's my question: why is she being arraigned on and bailed at if she's got an alibi from three firemen?"

"Because my boss reckons a timing device was removed postmortem."

"Wouldn't she need to be there to remove it?"

"Someone would," Mike said. "Thank your stars there's a camera on that office doorway."

That shut me up. *I* knew I couldn't have gone up to a body blown apart like some kind of X-rated Tom and Jerry gag and fiddled with the wiring to make an alibi. But the cops didn't seem to know that there was a back way out of the office building into an alley. Or to have considered the possibility of me leaving by the balcony and shinning down a very convenient pepper tree inches away.

"You know there's a back door into the alley, don't you?" I heard myself saying. "And a pepper tree to climb down."

Mike said nothing for a minute or two. Then she sighed. "Yeah, we were hoping you wouldn't think of that," she answered eventually. "Truth is, the camera on the front door isn't what alibied you." I waited. "It's the camera in the room next door, filming you through the air vent."

"What?"

"We've been working on busting a little prostitution racket that uses those offices."

"Jesus Christ, I thought that was the motel!"

"With Noleen watching? Shehh, right."

"I was filmed the whole time I was in there? Isn't that a violation of something?"

"Did you read the rental agreement?"

"Of course not." I was thinking hard about the two hours I had spent in the room. Mostly I had been flinching, cowering, and yoga breathing. *Mostly.* "I picked my nose," I said.

"And wiped it on a Kleenex and put the Kleenex in the trash," Mike said. "Yeah, I know. Your momma brought you up right."

I slid down in my seat and looked out the window. Everyone picks their nose. The Queen picks her nose. And craps. And farts and lifts the sheets to sniff. There's no need to be embarrassed, and a trained counsellor is the last person on earth not to understand that.

"I burped at a funeral once," Mike said. "Through a microphone, in the middle of a eulogy."

"I once trailed a toilet paper tail all the way from the dispenser back to my seat in a restaurant. On a first date."

"I don't use a Kleenex when I pick my nose," Mike told me. "We done?"

■ ■ ■

The courthouse was bewildering: jammed with bodies, ringing from its shining floor to its buzzing strip lights with beeps, shouts, slams, laughter, weeping, and somehow, above anything else, a thousand whispered conversations, their intensity making up for their lack of actual volume so it felt, sitting in the long corridor, like being inside a beehive with a queen-off brewing.

The courtroom itself, when I got inside it about quarter to ten, was an oasis. Set up to hold a jury, press, public spectators, and lawyers as well as criminals (alleged criminals? defendants? prisoners? accused Americans?), this morning it was home to two bored-looking uniformed guys, one on each door, a secretary-type person, and a little rag bag of sorry-looking individuals in the front row — possibly lawyers, possibly their clients (clients! That couldn't offend anyone), possibly both mixed together. Then a door in the blonde wood panelling swept open and the judge swirled in like a dementor — black robe, black eyes, black looks for everyone. The uniforms and the secretary sat up and the little straggle of whoever-they-were in the front row cowered

59

even lower.

We all rose. Because the Honourable Judge Something I Didn't Catch was suddenly presiding. It was exactly like being in an episode of *Columbo*. Except that I usually understood *Columbo*, and every word uttered in Judge Dementor's court that morning was beyond me. People stood up, people sat down. They said things calmly, then a bit louder. The judge said numbers, banged his gavel, and it all started again. The only time I had ever been more mystified was watching American football. Here in the court there weren't even colour-coded pom-poms or people being stretchered off to help me decipher the doings.

So my attention was drifting a bit when, in the middle of a long string of numbers and letters, I heard "Visalia Maria Bombaro" and sat up. Mizz Vi being brought into court all in orange made even the most hard-bitten lawyers give a double-take and look at the judge. *Aw, come on,* they seemed to say. *What next? Stamping on puppies?*

She was on the arm of a buxom cop, at least a foot taller than her, who glowed with good health and copious bronzer, so it was partly by comparison that my client looked like such a withered little twig.

She had always been slight, her calves

60

thinner than her ankles above high-heeled pumps that made her totter as she walked, and her neck reedy above her collar, making me think of a baby bird stretching up, cheeping, out of its nest.

After a night in jail, though, one jaded sigh from a public defender could have blown her away. Her hair, usually a translucent mauve-tinged cloud, was lying flat on her head with stripes of her pink scalp showing through. Her lips wobbled, and even from where I sat, I could see that one corner of her mouth was wet with spittle. She sat down and folded her hands in her lap, not quite managing to stop them trembling. The Amazonian cop looked at how Mizz Vi's feet didn't reach the floor, turned, skewered the judge with that look I had learned was called *stink-eye,* and walked away with mouth pursed and head shaking.

This time, because I cared, I paid more attention and I gleaned some sense from among the streams of words. "Collusion in the unlawful killing of Clovis Alfredo Bombaro" was pretty hard to miss and also "flight risk."

The Amazonian cop tutted loudly and then, when the judge swung round to glare at her, she pretended she was sucking something from between her teeth, doing a lot of work with her tongue and one of her acrylics to convince him.

Bail was discussed, figures batted back and forth, and then one of the lawyers, a scruffy sort in a pale-grey shiny suit and brown loafers, pointed out that Mizz Vi's assets were, to all intents and purposes, frozen, since her spouse had just died. The judge rubbed his chin and I thought (although it might have been my imagination) that he turned slightly away from the buxom cop, who I also thought (and this was not my imagination at all) terrified him.

Recognizance, surety, property percentage . . . my mind was wandering again when all of a sudden I heard something that snapped me back like a bungee. Someone in the court had said my name. Whoever it was, was still talking.

". . . mental-health professional currently counseling Mrs. Bombaro and present in court today."

Mizz Vi was searching the room with her swimmy, pink-edged eyes. When she caught sight of me, she lifted a hand as if to touch me, although we were separated by twenty feet. A little cry escaped her and she mouthed "Lexy" too quietly for anyone to hear. Seeing a friendly face was just too much for her. Her bottom lip quivered and she fished a hanky out of her sleeve and pressed it to her eyes. There was a collective swishing sound in the court as everyone present said something that included the word *shame*. The woman on one side of me said ". . . should be ashamed of himself," and the man on the other said, "Damn shame." The overall effect was of twenty strangers shushing Mizz Vi gently. She cried harder, overcome by their kindness maybe.

"Ms. Campbell?" said the judge.

"M'lord?" I blurted. "Your grace-judge-justice . . . Yessir?"

"Honor," said the judge coldly.

"Of course," I said. "Your Honour. Your absolute and obvious Honour."

"You are Mrs. Bombaro's . . ."

"Marriage guidance counsellor," I said. Someone snorted. Who could blame them? "Family therapist?" I tried. "Yes, therapist."

"And you will continue to be available to Mrs. Bombaro if she is released on recognizance?"

"I . . ." I said, thinking of my missed plane. And maybe because I'm Scottish he thought I meant yes. *Aye, aye, captain.* Well, I suppose I'd just said *m'lord.*

"Good," he said with a curt nod. A nod that could have cracked a walnut under his chin. "And how would you describe your standing in the community?"

"Uh," I said.

One of the lawyers stood up. "Ms. Campbell is a legal permanent resident, the spouse of a prominent citizen, and a registered notary public."

"Who's willing to cosign a bail bond?" said the judge.

"Yes," the lawyer said.

"Hang on," I said, but then I glanced at Visalia again. She was peering over her hanky and her eyes, while mostly still glistening with tears, were also now shining with faint hope. "I'm divorced. But otherwise, what he said. And yes."

The judge nodded then went back to long knotted strings of total gobbledygook and numbers again. The lawyers understood him, clearly; they chipped in with argumentative strings of their own. Without anything that sounded like a resolution to me, suddenly His Honour banged the gavel again and Mizz Vi was helped to her feet by the Amazon, now grimly pleased — she gave the judge a look that said *lucky for you you did the right thing this time* — and the old lady went tottering away into the depths of the courthouse again, waving her hankie over her shoulder in my direction and making the court collectively say "aw" because everyone said something with the word *adorable* in it this time.

"You coming?" Mike was at my shoulder.

"Coming . . . back to Cuento?" I guessed.

"Coming to do what you said you would," said Mike. "Job one's easy. Job two's a doozy." She strode out of the court with me scuttling after her.

"Job two?" I said when we were out in the mayhem of the corridor again. I couldn't imagine what would ever make me bring a kid to a courthouse, but several local families seemed to think a trial was just an excuse for a picnic. There were children of all ages from infants to hulking, sulking teenagers all over the benches now, little ones marching up and staring at other little ones, big ones stealing surreptitious glances at other big ones. Aunties and grannies were cracking out the Tupperware left and right, passing round paper napkins, pouring Coke into red plastic cups. People had cut up fruit. I wouldn't have been surprised to see an uncle wheel in a grill and start some burgers.

"Mizz Vi has to ID the body," Mike said. "And you need to hold her hand. Like you said you would. To the judge."

"I . . ." I said again.

"Yeah, like that," Mike said and walked

away laughing.

When she came out through the metal door twenty minutes later, though, I'd have needed a heart of stone wrapped in lead to deny her anything. I was feeling a bit better anyway, because the whole bail bond deal took less than fifteen minutes and got done right there in the hallway. The bail bondsman cracked open a hard briefcase with a printer inside and showed me where to sign. It might have taken longer if I'd read what I was signing, but the guy seemed busy and I was filled with the milk of human kindness in the form of an egg salad sandwich donated by the matriarch of a family sharing the same bench. She'd poured me out a cup of coffee from an enormous flask too and shushed me with a wink when I realized it was only half coffee and the other half was rum. I soaked up some of it with a slice of warm banana bread and was dabbing my lips with a Snoopy napkin when Mizz Vi, in a pink dress and a little pink cardi now, but still on the strong arm of the buxom cop, came pattering my way.

"Lexy!" she said. "Oh, Lexy! Oh, Clovis! Oh!"

"Now you take care, won't you?" said the cop. Her face was made for scowling at prisoners — I imagined her whole résumé to snag this job could have been just a mug shot — but she was smiling at Mizz Visalia, a fierce and toothy smile that didn't reach up as far as her frown to lift it.

"Oh, Val!" said Mizz Visalia. "You've been so kind! Everyone's been so kind! Tell the girls in the back there I said goodbye, won't you? I feel just awful that I didn't get to go back and visit with them again. They were so very sweet to me in the night. I couldn't stop crying, Lexy. I disturbed them all and some of them were very . . . drained."

"Hammered," said the cop.

"But they were so kind! Oh! Oh! What am I going to do?"

The short answer was that she was going to go and look at the corpse of her husband that had been blown apart. To what extent I didn't really care to imagine, although I knew I'd find out for sure pretty soon.

"Now, now," I said. "Take a couple of deep breaths, Visalia. Big breath in and let it all go."

Mizz Vi took a big breath in and used it to say, "Is that banana bread I can smell?" She clapped a hand over her mouth, but it was too late. The keeper of the Tupperware had heard her and pressed a slice on her, with a cup of the "coffee" to wash it down.

"Oh! You are so kind!" said Mizz Vi. "The

police do their best, I'm sure. But dinner last night was a protein bar and breakfast this morning was . . . well, they called it oatmeal." She took a bite of the bread and slurp of the "coffee" and smiled. "Just the way I like it," she said.

I believed her. We had touched on it in therapy, the way Visalia medicated with peach slings when Clovis got "that way he gets." She called them smoothies and said they helped her "cleanse." Clovis told me they were three parts gin to any peach involved and "that way he got" meant anytime he tried to resume the marital relations that she'd renounced in the early nineties. I was never sure if she blunted her sense with booze and then welcomed him back or if she drank till she passed out and that made him stop asking. It wasn't the healthiest marriage I'd ever seen, put it that way.

In the back of Mike's unmarked on the way to the morgue, Mizz Vi certainly seemed pretty cleansed by the coffee. She had stopped yelping and I had never heard her speak so highly of her husband.

"I can't believe Cousin Clovis is gone," she said.

"Clov—" I began, but since he was dead I was no longer their marriage guidance counsellor, so it was no longer my business.

"He was always so very alive," she said. I nodded. If it was none of my business, then it wasn't my place to contradict her. Two weeks ago she had thrown a cushion at him in my office and called him a slug. "He was a force of nature," she said now. I nodded again. Forces of nature technically included drizzle and ground fog. "I don't know what I'm going to do without him."

"Go to your sister in Bend, Oregon?" I suggested, since that was what she had been planning, quite gleefully, to do without him twenty-four hours ago.

"I wasn't going to sign," she said. "I was going to agree to what he had asked me."

"You weren't going to sign the divorce papers?" I said. I caught Mike's eye in the driving mirror. "What had he asked you?"

"To go back to Trapani with him and spend our golden years where we belong."

"Back?" I said. I knew both Clovis and Visalia had been born in central California, in different branches of the same family of exuberant recent immigrants, hence the names.

"Back," said Mizz Vi firmly. "Back to the true life of our hearts. To the lemon groves, to the harbor side, to the shade of the olive trees . . . with white-glove concierge service and a full spa."

"Clovis and you were going to Sicily?" I said. "What about . . . ? Now, don't react. Remember what we talked about. There is nothing talismanic or dangerous in the speaking of a name. Agreed?"

"I never disagreed," said Visalia, for all the world like she hadn't spewed pea soup while her head spun any time I'd raised the subject before.

"What about Barbara?"

Mizz Vi hissed like a snake. Like a set of straighteners on damp hair. She drew back her lips and hissed.

"Have it your own way," I said. I wasn't on the strongest ground anyway, because of course "Brandeee" didn't really have three es. I just pretended it did because I hated her. "But I thought Clovis was meeting Barbara at the San Francisco airport and going to the Cayman Islands?"

"He dumped the bitch," said Mizz Vi. "He told her the store was closed, he was renewing his vows to me, his wife, and together we were going home."

Home. To a place they had never been except on holiday. To a place their ancestors had left. It was the American way, and it bugged the haggis out of me. I had lost count of the number of times someone had

70

found out I was Scottish and cried, "Me too!" Then I'd ask how long they'd been in the States and they'd clarify: one of their great-grandparents hailed from Paisley; the other seven were from God knows where and my "fellow Scot" had been born and raised in Missouri. I blinked at Visalia trying to remember what we were talking about.

"So . . . why were you driving to our therapy session separately?" I said, but Madding isn't a big town, so Mike was slowing and turning already.

California. The missions were painted the colour of clotted cream with gingerbread pan tiles and verdigris window frames. It's very pretty and, having found a look that worked, California — like Her Majesty and Anna Wintour — stuck with it. High schools, nail bars, Whole Foods, dog pounds . . . there's nothing that doesn't look better Mission-style. Including, as we now saw, morgues. Mike pulled up at what would be valet-parking for check-in if this were really the resort hotel it looked like, and I hopped out and ran round to haul Mizz Vi to her feet.

The hairdryer was set at blowtorch now, at nearly lunchtime. We stepped inside to the air-conditioning and stood waiting under the safe disposal of sharps poster for Mike to park and join us.

"I want to thank you, Lexy," Visalia said.

"No need," I assured her.

"First you saved my marriage and now you're saving me from going through this alone. I can't tell you how much that means. I thank you from the bottom of my heart."

"Shoosh," I said. "That's what I'm . . . the saving the marriage bit is what you paid me to . . . and this is . . . don't mention it."

"I've never been more truly grateful for anything in my life."

"Stop."

See, the thing American people forget with their rampant sincerity and their open expressions of heartfelt gratitude is that whoever you're thanking has to think up something to say back. In Dundee, if you were waiting at the mortuary with a pal to ID her husband's body, she'd have said:

"You sure you've got time to hang about? You can go, if you like."

And then I could have said:

"Nah, you're all right."

Which does the same job and nobody's squirming.

Six

The foyer of the Beteo County coroner might have been trying for Holiday Inn Express, but the morgue itself — in the basement, since heat rises and cold sinks — was the real, green lino, crackling strip-light, whiff of formaldehyde deal. A short, taciturn man in grey scrubs and squeaking wellington bootees led us along a corridor into colder and colder air and then ushered us into an operating theatre. Of sorts. The more I looked around, the more *of sorts* it got. The floor drain didn't help. The rotary saw sitting on the side didn't spark thoughts of bunnies making daisy-chains either. But worst of all was that some of the equipment was draped in sheets. My mind boggled. What were they covering if they let us see the *saw*?

In the middle of the floor sat a gurney with a sheet-covered object we all knew wasn't a power tool. The topography of his toes, knees, belly, and nose was unmistakable. Here was Clovis "Boom!" Bombaro. Visalia let out a soft whimper and I put my hand under her elbow.

"Mike?" I said. "I've met Mr. Bombaro fourteen times. I could ID him, couldn't I?"

"We'd rather have Mrs. Bombaro's word on it," Mike said.

I frowned at her. He was clearly in one piece despite the cause of death. It wasn't as though she'd need to navigate by birthmarks. I didn't understand why she had to be put through it and I said as much, with my face. Mike returned a flat stare, her mouth a line.

Then I got it. If Mizz Vi was under suspicion, her reaction to Clovis's body was evidence. And once I'd thought of that, I kind of wanted to see it too. Her reaction. Looking at the body was the price I had to pay.

The little orderly in the grey scrubs didn't get any friendlier, but there was a comfort in his deftness. He had done this a thousand times and nothing had ever gone wrong, his spare movements seemed to say. The body was his business and he could handle it. We had one tiny part to play and he wouldn't let us fluff it and cause him any trouble.

As we walked forward, Visalia's steps getting shorter and shorter, the orderly folded the sheet back in a crisp V-shape so that only the face of the corpse could be seen, inside a sort of reverse wimple.

I glanced at it and had to smother a giggle. Horrified, I felt another one bubble up behind it and smothered that too. I wish I could say it was shock. But really, it was because Clovis looked so . . . surprised. So very, very, very surprised. His eyebrows were arched, his brow furrowed, his eyes wide open, and his mouth a perfect O.

"Can't you —" Visalia said and reached out a hand. Mike cleared her throat. "Can't you close his eyes at least?" she asked, although she drew her hand back again.

"The next time you see him, he'll be more peaceful," Mike said. "For now, can you confirm that this is Clovis Bombaro?"

"Oh!" said Visalia. The coffee had worn off; the yelp and the tremor were back in her voice. "Yes, of course. Yes, that's Cousin Clovis. We met when we were twelve. At a family picnic at the Creek House. Such a pretty day."

It seemed like a bit of a tangent and I had no reply, but Mike stepped in with a good old "I'm sorry for your loss."

"I want to go home," said Visalia. "Lexy, will you take me?" She turned to me with a searching look. She had always been a big eye-contact kind of client. And she had great eyes to work with. The brows were drawn on in dramatic slashes with an eyebrow pencil that must once have matched her hair but now bore no relation. Her lashes were short and stubby and she gunked them up with thick blue-black mascara. The eyelids were hooded, with prominent blue veins. Somewhere between Bette Davis and Garfield. Right now, they swivelled back to take another look at Clovis.

"*Can* I go home?" she said. "Is it covered up with yellow ribbons?"

"Crime scene tape?" said Mike. "No, they're through. You . . . You don't want to go in the garage until the cleaners have come. You got the card for the cleaners, right? But sure, go home. Rest up. I'll speak to you later."

But when we got in the cab, Visalia gave the driver not the address of Casa Bombaro, but the name of a bar in what passed for Cuento's financial district. That is, three real estate agents and a CPA.

"We need to send him on his way," she said, sinking back into the taxi's split vinyl seating. "With a daiquiri."

Mizz Visalia Bombaro clearly marked

76

more things than the death of a spouse with daiquiris. As soon as we pushed open the door and stepped into the cool dark, the barman was reaching for his shaker.

"Watermelon times two, Chico," she called to him. "What are you having, Lexy? I recommend the watermelon daiquiri, but Chico can make anything you've ever heard of and a few you'll wish you hadn't."

"Can you call people 'Chico'?" I said.

"That's his name," said Mizz Visalia. She shrugged off her little pale pink cardigan and dropped into an armchair. "Two each and keep 'em coming."

The cocktails arrived quicker than seemed possible and the first sip turned into a glug that left me tingling from lips to hips to fingertips.

"I didn't do it," Visalia said.

"Of course not."

"They think I did it. I don't want to go to jail, Lexy. Last night was enough."

I didn't want to remind her that jail wasn't the only possible outcome. This was America and one of the biggest chasms between the old country and the wild west was staring Visalia in the face. Bigger than the missing walls, bigger than the paper plates, bigger than Christmas being flavoured with peppermint, even. She could fry.

"So, who do you think *did* do it?" I said.

Visalia shivered. It might only have been the crushed ice in the daiquiri, but she rubbed her gnarly old hands, bristling with diamonds, up and down her scrawny liver-spotted arms. She was California through and through: no truck with the idea that an old broad's arms should be covered.

"Barbara?" I said. Visalia hissed while drinking and made herself snort. She coughed her airways clear and glared at me. "I mean, if he dumped her, she must be angry."

"Are you kidding me? I bet she heaved a sigh of relief that changed the tides in Hawaii."

"What about the what were they called . . . the Dolshikovs?"

"Oh that man and his goddamn conspiracy theories!" said Visalia. "If I've told him once!"

The Dolshikovs were well-known to me after fourteen sessions. They lived in New Jersey and they manufactured fireworks there. They had field offices and outlets all the way to Colorado. Bombaro Pyrotechnics (Nothing goes *Boom* like Bombaro!) had the West Coast in hand. Then Dolshikov's Pyrotasia opened a Dallas branch and

Clovis Bombaro doubled his order of Pepto-Bismol.

"Dey own da whole a da Eas Coas," was how Clovis explained it to me. His birth in the Sisters of Mercy hospital in Bakersfield and the certificate that declared him one hundred percent red, white, and blue went right out the window when he talked about the firework business. It was bye-bye Bakersfield and *ciao Sicilia*. "I own da whole a da Wes Coas. Texas is da Wes."

"Well," I had said once, "Texas is east of Colora—"

"You're wasting your time," Visalia had said.

"You gonna go downa Texas and tellem dey not in da Wes?" Clovis demanded.

"Better take backup," said Vi.

I stared at her now over the rim of my daiquiri, mildly astonished by how far I had to tip the glass to take a sip. I had really chugged this. Chico put another one in front of each of us and melted away.

"Clovis and his Dolshikov obsession!" Visalia said. "You only had it an hour a week, Lexy. I had it all day every day."

"But the thing about a conspiracy theory," I said, "is that being murdered kind of adds a bit of weight, wouldn't you say?"

She stretched her neck hard one way and

then the other. I thought she was trying to get out the kinks of a night with a jailhouse pillow, but then she scooted forward on her chair and gestured to me to do the same.

"I know who did it," she said, once our faces were inches apart. "I just don't know how they found out so fast."

"How who found out what?" I said. "Wait. I mean, how who found out what. Oh, I was right the first time." I blinked. What exactly was in a daiquiri anyway?

"This has got Poggio written all over it."

"What does that mean?"

"The Poggios killed Cousin Clovis," said Mizz Vi. "They heard we were coming back to Sicily and they sent a message."

"That," I said, after taking a moment to look as if I was considering it, "sounds quite a bit more mad than the Dolshikov theory."

Mizz Visalia sipped her drink a while then sighed and set it down. "I should be flattered," she said. "I remember when that would be the first thing anyone thought about any Sicilian American dying suddenly. The first and *last* thing the cops thought. I should be happy it's changed."

"It's just . . . When did your parents come to California? And Clovis's parents?"

"Our mothers came together when they were six and seven. They were sisters. You

80

know that."

Of course I did. But I didn't dwell on it because, to use the formal language of my clinical psychological training, it was icky.

"That was 1912," she went on. "The blink of an eye. And my grandfather didn't give up his interest in the farm when he left. Cousin Clovis still owns — *owned* — a sixteenth share. Say what you like about America, but we managed to buy out all of our cousins *here* until we owned the Creek House outright. No such luck in Sicily."

"I dunno," I said, draining my glass. Again. "It's just . . . the way he died. I don't want to upset you but, the way he died, it seems more likely that someone who knew something about the firework business would have done it."

"Lexy, how much do you think you need to know about the firework business to . . . to . . . ?" We stared at one another for a while trying to think up how to refer to his cause of death with even a pinch of dignity. Unfortunately, running through the options made me remember the look on his face — the O! — and I could feel my cheeks begin to twitch again.

"To . . ." I said. I could think of nothing even vaguely useful. Phrases like *park a stick* and *sun don't shine* weren't going to help.

"To . . ." said Visalia, "place a lit firework too close for comfort."

I knew I clenched my buttocks and I thought I saw her tilt a little as she worked her own.

"Only it wasn't lit," I said.

"Well, introduce it, light it, and run then."

"No," I said. "The cops think it had a timer on it. Didn't they say that to you?"

"They *think*?" said Vi. Then she added, "A *timer*?"

"They think someone removed it afterwards," I said. "That's why . . . I can't believe they didn't tell you this! That's why you're out. Because you had three firefighters to vouch for you when Mr. Bombaro went b— Um, at the time of death, I mean. And you had an alibi from then on in." She was staring at me as if her two double daiquiris had been little cups of Earl Grey tea. She was steady and clear-eyed, and behind her gaze I could see a thousand little sparks firing, a tiny firework show going on right there in her head.

"A timer?" she said again. "And then someone *removed* it?"

"So," I repeated, thinking she might look steady but she was eighty-six, she'd spent the night in jail, and I could attest to the daiquiris. "So it seems much more likely to me that someone who knows something about pyrotechnics is involved."

"Like who?" she said. "Did the cops tell you *that*?"

"No," I said. "But it's got to be either someone from Bombaro's, someone from Dolshikov's, or someone close enough to Clovis to have picked up the basics. During pillow talk, for instance."

Her eyes opened so wide that I could see the whites (the pinks, actually) all around the warm brown irises. The *usually* warm brown irises. Right now, they were as cold and black as two lumps of coal that had fallen off the lorry and rolled into a puddle of slush at the side of the road. I blinked. Puddle of slush was right. Her face had gone grey.

"Pillow talk?" she said. "You think it was *me*?"

"Barbara," I told her. Now her lips were blue. "Are you okay?"

"I think it's just hit me," she said, hoarsely. "I need to go home." She rallied a little and called over to the bar. "Put it on my tab, Chico, and call a cab for me."

I helped her out and into the back of a taxi. I had never wished so hard for a proper black London taxicab. They're so roomy. As I stuffed Mizz Vi into the back of the low-slung Chevy that had turned up to take her home, I didn't see how she would ever clamber out again. So I got in after her and went along for the ride.

Casa Bombaro was in The Oaks — Cuento's ritziest neighbourhood, comprising six blocks of stucco wonders and other assorted McMansions, right at the edge of town, just before the start of the dusty tomato fields.

Clovis's garden gates were visible as soon as we turned onto the block. They had obviously been commissioned by Clovis himself; perhaps even designed by him, judging by the fountains of enamelled iron on them. They looked like whale-spouts, maybe badly uncorked Champagne depending on how the light caught them, but I guessed that they were fireworks.

"Pull forward," said Mizz Vi weakly. "Lexy, key in the code." She leaned towards me and whispered it into my ear, earning a look of disgust from the taxi driver.

"I know key codes for bigger estates than this," he muttered and he turned his wheels away from the box so that I had to take off my seatbelt and hang out of the window to enter the PIN.

Inside the gates, against a background of pillowy green lawns and perfectly kept paths was a display of every plant that either already looked or could be trained to look like a firework. There were palm trees, yuccas, and agaves, naturally, and — less naturally in every sense — roses pruned to the shape of fright wigs and bougainvilleas cascading from pots held up by wires so they looked as though they hung in mid-air. And, of course, the fountains. Coloured water fired up and out from an elaborate system of jets and spouts and foamed and fizzed down from an even more elaborate system of chutes and funnels.

"He called it his Garden of Eden," said Mizz Vi.

"If God *puked* Eden," I said.

The taxi driver snorted and Mizz Vi nodded her head, unable to disagree.

The house, hidden from the gate by an unnecessary curve in the short drive, was another terra cotta, cream, and verdigris extravaganza. Bigger than the morgue, bigger than any of the missions I had visited so far, and with cathedral windows and a quadruple garage, it didn't look like the sort of place a tired and lonely old lady could be abandoned. The tatters of crime scene tape still clinging to either side of the roll-up garage doors didn't help.

"Are you going to be —" I got out, but

then the door opened and a middle-aged woman stepped out. She didn't look like a housekeeper. She was wearing a dress. She looked slightly firework-related, actually, from the way her hair was gathered in a ponytail right on top of her head, exploding in all directions. Under it, her face was blank.

"My niece is here!" Mizz Vi said. Then, "I didn't think she'd be able to get a flight this soon. I only called this morning!"

"That's wonderful," I said. "Isn't it?"

But Visalia didn't seem so much soothed or comforted by the sudden appearance of a loved one as she seemed . . .

"You seem . . ." I said.

"That's my niece, Sparky," said Vi. "She was *very* close to Cousin Clovis, Lexy. You should probably try not to mind what she says."

"Seriously?" I asked. "Sparky?"

As I got out and walked around to help Visalia, the woman came plodding down the steps. *Plodding* was the only word. I stretched out a hand to greet her.

"I'm Lexy Campbell," I said. "I'm your aunt's therapist. I've been looking after her." This I delivered with a ghost of a glance backwards to where Mizz Vi, half-cut and dishevelled, was beginning to wriggle out of

86

the car. The driver, not trusted with the code, was looking stolidly forward and offering nothing.

"Serpentina," said the woman.

"How did you get here so soon, Sparky?" Mizz Vi called over.

"We were coming anyway," Serpentina said.

"Who's *we*?"

"I've got some news, Auntie." She turned back towards the open door. "Allow me to present my husband, Jan."

A tall, slim, kind of catalogue-modelly man in overstarched casuals came out and stood frowning on the doorstep. "Call me Bang-Bang," he said. His shirtsleeves and chinos crackled as he moved towards me and shook my hand.

"You're married?" said Vi. "Oh, Sparky. That's . . . Oh, that's . . . Bang-Bang, come and kiss your auntie!"

Jan went trotting over to the taxi with his clothes crunching.

I didn't know what was causing *her* such surprise, but using my professional experience, I found this couple way bogus. Bang-Bang-Jan should have had a skinny wife with life goals and two hundred dollar flip-flops. This dumpy woman in the muumuu with the comedy hairdo wasn't in his league.

"And these are Jan's cousins, Alex and Peter," Sparky-Serpentina went on, as a pair of thugs from central casting sidled out and stood with their hands clasped behind their backs watching me from behind sunglasses.

The starched man had plucked Mizz Vi out of the taxi and was ushering her — practically carrying her — past me, into the house.

"Lexy," she said. "Thank you again. I don't know where I would have been without you today."

"Please stop thanking me," I said. "You need to rest. I'll see you soon."

"Yes," she said, turning to face me while Bang-Bang-Jan kept pulling her, backwards now, into the house. "Maybe tomorrow. I can come to you or you —"

"I'll come here," I said. "In case you're tired. After lunch? Two o'clock?"

"You remember the key code?" she said as she disappeared into the shadows of the dim hallway, with Bang-Bang's arm firmly around her.

"I remember," I said. "I'll see you soon."

The two thugs turned smartly and disappeared after her. Jan came back out and sort of bowed. He might even have clicked his heels, except that he couldn't possibly have clicked his heels, could he? Then he gave his bride a look and once again disappeared.

"Thank you again for everything you've done," said Sparky, her face about as sparky as a dead halibut. She looked numb with misery.

"Are you okay?" I asked. Occupational hazard.

"Not really," she replied. "I loved Uncle Boom. I owed him everything. And I . . ."

"What?" I said. *Killed him,* I thought.

"I betrayed him."

"Oh?" I said. "How'd you do that then?"

"I hope you'll forgive me being rude, Lexy," she said, "but this is a time for family."

"Of course," I said. "But let me give you my card."

I had about five thousand of them left and anyway it wasn't as crass as it seemed because Americans give you their card *all the time.* I've been given cards by taxi-drivers whose sisters-in-law run scrapbooking classes and by pizza delivery guys whose college roommates are trying to kick-start climbing gyms and by antique dealers who sat next to me in the hairdressers and by hairdressers who outbid me at antique auctions and by the sisters-in-law of climbers who were raising money for pizza ovens by auctioning scrapbooks. When I shared a taxi with them.

Sparky pocketed mine and handed over hers. See? She was at her auntie's house to console the old lady about her new widowhood, but she had a few business cards on her.

She stretched her lips at me and then stepped inside and shut the door. It was spring-loaded and well-insulated so, despite her determination to make her meaning clear, it closed with a soft *pafp* rather than a *slam,* but I got the message. I felt as if I'd just watched a little fish swim into the mouth of a shark and heard its teeth mesh.

Even the taxi driver, not Visalia's biggest fan, looked worried.

"Bet you twenty that key code's changed before tomorrow," he said. He was right. Hell, he was *more* than right. We stopped and checked on the way out and the gate remained closed, telling me I had two more tries and one more try and then I was out of tries and my license plate had been photographed and would be held on file.

Back at the Last Ditch, Noleen was backing out of the room underneath mine with a maid's cleaning cart.

"Cops have been back," she called in

greeting as I was paying off the cab. "They were in your room."

She strolled over to the rank of dumpsters that cut off the view of the pool from the street (Feng Shui wasn't the Last Ditch way) and tossed two empty Clorox bottles into the blue one. "I tell you," she said. "Every time I think I've seen everything . . ."

I didn't want to know what a motel guest might have done that needed two bottles of bleach and surprised an old-timer like Noleen, but before I could escape, someone shouted from the open door of the Skweeky Kleen.

"Did it come out?"

"My partner, Kathi," said Noleen, then called back. "Like a dream. Still no clue what it was, but it washed out."

"Some people!" Kathi called back and then withdrew as a telephone rang inside.

"I thought it was a menstruation incident," Noleen said. Not that I asked. "Or it could have been beetroot," she went on, even though I had started backing away. "Plus a blocked drain," she added, despite the fact that I have never had a less interested look on my face in my life. "But I tell you . . . I don't know *what* it was," she concluded.

"Good," I said. "I mean, oh. I'm glad to

hear it came out. So, anyway, it's getting kind of warm for standing around."

Noleen looked at me and then at the sun, beating down mercilessly onto the concrete. "Warm?" she said. "It ain't even ninety."

I turned and headed up the iron staircase towards my room. After a day of court, morgue, the empty midday bar, and those creepy nieces and nephews, I wanted nothing more than its blankness and the chance to wash my single pair of knickers so's I didn't have to wear them for a third day.

I was in for a surprise. First off, someone — I guessed the Cuento cops, on a break from their prostitution-ring stakeout — had sprung my suitcases from the office where I'd abandoned them the evening before and left them sitting just inside the door. The door of the *unrecognisable* Room 213. It was transformed. There was a pale pink velvet chaise longue scattered with silk cushions. More silk cushions in pink, grey, and blue covered about a third of the bed, heaped up on top of a dove grey coverlet. The lamps had birds on the bases and clouds on the shades, and an oil painting of a foggy lake with ripples spreading out calmly from behind a solitary swan was on the wall.

I sank down on to the chaise just as the

door opened and a strange man walked in as if he owned the place. Or me. Or both.

"Lexy, isn't it?" he said. He was chiseled and gleaming, his hair shaved down to no more than a shadow on his mahogany skull and his perfect teeth almost blue as he flashed me a perfunctory smile. He wore a pink shirt cut like ice-skater's spandex and grey trousers I could tell cost more than my entire wardrobe.

"It is," I said.

"I'm Roger," he said. "I understand you had some trouble earlier."

"Are you a lawyer?" I said. It was partly the trousers but mostly the brisk confidence.

"I'm a pediatric surgeon," he said. "Why?"

"I . . ." I said. I've had a lot of communication training one way and another, besides starting out pretty gobby. I don't think I'd ever been at a loss for words so often in my life before as the last twenty-four hours.

"Todd said there was a spider?" Roger went on.

"A tiny little one," I said. "It was nothing."

"Right," said Roger. "Exactly. You see," he went on, with a look over his shoulder, "Todd is halfway through a program and whilst I understand that you meant to be

93

kind, we're trying — his doctor and I — to challenge the confabulations rather than confirm them."

"What?" I said.

"I know there was no spider," Roger said.

"Oh!" I said, light dawning. "Cleptopara-sitosis?"

Roger sat down — *flump!* — onto the grey silk coverlet as if I'd punched him in the solar plexus. "Glory be," he said.

"I'm a clinical psychologist," I told him. "Well, in Dundee I am. Here I'm a generic therapist working towards a licence. But see, the thing is there really was a . . . Wait though. He said there was a great big hairy one in army boots, in the bath. And I found a tiny little brown one like a gnat with spare legs, on the windowsill. Coincidence, prob-ably, eh?" I kicked my shoes off, but Roger glanced at my feet and I'm sure his nostrils flickered so I wriggled them back on. "So how bad is he?"

He rubbed one of his perfect hands, Rolex just peeping out from a pink cuff, over his perfectly stubbled jaw and groaned. "Well," he said, "we're living in the Last Ditch Motel. We left the house about a year ago. We rented an apartment, then a suite at the Hilton Garden, Best Western, DoubleTree, La Quinta, and . . . here we are. If this goes toes up, we'll be camping."

"Doesn't medication —" I began, but Roger knew the Last Ditch's noises better than me and shushed me as Todd appeared round the open door.

"You're back!" he said. "I came to leave your key. Tah-dah! What do you think?" He did a slow turn in the middle of the room, showing off the painting, the pillows, the lamps, and then stepping off the Aubusson carpet — I hadn't even noticed that! — and tidying the fringe.

"Where did you get it all?" I said.

"I had it in storage," said Todd. "We've got tenants in our house and they wanted it unfurnished. You're doing me a favour, really. This way if I come to borrow a cup of sugar I get to see all these pretty things."

"Are you a designer?" I said. "It really is gorgeous."

"A designer?" said Todd. "No. I'm an anesthesiologist."

"Sorry," I said. "God, I'm sorry. That was really offensive."

Todd waved it away. "And so anyway," he said, "what happened with your friend? Is he out? Is he with you?"

"She," I said. "Yep, she's bailed. No, she's gone home." I think my face must have clouded as I remembered the door closing on Mizz Vi, the instant change of the key code at those towering gates.

"What happened?" said Todd.

"Her husband was killed last night. Don't ask me to tell you how. You really don't want it in your heads, believe me."

"Get out!" said Todd. "Is your friend the firework lady? Oh Em Gee. It was all over the front page of the *Voyager.* She murdered her husband, and she's out on *bail*?"

"I cosigned the bond," I said.

"You . . . ?" said Todd. "Well, for God's sake pour us a glass of Chablis and tell us all!"

"I haven't got any Chablis."

"He's probably filled your refrigerator," Roger said. "As you see, Todd doesn't really do boundaries."

"As you see, Roger tends to overpsychologize everyday life," Todd shot back.

"My apologies," said Roger. "As you'll find out, Todd likes to take care of people."

"As you'll find out, Roger is troubled by normal amounts of everyday kindness."

"Normal?" said Roger. "What about when you fostered those hedgehogs?"

"What about it? The PETA website linked to my Facebook post."

"Todd, you bought a stroller."

"I *customized* a stroller," said Todd, reaching his phone out of his back pocket and scrolling through the photographs. "I Bento-ized it. Six little compartments. It was adorable. It went viral."

That was when I stopped listening. I had opened the fridge and my eyes filled. There *was* a bottle of Chablis, that was true. And on the counter above the fridge there were six beautiful wine glasses with spindly stems and the soap-bubble irridescence of really good crystal. But what had put the lump in my throat was the six-pack of pork pies and the three bars of Cadbury's Whole Nut.

"How did you find . . . These are genuine Melton Mowbray."

"I have connections," Todd said, sepulchrally. "But they're all pharmacists. When it comes to charcuterie, there's a deli in Sacramento."

So, over pies, chocolate, and Chablis, I told them everything.

Halfway through, Kathi from the Skweeky Kleen joined us. She was pretty much identical to Noleen, only years younger: her grandma haircut still dark and nothing on her t-shirt but a small SK logo. I looped back to clue her in and she listened, nodding all the time and showing, from a couple of short questions, that she was as sharp as a shiv.

97

Later, as the sun sank, Noleen followed the squawks and shrieks to their source, and made a fifth, bringing a jug of margaritas with her. So I had to go back over it again. Noleen said plenty: Vi was a fool, Clovis was an asshat, Sparky was a bitch, Bang-Bang was a creep, Sicily was a dump, love was a mug's game.

By the time they left, some things seemed clear. Clovis "Boom" Bombaro was planning to skip out on his wife without even signing his divorce papers. Of course he was. He had fooled her into believing they'd start again in Sicily and she'd swallowed it whole. There was no age-old Sicilian family feud at the heart of this. Of course there wasn't. What there *was* was a woman still in love after sixty-odd years and an old man too cussed to split his wealth with her. As to who had killed him . . . I couldn't get past the idea that if Sparky was Clovis's heir, she came to Bang-Bang with a hell of a sweetener besides her well-hidden charms. And he'd got that perfect nickname up and running pretty sharpish. Plus there was the two nightclub-bouncer cousins too.

Because what kind of family goes to the house and waits for a therapist to bring their dear old auntie home? Why weren't they at the courthouse, paying for a swanky lawyer for her? Why weren't they at the jail, pounding on doors and demanding that she be set free?

And how could I get her to wise up before they got rid of her too?

SEVEN

Life's too short to count threads, if anyone's
asking me. Still, the first night between
Todd's dove-grey sheets slipped by me like
a greased eel and when I woke up, with the
sunshine slicing through the gap in his lav-
ender window-treatments, my head resting
in a cloud of goose-down on one of his big
square pillows, and all my stuff on his padded satin hangers behind the doors of the
fitted cupboards, life felt immeasurably better than it had only twenty-four hours before.

I needed to see Mizz Vi, to set my mind at
rest. And I wanted to speak to Mike again
too, to point her in all the directions that
led away from my sweet little old client and
towards manifest villainy. And, I supposed
as I turned over for the sheer joy of feeling
all those counted threads against my bare
skin (I didn't have any nightwear worthy of
the new linen and so I had done without), I

should really phone home and let my family know that my shamefaced return had been postponed. Or I could email Alison. She was such a gossip she'd be round at my mum's before her laptop went to standby. And then, even though I'd have to field a million tearful questions, at least I wouldn't have to find a way to break the news.

I worked at convincing myself for about five minutes, then I put on a pot of coffee and lifted the phone.

"Change of plan, Mum," I said, when she answered. The coffee smelled even more like heaven than usual, and the smell of the first cup of coffee is sometimes the highlight of my day.

"Oh, Lex! I knew it. You've worked it through. I told you if you just stuck at it, things would look brighter soon. Didn't I? How many times did I tell you?"

"Seventeen including this one," I said. "But listen —"

"Keith?" my mum shouted. "Ke-ith! It's Lexy. They've worked it out. She's staying. We can go over for Christmas."

"Mum!"

My dad lifted the dining room extension. I could see him, bent over the table working on his fishing flies.

"There!" he said. "What did we tell you?

Every marriage has a few bumps in the early days, but you work them through."

"Dad. Mum. I'm divorced. It's final. He is remarried to his first wife. I'm sorry about Christmas and the pool and the side-trip to Vegas. Although, nothing is stopping you going to Vegas for Christmas, you know."

"Now why would you get our hopes up?" said my mum. "What are you playing at now?"

"As I was saying: a change of plan. I'm stopping on a for a bit to help out a friend —"

"You've met someone else!" said my mum.

"What's his name?" said my dad. "Another dentist?"

"*She*'s a retired pyrotechnician," I said. The pronoun stopped them both dead. "She's a former client and a friend. Well, actually maybe she's a current client if I'm sticking around a while, so I probably shouldn't say any more. She's a recent widow. Very recent widow. And she needs some help with some . . . things."

"And as long as you're there you can spend a bit of time with Branston," my mother said. "See if you can't iron out some of your differences, eh?"

There was a sharp rap at the door of Room 213. It sounded like Roger. He sounded cross again. But Roger pissed off with me was infinitely preferable to my mum and her fantasies, so I opened up. It was Plainclothes Mike and Mills of God, the uniformed cop.

"Mum," I said. "I've got to go. I'm going to start telling you why. If I get to the end of the sentence, you'll understand. If you interrupt me, you won't. Okay?"

"What are you talking about?" my mum said.

"Don't treat your mother as if she's one of your patients," my dad said.

"The police are here," I said. "I need to give a statement about —"

"NO! Oh Lexy, what have you done? Have you got a lawyer? Don't say anything. They've got the death penalty in California and —"

I hung up quietly and smiled at Mike and Mills. "Coffee?" I said.

When we were settled with our coffee mugs (bone china, plain white with a fine gold line), Mike flicked through a notebook.

"So," she said. "You had an appointment with both Bombaros at seven p.m. on the fourth. They didn't show. They didn't call you. You didn't call them. You didn't leave your office. Right so far?"

I nodded. "I was staying put, avoiding the

fireworks," I said. "I hate fireworks."

"And who made the appointment?" Mike went on. I frowned. What was she getting at? "Was it you, or Mr. Bombaro, or Mrs. Bombaro who suggested a meeting at sundown on the Fourth of July?"

"Ah," I said. "I'd have to check. Oh — actually I can't check. I've closed my practice account because I've closed my practice." I had deleted everything and shredded what I'd printed. I was one county permit away from a great big symbolic bonfire, really.

"Cast your mind back," said Mike, dryly. The dryness intrigued me. The look that went with it intrigued me enough to make my pulse race. She thought I was playing her in some way. I was so far from playing her I couldn't even work out what the game would be.

"Well, typically," I said, "one or other of the Bombaros emailed me from their joint account. That last appointment request" — I screwed my face up, trying to remember — "came from . . ." I shut my eyes and tried to visualize the end of the message. Was it *Yours, V* or *Boom!*? But, honestly, who reads to the end of an email? I don't even open them if I can get the gist from what shows in the inbox. "I can't remember," I concluded. "I'd be guessing if I picked one."

"What a surprise," said Mike, dryer than a cornflour desert.

"Ah," I said. "You think . . ." I paused to let my brain catch up. No luck. "Sorry, what do you think?"

"Next question," Mike said. "You said you were leaving town?"

I nodded.

"You look pretty cozy for someone who's leaving town," she said. "We delivered your luggage so you wouldn't need to go to Target and buy panties. Quite a surprise when the owner let us into your room."

"We?" I said. "*You?* A detective delivered my luggage to my motel room? That's a bit odd, isn't it?"

"I thought I might learn something," she said. "I was right." Then she glanced down at her notebook. "And after the appointment was made, did you have any communication with Mr. Bombaro about it?"

"Uhhhh, no," I said. "But that's not unusual. I gave them tasks at first. You know, listening exercises, quizzes, that kind of thing. But by yesterday . . . no."

"And how was the arrangement made for you to witness the divorce papers?" she went on.

"Oh well, *there* I can be much more help.

Mizz Visalia called and asked me."

"No communication with Mr. Bombaro on that either?"

"No," I said, "but I'm assuming he was fine with it."

"And do you have any idea why they were traveling to your office separately? I mean, why Mrs. Bombaro was traveling alone?"

"No!" I said. "And actually I meant to ask her about that but I got sidetracked."

"Oh you did, did you?" said Mike. A hot wind had blown across the cornflour desert and baked it just a little drier.

"I did," I confirmed. "I will ask and I'll let you know, if I see her before you do. There's a lot of things I'd like to ask her, actually. Barbara's full name and address for one thing. Oh but wait. Actually, that would be better coming from you lot. But, you see, it occurred to me that if Clovis and Visalia had made up and he'd ditched Barbara, she'd be pretty angry. You should definitely speak to her. And there's the Dolshikovs too. Business rivals. And there's family. They've turned up and I got a very bad vibe from them yesterday. They're at the Bombaros' house out on — Oh, but you probably know the address."

"Do you have their names?" said Mike. "The family, with the bad vibes?"

"Serpentina," I said, "and Jan."

"Bombaro?"

"No," I said. And then I remembered the card swap. I fished in my wallet for it, smoothed it out, cast my eyes over it, and dropped dead from the shock of what I saw there.

At least, it took a minute before I could speak again.

"*Not* Bombaro," I said. "Serpentina Dolshikov, chief financial officer of Dolshikov Pyrotasia. Contact numbers are for Dallas, Texas."

"Dolshikov the business rival?" said Mike.

"And her brand-new husband Jan. And the two cousins were called . . . Oh God, I want to say Ivan and Boris. Definitely Dolshikov-compatible. They weren't Angelo and Dario, anyway."

"And all these people are staying with Mrs. Bombaro at the house?"

"Yes!" I said, loud enough to wake Mills of God out of his daydream. "And this is interesting. Visalia was surprised by how fast Sparky had turned up and —"

"Who?"

"Serpentina. It's a nickname. She's beating herself up about something or other she thinks she did to her uncle. Oh yes, very definitely worth looking at the family, I think. And speaking of family —"

"Yes?" said Mike. One of her eyebrows was a good two inches higher than the other. It's a useful skill for a detective. It might have been what made her join the force in the first place. It worked on me, anyway. There was no way I wanted to tell that eyebrow anything so cheesy as Mizz Vi's Sicilian mafia theory.

"Don't you think it's a bit odd that they didn't come to the court or even the jail?" I said, substituting pretty adroitly, in my opinion.

"I do," said Mike. "It's very strange indeed. An old lady relying on a therapist for support while her family waits at home? There's no way that would happen without someone planning it and laying down the law."

"Exactly," I said. "So. Barbara and the Dolshikovs. Both worth a look, eh?"

"We'll get right on it," Mike said. I blinked at her. The eyebrows had changed places. Many people have made a good living from their eyebrow work — Nathan Lane and Nicolas Cage, for instance — and a subset of *them* can quirk one eyebrow at a time — Roger Moore and Sarah Jessica Parker do it all the time. But until I met Mike, I had never seen anyone truly ambisupercilious.

She drained her cup and stood. Mills of God, who had not said a word yet, set his cup down, the coffee untouched, and joined her.

"You're not still 'leaving town,' are you?" Mike said.

"No," I assured her, ignoring the quotes. "For one thing, there's the bail bond. And anyway, she might need me again, you know?"

"She 'might need you again'?" Mike shook her head and left, laughing. I watched her go and wondered about the laughter for a minute or two then headed into the bathroom for a shower.

Todd was sitting on my bed when I emerged wrapped in a bath sheet from armpit to ankle. He had fluffed the covers and reapplied the seventeen cushions in order of size.

"Have you got a master key?" I said.

"No," said Todd giving me a look as if I'd asked a weird question. "Kathi gave me hers. Why?" He shook it off before I could answer. "Listen, I've laid out an outfit for today." He waved a hand at the back of the wardrobe door where a skirt, shirt, bra, and pants were hanging on a satin hanger. "But you really need to go shopping. I can take you to Nordstrom's Rack if we leave now."

Boundary issues, Roger had said.

"Aren't you working today?" I said.

"Get your clothes on quick before your hair dries and I'll blow it out for you," he said. "I'm not looking." He was gazing straight at me without a hint of a smile.

"Are you on a late shift?" I said. "On call?"

"I'm out sick at the moment," he told me. "I'm surprised Roger hasn't delivered the propaganda already. He's had a whole day and he likes to get in quick. Roger, for reasons known only to himself, has decided to convince the hospital board that I'm suffering from a mental condition."

"You're not?" I said

"I'm not," he said. "We had termites at the house and we moved out while they were treated. Then we had a wasp nest at the Hilton Garden, mosquitoes at the Double Tree but we couldn't find the hole in the screen. We had bedbugs at the Four Points and roaches at La Quinta. If you want to live with roaches, you go ahead. I'll stay here."

"So are all those hotels closed down while they deal with the problem?" I said.

"People are pigs," Todd said. "Did Noleen tell you about the tomato juice in the toilet? But she and Kathi know how to clean. I mean, say what you like about the hair-dos,

110

those gals can *clean!*"

"Right," I said. "Can I ask you something?" He nodded. "Would you let me interview Roger to see where his delusion is coming from? You can sit in on the sessions if you like?"

"Why, Miss Lexy!" he said. "You have caught me in your clever web and I can't escape. You wouldn't be trying to get me into therapy to see if you can cure me while I think you're working on Roger, now would you?"

"Okay, scratch that," I said. "Can I ask you something else?"

"And then we go to Nordstrom's?" he said. "Your lingerie is a sin against God."

"Agreed," I said. While I dressed, back turned, I related the whole of the morning's interview with Mike, eyebrows and all.

I turned back, fully dressed, to find him staring open-mouthed at me.

"You are not safe to be out alone!" he said. "Oh my giddy aunt. You need supervised care! What were you thinking?"

"What are you talking about?" I said, taking the earrings he had selected for me and sitting down so he could start work on my hair.

"The Sicily story is obviously garbage. The old guy obviously wanted a divorce. So

Visalia killed him. He was never coming to your office. She cooked that up alone. And the niece is in on it — or at least *someone* took the timing device away. Maybe the niece gets the business as a reward for playing her part. It's too much of a coincidence that she just happens to have married another firework guy exactly when her uncle exits the scene. And now they're all hanging back and letting the spotlight stay on you."

"What did *I* do?"

"Provided an alibi. And I *think* the *cops* think Visalia paid you for it."

"What?" I said, spinning so that the section of hair he had wound round a brush was yanked hard. "Ow! *What?* She didn't pay me. Well, I mean yes, she paid me for our sessions and she paid me extra for the last night, because it was a holiday and I was doing notary work, but she didn't *pay* me."

"If I were you, I would steer clear of all Bombaros and Dolshikovs from here on in. Can I trim your bangs?"

"I can't steer clear," I said. "I've dropped Mizz Vi right in it. The only good thing is that I didn't tell the cops the Sicily bit in case it sounded unlikely. But I need to straighten this out. Without making it worse. I need to — Whoa! I look great."

We agreed there was too much going on for me to take off on a shopping trip, but I noticed Todd entering my bra size into his mobile as I locked the room (Why? If Kathi shared the master key willy-nilly?), although he assured me he would only buy unmissable bargains.

There was some kind of altercation going on in one of the rooms on the ground floor. Kathi, in her Skweeky Kleen overall, was standing in the open doorway of the room like a Viking warrior. With a wet vac. From inside came high-pitched but inconsolable wails.

"They're not!" a child's voice was yelling. "They're pets, Mama! They're my pets!"

"No pets," Kathi said. "You signed the forms, Della." She pulled the cord of the wet vac and plugged it in to an outlet on the walkway.

Todd clutched my arm. "Kathi?" he said. "What's going on?"

Kathi shot a poison dart of a look into the room and then turned and gave Todd a tight smile. "Nothing. Absolutely nothing."

A woman appeared in the doorway. She had the sobbing child on one hip.

"Della?" said Todd. "What is it? An ant farm? Stick insects? Bees?"

"It's not insects, Todd," Kathi said. "It's

really not. I would never lie to you about that."

"They're my pets!" said the child. He was about three with a mop of black curls — sweaty at the edges from crying — and impossible, enormous brown eyes, bigger than Disney, brimming with tears.

"Let me see," said Todd. "Show me."

"They'll be gone in five minutes," Kathi said, wielding the hose of the wet vac like a sabre.

"Pe-he-hets," the child sobbed.

I could feel Todd's hand on my arm getting slick as his temperature rose and when I turned to glance at him, his face was flushed and a pulse was fluttering in his throat.

"I can help you," I said, and I slipped my hand into his and squeezed. "What kind of creatures are we talking about?" I asked Kathi.

"I hashed them," said the kid, laying his head against his mother's shoulder.

She kissed him and gave a sad smile. "It's frogs," she said. "He hatched them from the eggs."

"Frogs?" said Todd. I felt his hand go limp in mine.

"I came home and found the egg jelly in the bathroom," the child's mother said.

"Where did you get frogspawn?" I asked the kid. It seemed an old-fashioned kind of thing for a twenty-first-century California child to do. Like catching tiddlers in a jam jar or scrumping apples over a garden wall.

"From the slough," said Kathi. "At a guess."

"What's a *sloo*?" I said. All four of them, even the kid, stared at me.

"Don't you ever look out of your windows?" said Todd. "Last Ditch Slough. The river? That runs along behind the motel?"

"I've been busy," I told him. "What's your name?" I asked the child.

"Diego," he said. "And I knew what a slough is."

"Well, see the thing is, Diego," I went on, "those frogs you hatched need to go back and live in the slough now. You did a great thing taking care of them, but now they need to go and live in the river. They won't be happy out of it. You need to set them free."

"Like Nemo?" he asked. His eyes grew wider and a couple of the brimming tears brimmed properly and splashed.

"Lose the Hoover," I said to Kathi out of the corner of my mouth. "Just like Nemo," I told Diego. "And speaking of Nemo, I bet Kathi and Noleen wouldn't mind if you had

115

a pet goldfish, would they?" I turned and glared at Kathi. "Would they?"

"But if a goldfish turns into a hamster . . ." she said.

"We'll all be in the news," I finished. "Diego, if you and your mama can put the froggies back in the slough this morning, I'll bring you back a goldfish this afternoon. Or we can all go to the pet shop and you can choose one."

"Chihuahua adoption event," said Della, out of the corner of her mouth. She was better at it than me.

"I'll bring one for you," I said firmly and, still holding Todd's hand, I walked away. "Can I borrow your car?" I said. "And can you tell me where the nearest pet shop is?" I gave his hand a squeeze. "And will you let me help you?"

"Three yeses," Todd said. "But I get to buy bras and you have to wear them."

While he went to fetch the keys to the spare car that he and Roger only used at the weekend, Kathi came back from her cleaning cupboard, minus wet vac.

"Okay about the goldfish?" I said.

She nodded. She was a stern-looking woman. Could have given Korean dictators hot tips for their headshots. "Nolly said you were some kind of shrink," she said. "You helping Todd?"

"I'm going to try," I said. "I'm not a psychiatrist, though. I'm a psychologist. In Scotland. Here I'm not even that. Just a friendly ear."

Kathi shrugged. "Psychiatrists just want to fill you full of drugs and write papers," she said. "One friend is more use than every shrink in America stuck on the same skewer." I nodded as if it was an expression I heard every day. "I help Todd and he helps me, you see," Kathi said. "I want him to get better, sure I do, but I'll miss him when he's gone."

"Helps you do what?" I asked.

"Keeps Noleen off me," said Kathi. Then Todd was back and I couldn't press her any more.

The "spare car" was a black Jeep glittering with chrome and without a speck of dust on it anywhere, even in the wheel arches. If Todd and Roger used it to go off-roading, they must put carpet down first. Todd waved me off, perfectly unconcerned about me being in charge of it, and thankfully I was out of his sightline before I turned the wrong way onto the main road and had to swerve out of the way of a UPS truck.

"Drive on the right," I told myself. "Drive on the right and stop at the stop signs."

As long as I remembered things like that, I would be okay.

EIGHT

I was half convinced that either no one would answer the bell at the gate at all, or that they wouldn't let me in once they heard it was me. I was hatching a plan to threaten them with a call to the *Cuento Voyager*. Elder abuse and false imprisonment would put a kink in Clovis Bombaro's will no matter which of them he had meant to take over the fizz-bang now he was gone.

To my surprise, the voiceless presence who answered my ring buzzed me in and when I arrived at the top of the drive the door was open.

I had never seen the inside of the Bombaro residence since, the last thirty-six hours aside, I usually try for a bit of professional distance. And even the gates and landscaping hadn't prepared me. On the one hand, the depiction of actual fireworks was restricted to an oil painting above the sitting room fireplace, the embroidery on a few cushions here and there, and, well yes, the fountain in the stairwell. On the other hand, the overall approach to décor made fireworks look a bit drab in comparison. It was as if the decorator Saddam Hussein had fired for vulgarity had come straight here and doubled down.

More things in the house were gold than I would ever have dreamed *came* in gold. Door handles, window latches, and light switches I was ready for, but there was a gold fireplace, a gold remote control on a gold-and-glass coffee table, and, when I followed the coffee aroma into the kitchen, I saw a gold dishwasher. That's only four things, but as well as the gold there were a lot of mirrors, so it seemed like more.

My hair looked fantastic, I noticed, as I walked along a mirrored hallway between the public rooms and the service area. My fringe was shorter than I'd had it before, a kick off a Lisbet, but because Todd had plucked my eyebrows too, I looked pretty sharp.

Mizz Vi was sitting at a round table in a round bay that bulged out of the kitchen and overlooked the back garden, with its rose terrace, koi pond, and the inevitable, enormous, bright-blue swimming pool. She looked even smaller than she had in the

120

courtroom the day before and her eyes were red-rimmed and baggy-looking.

"Oh, you little love!" I said and surged forward with a hug. Professional distance has its places and this wasn't one of them. "Did you sleep at all?"

"I drifted," said Visalia. "I kept dreaming and waking up again."

"You know what I'm going to say next, don't you?"

"Go to the doctor, get some pills," she said, nodding. I had advised it even for the stress of divorce. I'm a great believer in the wonders of modern medicine and I never understand why the same people who get their flu shots like lambs every autumn and take an aspirin for a headache won't take the edge off misery with a little tab of magic that's been tested and retested and works every time. And then they do it with daiquiris anyway.

"Have the police spoken to you again?" I asked her. She shook her head and I could tell from the way she moved that it was pounding. "They came to me," I said.

"And what did you tell them?"

"Well, Vi, to be perfectly honest, I didn't know what to tell them. You could have fanned me flat with a flapjack when I looked at Serpentina's business card and saw her married name."

"I never thought I'd be happy Cousin Clovis was dead," said Vi, in a tiny voice, "but I'm glad he didn't live to see his own niece marry his bitterest rival." She heaved a mammoth sigh and lay back against the cushions of her seat with her eyes closed. "So *what* did you tell the police?" she murmured faintly.

"Well, I told them about what Clovis suspected about the Dolshikovs," I said. I thought she would be angry, but if anything her face smoothed out a bit. "And told them about Serpentina marrying into the Capulets and bringing a contingent of them here to your house." She looked positively serene now. "And I told them about Bar— the other woman." She was smiling. "But I didn't tell them about the Poggios."

"You didn't?" she said, snapping to attention. "Why not?"

"It seemed kind of . . . . How can I put this? Beyond nutso. I will, next time I see them, if you want me to."

"Of course I *want* you to. The Poggio family have murdered my darling Cousin Clovis, Lexy. And not only do the police not know that, they're actually trying to build a case against me. *Me!* A little old lady who loved him more than her own life."

122

"Not just you," I said. "They think I'm involved too. So, listen. Here's one thing we can do to get them off of us both. Have you got any evidence that Clovis knew about the Fourth of July appointment? Did he set it up?"

"No," she said. "That was me. Why not just tell them it was the Poggios?"

"Well, is it written on your kitchen calendar or did you forward the email to him?" I said, ignoring her.

"You youngsters," said Mizz Visalia. "We've never emailed each other in our lives. We lived in the same house. We slept in the same bed."

I knew this to be true, odd as it seems. Even at their worst moments, Clovis and Vi Bombaro shared a bedroom. Sometimes they rowed all night and came to therapy exhausted and still furious, but they had never moved to separate rooms. Of course, now that I'd seen their house, I reckoned the bedroom was probably big enough to hold a dance in and the bed itself might have space for two separate fiefdoms with a pillow border in between.

"Or have you got ticket receipts or anything pertaining to your upcoming emigra— What?"

She had shushed me. "Sparky doesn't

123

know," she breathed. "She doesn't know we were planning to leave."

"What's the problem with Sparky knowing?" I breathed back. When she didn't answer, I went on, "But *do* you? Because as of now, the cops think you masterminded the whole thing and set me up as your alibi."

"Why would I make such a mess of removing the timer if I had set up an alibi?" she said. "That's what they're saying, aren't they? That there was a timer and then there wasn't?"

"Yeah, about that," I said. "How do they know?"

"You think they tell me?" She had never sounded more like Clovis.

"Can't you guess, though?" I said. "How much do you know about the technicalities of setting fireworks?"

Mizz Visalia shrugged. "I never took an interest in that side of the business," she said. "Helped out a little in the early days, mostly bookkeeping, then I did the galas and luncheons once things looked up. If I had tried to . . . do that, we'd both have blown to smithereens."

"Well, but cast your mind back to those early days," I said. "What would the signs of a timer be?"

"Wire," said a voice, making us both jump.

124

Serpentina Dolshikov — was there ever a name that sounded more villainous? — was standing in the archway that led to some kind of dining room. I knew it wasn't *the* dining room, because I had walked through that, and clearly Vi and I were sitting in the breakfast nook, but since posh Americans need three different places to watch telly — a living room and a family room and a den — no doubt they needed three different places to never use while they ate out every night.

"It's not that complicated," Serpentina said. She was dressed for a practice round of golf. It was a look I knew well from Branston and Brandeee: visor, cargo shorts, polo shirt. This particular polo shirt had a logo that looked like a whale's spout (I was learning that fireworks were hard to depict in wrought-iron, floral bedding, or — as here — silver thread) and the wordoid *BOOMSHIK-A!* printed underneath in metallic lettering.

"Boomshik-a?" I said, nodding at her bosom.

"Unity," said Serpentina. "I united the two families and I'm working on the businesses. Bombaro Pyrotechnics plus Dolshikov Pyrotasia equals Boomshik-a!"

I turned to Mizz Vi. I wish I had Mike the

cop's eyebrows. Even one of them.

"Sparky isn't that . . . street," said Vi. Like she was.

"So," I said. "You were saying . . . wire?"

"An electric match with a remote switch would be the safest way," Sparky said. "A timer, an actual timer, is not something any responsible pyrotechnician would ever recommend."

"Neither is . . ." I said, then cleared my throat and stopped.

"Using an old man's butt crack as a launch stand," said Mizz Vi. It was her old man and so her call, I supposed.

"The cops probably said 'timer,' " Serpentina went on, "because they think in terms of bombs. But if all they're going on is something removed — a cut wire — there's nothing to say what it was. Wouldn't you think it was a remote switch, Auntie?"

"Talk me through it," I said. "The electric-match-plus-remote option and the timer."

"Timer first," said Mizz Vi. "Sparky, I wouldn't be so quick to assume the cops don't know what they're looking at. And a timer is much more . . . I mean, I would think a timer is something that every penny-ante crook in the world would know something about. An electric match and a remote switch is going to have the cops looking . . .

close to home."

"Everyone with a laptop knows everything these days, Auntie," said Sparky. She turned to me. "The electric match is a given, either way. Straight up and down little pack of pyrogen and a bridge wire. You could plug it into a wall socket on a timer — very dangerous, as I said — or you could plug it into a wall socket with a remote switch. Then you could walk the site and make sure no kids or dogs or gophers were around." She had completely forgotten what we were talking about. She was giving her bog-standard firework-safety speech. "Afterwards, if no one came back," she said, "you'd be left with a burnt-out wire still attached to the plug in the outlet. So if someone wanted to make it look as if . . ." she stopped. "That's stupid," she said.

I was trying not to think about it too much but even just peeking through my mental fingers with my mental eyes half shut, I got it.

"The firework wouldn't still be attached to the wire," I said. "It would get ruptured" — Bad choice of words; we all winced — "it would get *detached* when the firework went off?"

"Whichever way the fuse was joined to the wire, it would get blown apart," Sparky said.

"So whoever it was who went back would just remove the whole device. Unplug it and take it away."

"If they had any sense, yeah," said Sparky. She was standing with her hands on her hips, looking at both of us as if we'd forgotten we were doing the snacks at the PTA. Before Vi or me caved and apologised for affronting her, we heard what sounded like troops advancing. Actually it was only the three Dolshikov men, all wearing work boots, marching in lockstep along the tiled hall.

"Jan thought we'd go into the factory, Auntie," Sparky said.

"See if anything needs attention," Jan added. "What's the manager's name? Department supervisors? Passkey codes?"

"Just to take it off your hands-platemind!" said one of the cousins. Jan scowled at him and I found myself wondering if he had been given instructions, then fluffed his lines. And that made me think about the stupidity of the clean-up guy and if *he'd* failed to follow clear instructions too.

I liked these cousins. In the cop sense. I liked the way their necks were wider than their heads and the way they had gone with buzz cuts to look butch even though their necks were wider than their heads. I liked the way the one breathed through his mouth and the other cracked his knuckles and the way they refused coffee and went to the fridge for soft drinks. These were not men of urbanity. These were exactly the meat-head sort to remove half the evidence and turn it into a bigger clue.

"Alex," said Sparky. "Peter." I didn't feel so bad about considering 'Boris' and 'Ivan' now. "Are you coming with Jan and me?"

"We've been in touch with milk memo," said Peter. He had a light, clear voice with just a trace of Boston about it so I was sure I hadn't misheard the words. As to what the Hecate's hat he was on about . . . I kept listening. "We need to lodge our Clarence ducks but then we thought we'd go visit. They're having great results with their tee-moprawg." At the end he totally lost me.

"With their what was that?" I said.

"Teen mom prog," said Peter. "Program to retain teenaged mothers until graduation?"

"Clearance docs!" I said. I aimed my brain at 'milk memo' but got nowhere.

"Alex and Peter are co-founders of a nonprofit for troubled kids," Sparky said. "Harvey Milk Memorial High School right here in Cuento is ground-breaking in the area of retention and accelerated graduation, you know."

I didn't know. I was the kind of person who would look at a short haircut and decide a guy probably wasn't allowed near the business end of a firework factory when in fact he was a renowned philanthropist. I knew *nothing*.

Anyway, Mizz Vi had another candidate for the moron who cut the wire. Once the Dolshikov contingent had scattered, she took up the topic again. I didn't know that to begin with, mind you.

"The Poggios have been living on the same hillside since God made dirt," she said.

"Uh huh," I said. "And so . . . Can you nudge me into a category, Vi? They stay there because . . . house prices, homesickness?"

"Small gene pool," she supplied, for all the world like she hadn't married her cousin. "The Poggios are not the brightest stars in heaven. Although, now you mention it, they do hang on to their property and ride out boom and bust just the same. All the same, they're dumb enough to be wire cutters."

"Right," I said. "I'll be sure and mention that to the detective when I see her. And I'll be sure and see her soon. And while I'm at it . . . Now, don't get upset. Promise me?"

"Why would I get upset?" she said, fishing a balled-up Kleenex from inside her cardigan sleeve and touching it to her eyes. It was a stagey gesture but her eyelids were crushed and fuchsia-pink and the Kleenex had been well-used for something.

I reached out and stroked her shoulder gently. "What's Barbara's second name?" I said. "I'm going to track her down and grill her."

Mizz Vi made a fist and brought it down with a thump on the tabletop so hard that Alex's drained Coke can wobbled and fell off to roll across the kitchen floor sprinkling little droplets of Coke like a string of beads.

"You can mop that up," Vi said. I hopped to my feet, pulled a skein of kitchen roll off the dispenser and then skated around on it with one bare foot until it stopped sticking.

"It's almost as though you're protecting her," I said. "You won, Vi. He chose you. He gave her up and came back to you . . . briefly. You really should try to let this anger go."

"I'm not protecting her!" Mizz Visalia said. "I'm not even angry with her. I'm angry with him. I'm going to have him cremated and scatter his ashes at . . . at . . . Where should I scatter his ashes, Lexy?"

"To bug him, you mean? After you've gone to his funeral in a red dress?"

"Pants!" she said. "Red leather pants. And I'll scatter his ashes at Ikea. There's nowhere on Earth he hated more."

"It's healthy for you not to bottle things up," I said, "but as your therapist and your friend, I want to encourage you not to make any decisions you might come to regret."

"Oh, phooey!" said Visalia. "I don't mean it. His funeral is going to be spectacular and my dressmaker is coming to fit me for weeds after lunch today. Unless it's an orange jumpsuit I'm in for."

"Tell me her name and let me track her down," I said again, insistently. Therapy is half listening and half nagging, when you get right down to it.

"Her name is Barbara Skanky-Ho. And I can give you the address of the Duplex of Shame. She was on my Christmas card list for five years before I knew he was . . . Oh! If he wasn't dead already, I'd kill him."

She had risen while she spoke and now was rootling through a junk drawer at the far end of the run of kitchen units. I was glad somehow to see that even in this Taj Mahal to the optional nature of taste (with its gold dishwasher) there was still a junk drawer in the kitchen. Mizz Vi dumped out phone chargers, cigarette lighters, empty blister packs from batteries, cable ties, playing cards, and three different shapes of novelty pickle forks before she found what she was looking for. An address book of great vintage with envelopes tucked inside the front cover and a pocket for stamps. The second page of the Ts had been gouged through with the point of a pen. She snorted at it and sent it up the table towards me like a curling stone.

With a bit of patience and some Sellotape I managed to repair the tattered shreds and decipher that Barbara's last name was actually Truman and that the Duplex of Shame was on one of the flower streets right there in Cuento. I asked Vi if she wanted to come with me, ducked the look that came in return, and then left. Her hairdresser was coming at ten, she assured me and she would be fine with the TV until then.

Again the thought passed over me that Sparky and the Dolshikovs were absolutely bloody useless at succour; no way they should be visiting high schools and factories today. Then I was putting 357 Gerbera Drive in my GPS and I was on my way.

NINE

A duplex, it turned out, isn't some kind of futuristic living pod with nutrients piped in and wastes piped out. It's a semi-detached house. Well, it's a California semi-detached house; that is, a garage with living quarters included. The joined-on house next door, 355 Gerbera Drive, had green grass, geraniums in ceramic pots, red-white-and-blue bunting along the porch, and a little covered wagon at the entrance to the drive with surplus courgettes and tomatoes FREE!

357 Gerbera Drive, where Barbara S H Truman was (I hoped) to be found, had brown grass, Tibetan prayer flags along the porch, dried twigs in plastic pots, and nothing at the entrance to the drive except two yellowed newspapers, still rolled up inside their elastic bands, one of which had been driven over.

I picked them up as I walked towards the door, but two days in the sunshine had made them more like pastries than reading matter and after some bits flaked off and fell to the ground, I lobbed them into the heart of a rosemary bush and wiped the dust off my hands.

She answered my knock after about the length of time it would take to put down a whisky bottle, pull your bathrobe shut, and shuffle to the door. She still had the glass in her hand, and when she saw it was a woman she let her bathrobe drop open again. Underneath she was wearing a halter-necked playsuit in a print of orange-and-black hibiscus.

"Barbara?" I said, looking into her eyes. Her puffy, mascara-streaked, sleep-deprived, and slightly crossed from all the whisky eyes. "I take it you've heard? About Clovi—"

"Don't say that bastard's name to me," she said. "He dumped me. He led me on and got my hopes up and then . . . he dumped me. He didn't even have the guts to tell me to my face. So you can go right back to . . . who are you anyway?"

"I'm Clovis and Visalia's . . ." I considered it. I should have checked with Mizz Vi that it was all right to go public. But therapy isn't as embarrassing in California as it is in Dundee. And being in therapy isn't as embarrassing as being arrested for murder *anywhere.* "I'm their marriage guidance counsellor," I said and then gasped as the whisky hit me.

"Thanks for not throwing the glass," I said, dripping.

"So you helped them work it out?" said Barbara. She spun away to get a refill and bounced off a couple of walls en route. Looking at the trailing dressing-gown belt, I thought I should follow.

"Apparently," I said. "I thought I was helping them through an amicable divorce. I'm sorry."

"And was it your idea for him to let me know by *not turning up at the fricking airport*?" she said, slopping a good belt into the glass and then holding the bottle out to me. "Want some?" she said. "More?" she added, with a smile.

"I'm driving," I said. "Are you telling me you didn't know? You actually went to the airport?" I took another look at the hibiscus-printed playsuit. It was exactly what someone might wear to run off to the Cayman Islands with their sugar daddy. She must have been sitting drinking and crying nonstop since she finally gave up and came back here.

"Four *hours* I waited," she said. "And he hasn't answered his phone since I got back.

So you can go tell him from me that he's an asshole and a jerk and he *does* look his age and his hairpiece *is* lame and his breath from those cigars could stun a monkey."

"Oh God," I said. "The newspapers on the drive!"

"Oh gimme a break," said Barbara. "I get it every day from little Miss Yoga Pants next door. The yard, the mail, the raccoons in the attic."

"Ha!" I said. "*Grey Gardens* fan?" As a marriage guidance therapist, I don't approve of infidelity. And as the recent dupe of Branston and Brandeee, I wasn't too keen on mistresses at a personal level, either. But it would be pointless to deny that I quite liked Barbara on first impressions, whisky-throwing and all. I didn't relish what I was going to have to do to her.

"The thing is," I said, sitting down so she would sit down, "Clovis didn't stand you up." It was a technicality, but it might help. "He met with a mishap on the Fourth of July. Around teatime. Happy hour," I translated. I had seldom felt so disoriented (strictly, disoccidented) as the day I realised no one knew when teatime was. It was like being on another planet, where the days didn't have twenty-four hours anymore. How could there not be teatime? I shook

137

myself back to the dim little living room where Barbara, eyes focussed, was waiting to hear more.

"He was very seriously hurt," I said. "By a firework."

"But he's okay," she said. Then, when I didn't agree, she turned it into a question. "Is he okay?"

"I'm afraid not," I told her. "He didn't survive."

It took her a blink or two to process that. It always does. That's what makes it such a good way to break the news, a nurse once told me. "He died instantly," I added, once she had taken in the first fact. Why not say that if you possibly can, is my philosophy. "He didn't suffer," I added. And in this case it was true. Clovis's face — I would never get it out of my head if I lived to be a redwood — had clearly shown that he died thinking "What — ?" and hadn't even made it to "the — ?"

"Clovis is dead?" said Barbara. "A firework accident? I don't believe it! He was killed by a firework? After seventy Fourth of Julys? Fourths ofs . . . No way. I don't believe it. He was a lot of fun to hang out with until — until! — you got him on to firework safety and then you wanted to tear your own arm off and beat yourself to d— I don't

138

believe it. And he wasn't working this Fourth anyway. He was coming away to the Caymans with me."

"It wasn't an accident," I said. "Barbara, you need to prepare yourself for a shock." She blinked and then took a slurp of whisky like a good girl. "Clovis was murdered."

She nodded, took another healthy glug, and then smacked her lips. "Have you found his will?" she said. I managed not to look surprised, but she went down in my estimation a little.

"I'm not sure what paperwork the family has gone through yet," I said.

"Because I wasn't interested in his money," she said, surprising me and going up again. She didn't quite get the syllables dispersed around the words in the usual way, but I could tell she meant it. "I was adamant that he shouldn't leave that twisted old bitch penniless while he came off with me to enjoy the rest of his life."

It was halfway to being kind. In a nasty sort of way.

"So I had no motive, you see," she said.

"But you've got an alibi anyway," I reminded her. "Were you checked in?"

"Are you kidding?" said Barbara. "I was so angry with him for standing me up, if I was checked in I'd have got on the plane without him. I'd be there now. No, I hadn't gone through security yet. I have no alibi."

"But someone must have seen you," I said. I glanced down at the play suit and up at her face again. She was sixty if a day and either she spent a lot of time outdoors or she'd worked on her tan in preparation for the trip, but she did look quite memorable.

"San Francisco airport on the Fourth of July?" she said.

"Have you got that Fastrak in your car?" I said. "For going over the bridges? That's always giving people alibis in Harlan Coben books. The New Jersey one, whatever it's called."

"Cash lane," said Barbara, shaking her head.

"But I bet there's loads of cameras on the freeway," I said. "I really wouldn't worry if I were you. If you didn't know he had changed his mind about the divorce and you were waiting at the airport, you had no motive, alibi or not."

She had gone very still. I wondered if she was going to throw up. From the empty jars and wrappers strewn around, she had eaten quite a bit of raw biscuit mix and neat peanut butter and the level in the whisky bottle was low enough so's you'd put it on the shopping list for next time you were at Bevmo.

I was wrong. Drunk as she was, she was still thinking straighter than me.

"He changed his mind?" she said.

"Shit."

"He changed his mind about the divorce?"

"Bugger it."

"He only didn't dump me because he died before he got the chance?!"

"Barbara, I'm really sorry," I said. I had done so well with the *didn't survive* decoding task and the *died instantly* bullshit, and now I had destroyed her anyway. "Yes, I'm afraid so. Clovis and Visalia had reconciled in the days before his death and were planning to go to Trapani together."

"In the days before?" she echoed. "But he was round here on the third. We were online looking up seafood restaurants for our first night's dinner. Clovis was useless at all that. That's why we weren't checked in. He wouldn't let me pay and he couldn't do it himself. He was the only man in the world who still used a travel agent." She shook her head and smiled. Then she shook it faster, scowling. "I am so wasted," she said. "I forgot what you told me! The bastard went back to that swivel-eyed bitch for more, did he? And where's Trapani? If it's the resort we were booked in at, I will kill . . . Yeah, well, I'll dance on his grave."

"Sicily," I said. "They were going home to Sicily."

"Home!" said Barbara. "Unless Sicily is a neighborhood in Bakersfield they were no more going home than me heading for the Caymans."

I couldn't help myself, I still liked her.

"Can I make you a pot of coffee?" I said. "You need to speak to the cops and see if you can help them — they're baffled at the mo. But you know what they're like. If you go in hammered, they'll hold it against you."

"You make the coffee and I'll go and stick my toothbrush down my throat," she said. "Half an hour, I'll be good as new."

"You again," said Mike as I ushered Barbara into the Cuento cop shop not much more than half an hour later, indeed.

If Barbara had purged, she had done it quietly and without making her eyes water. She had emerged from her bedroom dressed in a black wrap dress and with her hair in a chignon. She added patent court shoes and huge dark glasses and looked like more of a widow than Jackie and Yoko combined. She drank the coffee I made like a drain drinks bleach and scarfed down a breakfast burrito she made me stop for and, by the time Mike clapped eyes on her, she was frail from grieving rather than wrecked from booze.

"I'm bringing a witness," I said and Mike, who had been crossing the foyer with a bouquet of helium balloons in one hand and a toddler's tricycle in the other, stopped, wheeled round, and came over. I wondered if she'd explain. I felt I was owed it for not mentioning the teddy bear the other day, but here's a newsflash: Cops never explain anything. You could find a cop sliding naked down a banister at the mall with a carnation up his . . . let's say *nose* . . . and he would just give you the cop scowl and tell you not to loiter.

"Witness?" she said, scowling. "You saw Clovis Bombaro die?"

"No!" said Barbara. "But I can assure you that he hadn't decided to stick with the devil he knew and go die in an olive grove. If you check his financials you'll see he had two first-class seats booked for Grand Cayman and a cottage right on the beach on Little Cayman rented for a month. He was divorcing her and coming away with me. She killed him. You can bank on it."

"Whoa!" I said. "Where did that come from? I didn't bring you down here to drop Mizz Vi in the shitter."

143

"We *did* find airline tickets," Mike said. "They were in his safe. Paper tickets in a cardboard folder, from a travel agent. Paid for with Mr. Bombaro's Visa card."

"There you go then," said Barbara. "And you let her out on *bail*?"

"Barbara," I said, "I know you're angry, but you have no evid—"

"We didn't find any divorce papers," Mike said.

"So she burned them," Barb said.

"Not anywhere at the house," Mike said. "There's no burn barrel and there was no ash in any of the fireplaces."

"She flushed them."

"We checked the drains."

"So she shredded them and put them in a dumpster at a rest stop on the freeway!" Barbara said. She was making a disturbing amount of sense, actually. I marvelled at Mike's thoroughness, going through bin bags and peering into drains, but I didn't see her point. If I had a pile of paper I wanted rid of, it wouldn't be beyond me. A dumpster at a rest stop on the freeway — exactly. I might not use those words but I could chuck a load of A4 in a big bin at a motorway services with the best of them.

"Let me take care of one thing," Mike said, presumably referring to the balloons

144

and tricycle, "and then if you have time right now, I'd like to interview you."

"I'm eager to help in any way I can," Barbara said. "Until the murderess is brought to justice my poor Boom-Boom won't really be at rest."

Mike nodded, did a bit of eyebrowology, and backed away.

I followed, calling over my shoulder to Barbara, "I'll get you a nice cup of tea, Barb." Quietly to Mike I said, "I'm Miss Truman's therapist. And she's had a severe shock. I'd like to accompany her to the interview."

"No way," said Mike.

"A very severe shock," I said. "And she's here without her service animal."

"There is no need and there is no way," said Mike.

"Unless you're actually detaining Miss Truman?" I said. "Of course if you Samantha her, I withdraw my request."

"Miranda," said Mike.

"Her too. Look, what's the harm in me being there to support her?"

"Ms. Campbell," said Mike, "Ms. Truman is a person of interest in a murder enquiry. This isn't a quilting bee."

"What is it you know?" I said.

"Well," said Mike, "I know you're not her

therapist and I know she has no service animal."

"I don't mean that," I said. "I can tell you don't believe her about the Caymans, but why not?"

"I can't share information about an ongoing investigation with my *mother*," said Mike. "Why would I share it with you?"

"Right," I said. "Good point. I'll get her that cup of tea."

"You wouldn't," said Mike. "What harm did she ever do you?"

I thought of a better information source anyway. After cooling my heels in the lobby of the cop shop for an hour, slowly learning that a Tuesday morning was the dead time in small-town law enforcement, when even the dispatcher is finding out which ten child stars grew up insanely ugly, I dropped Barbara at home, promised to tell her when the funeral was, and went back to Vi. I couldn't get the memory of her in that enormous gold kitchen out of my mind, so small and crumpled in her little dress and cardi, while her family left her to it.

I had forgotten the hairdresser had been. Visalia looked much more like her old self when she came to the door. She had heels on. Peep-toe slingbacks and bare legs, and as she turned and walked away again, leading me to the sun room, I could see that her heels were round and smooth. I felt my own scrape against the rubber of my flip flops with every step and marvelled at her. Her hair was teased up into the usual pastel cloud and she had put a little make-up on. More adeptly than usual, I thought.

"You seem more . . ." I said, sweeping my gaze all the way up and down. I stared at her toenails. "Have you actually had a pedicure?" I said. Her toenails were ten perfect little shells. No way a woman of eighty-six with her knees and her eyes could bend down and see to do that.

"My hairdresser," she said. "She stayed an hour and a half. Cancelled her next two appointments and straightened me out. A facial, a massage, mani-pedi, *and* my hair. It helps. You should know, Lexy. You don't look like yourself this morning, either."

"Well, good for her," I said. "People can be kind when push comes to shove, can't they?"

I was thinking of Todd and my new short fringe and whatever it was he did that helped Kathi, and thank God I did because it reminded me that I had to find a minute today to buy a goldfish.

"I could face the police now," Mizz Vi

said. "I hid when they came back yesterday with their warrant."

"Warrant?" I said. "Who did they arrest?"

"Search warrant," Mizz Vi said. "They opened the safe and took everything. Bank statements, house title, insurance documents. They took all the paperwork for the Trapani condo. I mean, they gave me receipts; I'm not worried. But they were everywhere, Lexy. They went through the trash. They took out the sink traps."

"Yeah," I said. "So I heard." What I *hadn't* heard was that Mike had found deeds for the Sicily property. That must be why she wasn't buying Barbara's story. Did the Trapani deed drop Barb in it? Who knew, but maybe it put Mizz Vi in the clear.

"Did they find airline tickets?" I asked.

"Everything is on the receipt," she told me.

"Does it say where the tickets are for?" I said, thinking he was maybe hedging his bets, buying the condo, renting the cottage, buying *two* sets of plane seats, hoping there'd be a sign at the eleventh hour to help him decide where to fly off to and with whom.

"We can check," said Mizz Vi. "I put it right in the safe as soon as they left and changed the combo. I think the receipt probably just says 'miscellaneous papers.' But then I guess . . . you see it on the police shows all the time. One crooked detective when no one's looking and poof! A suitcase of drugs with a street value of millions and it's gone, and the case collapses, and his partner doesn't trust him and he can't sleep and his wife is out of her head with worry and can't tell anyone what's wrong."

"I don't watch that kind of show," I said. "But I tell you what. Why don't I check the receipt and you can change the combination again after I've gone?"

She gave me a sharp look.

"I just want to save you running about," I said. "You look so much better. You should conserve your energy. You'll need it later."

"I will," said Vi. She smiled suddenly. "Father Adam is coming to discuss the funeral. And when Sparky gets back she's going to help me draw up the guest list. It's 1234. Upstairs in our — in my bedroom."

"1234?" I said. "That's a very bad idea, you know."

"I'll change it, like you said," she said. "Run along like a good girl and save my old legs. You're kind to think of it, Lexy. You were always so kind."

I got to my feet and headed back to the hallway. In truth, sitting in a conservatory

in California in July was extremely uncom-
fortable. The sun was beating in fit to
bounce off a watch face and start a wildfire
and so Visalia had the a/c cranked up to
'gulag.' I was freezing. It had been the one
argument that Bran and I had managed to
settle into properly during our short marriage. He kept the car like a meat safe and I
thought it was daft to have to put a jumper
on to drive when the sun was cracking the
flags. And we only had one car so we
couldn't go in a convoy.

I was halfway up the first flight of sweeping steps, feeling like Miss Ellie Ewing,
when I remembered what I had been forgetting to ask for two days. I turned back
before it popped out of my head again.

"Vi?" I said, as I reached the conservatory
door. Mizz Vi was sitting jabbing furiously
at an iPhone with her jaw set off-centre, her
mouth shut like a rat-trap, and her eyes narrowed to slits. She shrieked when she heard
me and flubbed the phone, sending it shoot-
ing up out of her death grip and trying twice
to catch it before it eluded her and fell to
the floor.

TEN

"Sorry!" I said. "I didn't mean to startle you."

"That was quick," Visalia said. "Did I get the number wro— Oh my God!" She stared at me and her face paled.

"What?" I said, darting a look behind me.

"If I've forgotten the number to the safe, what am I going to do?"

"I haven't —" I said, but she was up and away.

"I should never have changed it," she wailed. "The policeman told me I had to and he told me not to write the number down anywhere. He was very definite. But it's all right for him. He's not a poor old widow woman all alone in the world. Oh, Lexy, what am I going to do without him? What will I *do*?"

"I hadn't got to the bedroom yet," I said very loud and low. "I turned back. To ask you something."

Mizz Vi sat back and passed a hand over her forehead. "What?" she said. "What did you want to ask me?"

"Why were you and Clovis coming to see me separately on the Fourth? Why were you alone when your tyre blew out and when he . . . ?"

"Oh," she said. "Well, you might think this is silly. But we were . . . As far as we were concerned, we were starting again, you see. We wanted to come and meet. Like the first time we met. And really properly start again."

"Hmph," I said. "Right. Well, that makes sense." Except that the first time they met was at a family party when two sisters let their kids play together as cousins do. (Yes, it still bothered me, even if the state of California didn't mind.) "And whose idea was it?" I said, hoping the question wasn't too transparent.

"To drive separately?" said Mizz Vi. She screwed her face up trying to remember. "Mine, I think," she came back with at last. She smiled sadly. "But it wasn't hard to persuade him. He was always a romantic, my poor Clovis."

"Maybe," I began, "if the detective asks, you could say it was *his* idea. Beat yourself up a bit for agreeing. That kind of thing."

She regarded me for quite a while before she spoke again. Her eyes weren't quite the lumps of coal in the puddle, but they weren't pools of warmth either. "You really do think I did it, don't you?"

"What? No! Of course not," I said. "But it wouldn't do you any harm at all to help. Remember what's at stake? Starts with an *h*?"

"Hang?" said Visalia. "Is that what you mean? Hang, my fanny. I'd get life without parole in a country club. It would pretty much be free nursing care. And it's lethal injection these days, anyway."

"What makes you so sure?" I said. "And don't say 'fanny,' for God's sake."

"Sparky looked it up. And why not?"

"Never mind." I dropped to all fours to get her phone back, fishing it out from where it had gone skiting away under the table on the polished floor. I didn't hit any buttons or anything; nothing was further from my mind. Only, when I moved it, it came back to life. And so I glanced down. Of course I did. Because when something lights up in your hand, you look.

"I'll let you finish your text," I said. I didn't mean anything by it. It was two sets of speech bubbles on a phone. I never thought a thing.

"Text?" said Visalia. "Lemme see that. What text? I'm not sending any 'text'!"

"Sorry," I said, returning the phone to her and then putting my hands behind my back (never touched it, Mum, don't spank me). "It must have gone to an old one when you dropped it."

"I was looking at photographs of Cousin Clovis," Visalia said. She bowed her head and started muttering and fluttering over her phone as though it was a little square rosary. "What will I do if you've deleted them? How will I get them back? How many times did I tell myself to print them out and paste them in an album? Oh! Oh!"

"Vi!" I said. "Visalia! None of your photos will have gone. Don't upset yourself. Give it here and I'll find them for you."

"No!" she squawked, clutching it to her.

"I promise I won't —" I got out before she plopped the phone down the neck of her sundress and sat back.

"I'll check it later," she said.

I counted to ten in my head. Yes, dear reader, I counted to ten. After five years of college study, four hundred hours of accreditation and six years of clinical practice, nothing better had ever occurred to me. Count to ten, don't go to bed angry, and if you can't say something kind, write a memoir and hit the talk shows.

I only needed six anyway. I had liked Visalia from the very first time I saw her, borderline-incest notwithstanding, and given her current plight, I could forgive a lot more than a bit of intemperate random blaming.

"Vi," I said, gentle as a kitten whisperer, "I really do think you should try to speak to your doctor today. I'm sure your hairdresser helped a lot and of course *I'm* always here for you, but you're not yourself — How could you be? — and your doctor can help."

"Not myself?" she said. "What does that mean?"

"Upset," I told her. "Keyed up, strung out, done in."

"It's shock and grief," she said. "It's nothing medical. It's just sadness. Of course I'm sad."

"Of course you are."

"Who wouldn't be?" she asked. "And scared. The Poggios could be after me too."

"Who indeed." I ignored the bit about the Poggios.

"It would be stranger if I *were* myself. When the Poggios have broken my heart."

"Much stranger." I ignored the bit about the Poggios again.

And, as she talked of her sadness some

more and shut up about the Poggios at last, she seemed to settle into it. Her shoulders slumped and her eyes grew strained. She took a huge struggle of a breath and, as it left her, she sank back into the plushy, floral cushion of her rattan chair and seemed to slightly disappear among its buttoned bulges and splots of colour.

I gave her a small smile. Then I crept out, crossed the foyer, and took the sweep of stairs up to the bedroom landing.

It was obvious which door — real doors! — led to the master bedroom. It was pillared and there were urns of ivy and ficus set on either side. But behind it, at last, some of the splendour relented. Here in their bedroom the Bombaros had left off impressing and reverted to their roots. The furniture looked like family heirlooms; cheap veneer but well cared for and everything matching, even to the valet stand still with a pair of Clovis's suit trousers hanging on it. There were battered paper-backs ranged on both bedside tables: *The Godfather,* surprisingly, and *Eat, Pray, Love* as well as well-thumbed prayer books and Bibles. And, untouched — as pristine as the day they left the Amazon warehouse — the two copies of *Love for a Lifetime: the Journey of Marriage* that I had given Clovis and Vi in the early days of their therapy, that they had assured me they were working through, a chapter a night together.

I gave the books a rueful smile and started looking for the wall safe. It was so badly disguised, behind a generic reproduction of a poppy field that went with nothing else in the room and stuck out a good four inches from the wall, that it might as well have been sitting under a red sign that said SAFE. The picture swung forward and I opened the little door in front of the keypad and punched 1,2,3,4.

Irrcorrect, it read in blocky LCD. Two atterrrpts rerrrairrirrg.

"1," I said as I typed, "2, 3," I went on, "4."

Irrcorrect, it told me. Orre atterrrpt rerrrairrirrg.

"1234," I offered, rippling over the keypad like a concert pianist in case that was the problem.

Irrcorrect, said the display. Further atterrrpts will trisser alarrrr.

Softly, I shut the little door and swung the picture back. This, I thought, would send her right over the edge. Knowing she'd forgotten the combination would hammer it home for keeps that Clovis was gone and she was alone now.

157

She opened her eyes as I got back to the sunroom but she didn't lift her head.

"Well?"

"No luck," I said. "All the receipt says is 'plane tickets, house deeds, personal papers.' "

She closed her eyes again and was so still for so long that I thought she was sleeping. I jumped when she spoke at last.

"How about the stocks and shares?" she said. "Did they list them or lump them together?" I hesitated. "Or did they leave them behind? Why would they need to take away bonds and share certificates?"

"Um," I said. "For photocopying? To get a rounded picture?" I seemed to have dodged the question of whether they'd actually been taken, and before she could circle back to it the doorbell rang.

Kind of. It was the whistle of a rocket and the bang and shatter as it burst open, of course. I winced and went to answer.

On the doorstep stood a very young, very *California* priest, in cargo shorts, flip-flops, and pedicured toenails, all below a t-shirt depicting a black waistcoat, with a rosary peeking out of one fake pocket and a white dog-collar. His lean brown arms bristled with rubbery concern — *Everytown for Gun Safety; No Planet B;* even a slightly perished and faded *Yes, We Can!*

"Father . . ." I said.

"Adam," he offered, along with a warm and nicely judged handshake. "Are you Sparky?"

"I'm Lexy," I said. "I'm the —"

"Oh, yes," he said, waggling his sculpted eyebrows. "I don't officially approve of you, you know. Smoothing their way to dissolving a sacred union." I had no answer but thankfully he winked and went on, "But I'm glad you're here for her now."

"Ditto," I said. "I was trying to get her to see her doctor, but you're even better."

"I don't know about that," he said. "She was pretty insistent that she only wanted to talk about the funeral. She didn't want the sacrament. Well, actually, I can't offer it without her confession so —"

"Confession?" I said. "You think — ?"

"Her weekly confession," he said. "Saying 'shit' in the shower when she dropped the soap."

I couldn't help laughing. "Have you got your kit with you, though?" I said.

"My kit?"

"Travel pack? A miniature of wine and a snack-pack of crackers?"

Now he was laughing too. "You're not a child of the church, are you, Lexy?"

"I'm making a better job of God's work than he is here today. In my humble opinion." I jerked my head at the garage where the shreds of crime scene tape were fluttering in the thermals as the day drew breath to wipe us all out completely.

"It is hard to see His purpose in Clovis's passing," said Adam, suddenly sounding like any other purple-surpliced bishop.

I snorted. "That old chestnut!" I said. "Tell me this: if it's God's purpose, why do we punish the instrument? When we catch him?"

Give the man his due, he didn't roll his eyes. He took a deep breath and looked for all the world as if he was going to try to answer.

"Or," I said, "maybe now's not the time for debates. Come and see Vi. She needs you."

"Another night?" Noleen was back behind the reception desk at the Last Ditch.

"Do you do weekly rates?" I asked her.

"We do monthly rates too, if you're serious," she said. "And there's a Todd discount." I frowned. "When you're not using any of our furnishings or linens, I can knock off a Jackson."

"But then do I have to wash all my own

sheets and towels?" I said. "Although, I suppose, why not — with the launderette right there."

Noleen's face had clouded, though. "There's ahhhh . . . There's ahhhh . . . It costs extra if you don't take laundry and cleaning from the motel."

"You've got that the wrong way round, haven't you?" I asked.

But Noleen didn't answer. She hopped down from her stool and went to tidy the leaflet rack. Today's t-shirt had a splayed hand decal on the back. It looked like a friendly wave until you read the slogan: *Pick a finger.*

"Well, let's start with a week," I said to the hand. "See how we go, eh?"

I started out at a normal walking speed, but I was slowing before I even got to the stairs and then every step I took upwards brought me closer to where the window units were belching stale bedroom air out into the dead dog afternoon. I had enjoyed the spring here. Mornings warm enough to jump straight out of bed into the pool and afternoons never getting above thirty. Then I missed a bit. When I was family-packing and box-setting my way through the paperwork weeks I went straight from the hotel a/c to the car to the store to the a/c again and the short blasts of car park hell, I put down to disordered perception or maybe a stress-related virus. So I wasn't ready for this . . . this . . . *furnace* raging around me.

As a door in the bottom row opened, I looked down and slumped. I wasn't ready for *this* either. Della had emerged with Diego and he was holding a little banner made out of coloured paper and sticky letters: *Welcome NEMO*! He waved it madly.

"Where is he, where is he?" he said, bouncing up and down in his mother's arms. But she knew. She gave me a dead-eyed stare.

"Ahhhhh, he's still in the pet shop, Diego," I said, going back down. "I forgot to go and get him. It's just so hot. It's sapping my energy."

"Hot?" said Della. "It's nowhere near hot yet. What are you talking about?"

"I'll go and get him tomorrow," I said.

"You can go tomorrow and get him *and his little friend,*" said Della.

"Tomorrow?" Diego said, looking up at me, with his big eyes caught exactly halfway between trust and tears.

"Tomorrow," I said. "I'll bring Nemo and his little friend . . ."

"Gill," said Diego.

"Exactly." As I walked away from them I

scrabbled in my bag for a Sharpie to write *FISH!* on my hand with, until the sight of my half-open door distracted me. Senses thrumming and adrenalin giving me a heat-surge I truly did not need, I edged towards the gap and peered in. Todd had all of my drawers open and every stitch of my underwear was sitting in a pile on the carpet behind him.

"Oh good," he said, looking at me over his hipster glasses. "I've put a couple in the bathroom to check for sizing."

"I'm a 36C," I said.

"Yeah, no, you're not," Todd told me. "I got a 34E in the Passionata and a 34FF in the Heidi Klum because they run small. Typical supermodel. Go on."

"In return for information," I said.

"Deal," said Todd. He picked up a once-white Triumph boulder-holder that had been a good friend to me over the years and, holding it between thumb and forefinger, dropped it into the wastepaper basket. "Cough it up then."

I supposed it made some kind of sense that way round: he did my shopping and I paid him in gossip. But come on! He was determined to dress both my motel room and me for his own pleasure and in return for my compliance he was going to help me.

163

I went into the bathroom where two sets of lingerie, one grey and coral, one red and peach, hung on their satin hangers from the shower rail.

"So, Kathi," I said, starting to wriggle out of my skirt. "She said you —"

"What are you doing?" said Todd, appearing round the door.

"Uh, trying on underwear in comparative privacy?" I said.

"Okay, one," said Todd. "Don't up-talk. It sounds stupid in your accent. And, two: Bra first. *Obviously.*"

"Why," I said flatly.

"Well, go up on questions!" he said. "Why? Because if the bra doesn't fit there's no point in the panties. I got strings and boy shorts because I couldn't tell from that collection of granny cast-offs what you like." He gave me a curt nod and went back to the other room.

"So how is it you help Kathi?" I called, once I was sure he had gone.

"What are you doing?" he said. He was back. "Don't tell me you're a hook and swivel? You'll stretch them all to hell. Turn around and let me, if you truly can't reach. You need yoga if you can't reach around your own back to fasten a bra."

He tugged the band and snapped it closed,

low across my back.

"Ow!" I said. "It hurts."

"It *fits*!" said Todd, giving it an unnecessary twang that echoed off the tiled walls. "Now scoop and jiggle."

"What?"

"Bend over," said Todd, demonstrating with locked knees and a back as flat as a table. "Then scoop. And jiggle."

I hunched over, feeling my stomach roll over my waistband, grabbed the tops of the cups and shook my northern shimmy.

"It does not fit," I said. "It's far too bloody tigh—Wow." I had straightened up and seen myself in the mirror. "Knockerama."

"Try the boy shorts," said Todd.

"And you trust me to put my knickers on properly all by myself?" I said. "You won't barge in and take over?"

"You couldn't bribe me with Brad," said Todd. "I see that nasty disposable razor in your soap dish, Miss Thing. I've made an appointment for you with my waxing lady. We can go together and then have brunch, but until then . . . I would rather go blind." He swept out.

Boundaries.

But I still wanted info.

"How is it you help Kathi?" I asked again. "Is it the décor thing? Do you attract business?" But, even while I asked, I thought to myself that that would help Noleen too. And why would it make Noleen *um* and *er* like she'd just been *um*-ing and *er*-ing downstairs?

"Not exactly décor," Todd said. "If I tell you this, it's in the secret vault under the invisible cone, okay?"

I felt sure I could rise to Todd's standards of discretion and went out to show him the ensemble and tell him so.

"Ew," he said, pointing at my crotch. "Don't let me see the thong." I went back to the bathroom. I may have flounced. "I rent two rooms, you see," Todd called through to me. I let go of a big disappointed breath. The Passionata straps didn't so much as tremble. "Yeah, I rent two rooms, and Noleen thinks one of them is to run to in code-red bug situations."

"Why didn't you go there yesterday?" I asked, thinking of the tiny spider with the big build-up.

"I certainly could have," Todd said. "And then I'd have told Kathi she needed to move rooms. But I needed comfort and you were closer."

"Kathi 'moves rooms'?" I said. "Do Noleen and Kathi actually live in the motel like ordinary guests then?"

166

"They do," said Todd. "I've got your word of honor, don't I? About the vault under the cone?"

"Cross my heart and spit in my cocoa."

"They've got an apartment," said Todd. "Sure they do. Owners' quarters. But Kathi . . . Well, she likes things nice." He stopped talking. Stopped dead.

"I'm not with you," I said.

"She likes to keep the apartment clean," said Todd. Again he shut his mouth as if he planned never to open it again.

"So she moves out to a guest room if she needs to give it a good going over?" I said.

"She did," said Todd. Then turned Trappist Monk.

"She did once?" I said. "What does that have to do with your two rooms now, though?"

"Oh, for the Lord's sake!" said Todd. He said the next bit faster than a runaway train. "She cleans the apartment and lives in a guest room. Obviously."

"And how long has this been going on?" I asked.

I had my own failings in the area. I'd stayed in my rented hovel through three promotions and pay rises and so I'd missed my chance to be part of Dundee's property price boom. I just didn't care enough;

couldn't commit. I looked at big Victorian tenement flats and 1930s maisonettes, ex-council semis in nice areas and refurbed farm-workers' cottages on the outskirts. Then I thought about the faff of moving and shredded the brochures. I could do up the flat instead. So I bought DIY magazines and recorded make-over shows. Then I shredded them too and cleared the DVR. But half hearted as I was about the Tay Street flat, at least I lived there.

"A year. But she needs another guest room to clean while she sleeps in the first one, and Noleen said it was too much lost revenue. It nearly split them. That's where I come in. I rent a second room as a bolt hole but I promise to tell her if I use it so she can switch again. Now everyone's happy."

"I don't understand," I said. "What do you get out of switching rooms?"

"A happy friend," said Todd. "This is exactly why I have no time for shrinks. What you call codependence I call being a good person. I get a happy friend and that gives me a happy glow."

"And?"

"Boy, I'd hate to be that cynical," said Todd. "But okay, okay, if you insist. She has a contact in Costa Rica who sends up insecticide that's banned in California. She sprays my room, the rooms on either side of my room, the walkway between my room and reception, reception itself, and the parking lot around my car. *Okay?*"

"I'd really like to —"

"We don't need help," said Todd. "We don't need counseling, therapy, SSRIs, hospitalization, electric shock treatment, or a lobotomy."

"Aw!" I said. "It's been months since I got to lobotomise a client. Spoilsport."

"What we *need,*" said Todd, "is a clean room, a spare clean room, and some fly spray worth the name. And we have it. But that is classified information and it's In. The. Vault."

"Under the cone," I said. "Has Kathi ever explored the origins —"

"Oh my God!" said Todd. "What did I just say? Kathi is fine. I am fine. Have Roger and Noleen ever explored the origins of why they're such unsupportive rat bastards to Kathi and me? Why no, I believe they have not. So go and shrink *their* heads and leave us alone." He glared at me. "That bra and panties is super cute," he said. "Try the Klum."

No one goes into psychology for the money and not even psychologists go into family

169

therapy for two nice cars and skiing every spring. We do it because we want to help, and when we come across people in such dire need as Todd and Kathi it sets us off. Like a beaver when a tap's running.

Banned from trying to help a cleptoparasitosis case and a germaphobe who had clearly let her coping mechanism run completely out of control (with her backup room for her backup room, for God's sake), I redoubled my determination to help *someone,* if it killed me. I marched back under the railway bridge fixed on Clovis, Barb, and Vi like a death ray. And the contents of the safe, which might explain everything.

"Is Detective Mike in?" I asked the dispatcher.

"Detective Mike?" she said. "What is this, Mayberry?"

I couldn't answer. People talked a lot about Mayberry. And June Beaver. And some people called Brady, a whole bunch of them. And also a guy by the name of Bob Ross who sounded way creepy. And Julia Child, and Johnny Carson, and Bert and his friend Ernie. Then everyone smiled and stopped arguing.

"So?" Branston had said, the one time I mentioned it. "Just ask. What's the problem?" He spoke from his vast experience of exactly one month in Scotland when everyone treated him like a guest and no one talked to him about Weatherfield, Margot Ledbetter, Delia, Parky, or *Dangermouse.*

"If the wind changes, you'll be sorry," Mike said. The dispatcher had buzzed her. "What is it now?"

"You know the plane tickets you took into evidence in the Bombaro case?" I said, smoothing my scowl.

" 'The Bombaro case'?" said Mike. "Are you really trying to help me pick out which murder you're referring to? This is Cuento, Legacy. Not Miami."

"Lexy," I reminded her and, without showing a hint of it on my face, I filed away the news that she had been checking up on me, looking at the formal spelling of my name.

"Yeah, you're right," said Mike. "I looked up your residency just to dot the i's. Good poker face, though."

I made a mental note never to play it with her. She probably saw that on my face too.

"Okay then," I went on. "So the plane tickets you took out of the safe? Where were they for? Mizz Visalia wants to know and she can't check the receipt because she's forgotten the combination of the safe. She changed it and the new number's slipped

171

her mind."

Mike gave me a level stare. Her eyebrows looked like two stone mouldings above the darkened window of an abandoned building. Not a twitch in either or a flicker of light below. "Tell her to call us," she said.

"Ah. Problem," I said. "She doesn't know she's forgotten the combo. I didn't want to upset her."

"I see." The intonation matched the flat brows and the dead eyes. "I thought your type went in for facing facts and living in the bombed-out wasteland of your authentic life."

"Bombed-out waste . . . Mike, are you okay?"

"Peachy," she said, spitting the word out like grape pips. "And even if I wasn't, I still wouldn't share confidential information about an ongoing investigation with someone so heavily involved with one of the susp— Or with anyone. The financial rec— Any items we removed — Anything we did or didn't do at the Bombar—" She sighed and tried one last time. "Any activities associated in any way with the murder investigation are strictly confidential."

"Well done," I said. "You got there. Visalia didn't cut the wire, by the way."

"What wire?" said Mike.

"Really? No wire? Good to know."

"Watch it," Mike said. She turned away. Then she turned back. "And be careful. Clovis Bombaro pissed someone off, Lexy. Don't do the same. In fact, stay away from The Oaks altogether."

I gulped. "Thank you," I said and scuttled out. I stopped off at Swiss Sisters for a latte, standing in the drive-in queue between a so-called minivan that looked pretty maxi from this angle and a Saturn that was indeed planet-sized, shuffling forward with my flip-flops sticking to the tarmac and the maxivan's exhaust fumes baking me all down my front like a kebab on a burst spindle.

My mind was fizzing. If there was no wire left behind, then how did the cops know about the timer? Because if it was only the timer that put Visalia in the frame for any part of it, it mattered quite a lot that they were right.

But what I didn't know about fireworks was pretty much everything. There might be some other tell-tale sign and I'd have to grill an expert to get a clue what it might be. But just the thought of a firework factory was enough to put an extra film of sweat on me.

And all the pyrotechnicians I knew well

enough to speak to out of work hours were probably cold-blooded killers.

ELEVEN

Besides, something Mike had said to me was bothering me. And something I *hadn't* said to her was bothering me too. And the two bothersome things seemed connected.

Visalia had her theory and she was sticking to it, regardless of how outlandishly wackadoodle it might be. And even though it was too crazy by far to tell the cops, it made perfect sense, psychologically speaking. How much safer to lay the blame on a distant stranger, one of the mythic Poggios, than to wonder about someone closer to home.

How close, was the point. Because Mike hadn't said stay away from Barb. She hadn't said stay away from Casa Bombaro, or from the Dolshikovs or from fireworks. No, Detective Mike had said, "Stay away from The Oaks."

It stopped me like a stun gun. Like a freeze-ray. I stood staring back at my owl-eyed reflection in the bathroom mirror of Room 213. Todd had put in peach light-bulbs and the mirror itself was a vintage beauty, foggy and forgiving. Add the smoothing and plumping effects of the toiletries he had chosen for me and I had never looked better. It distracted me for a moment, but the new thought was too compelling to be quashed for long. The police suspected one of Clovis's neighbours. One of the residents of The Oaks.

As I prepared for bed, slipping silkily in between the thread counts in my brand-new posh nightie and pulling the chilled eye mask I had found in the fridge down over my smoothed, plumped, oxygenated face, I planned a day of advanced sleuthing for the morrow.

I'd definitely visit the closest neighbours under the guise of . . . something I'd decide later . . . and I'd find out if Boom Bombaro had an enemy. I'd lean on them like a tired horse. I'd work on them like a Swiss masseuse. And then I'd remember I was Scottish, and can the Raymond Chandler.

I would even, I thought to myself as I turned over trying not to think about the ten dollars' worth of night cream I was smearing onto my pillow, gas up Todd's Land Rover, a task I'd never quite got to grips with in my short career as co-owner of an Acura. If I wasn't trying to fill before paying I was forgetting which side the cap was on, giving myself carpal-tunnel because I couldn't remember the hands-free notch, rejoining the freeway blinded by bug splat because I kept forgetting the hands-free notch and never got the chance to clean the windscreen. And none of that was even close to the worst thing I'd done.

"Green is unleaded and black is diesel," I said to myself as I was falling asleep. "Diesel is black and unleaded is green. I am competent and purposeful. I will prevail."

Hoo, the day went wrong fast. I didn't even make it to the petrol station. I woke to screams, leapt from my bed, and bolted out onto the balcony into the smoke-grey dawn of a day already warm. Roger was just emerging from the room next door in nothing but silk boxers and his wedding ring. Two sleepy tourists in Mickey Mouse pyjamas and LL Bean yard boots — my guess was they were breaking their journey back to Oregon from Disneyland — stumbled out of the room on the other side, and all up and down the balcony, like munchkins when the witch is dead, people were blundering out yawning and scratching. Some of the more obvious tourists had their phones on ready to film whatever mayhem was in the offing, but the long-term residents looked angry rather than alarmed. Della came out of her room below and called up to Roger.

"You wake Diego, you take him to the playground and push him on the swings."

From the room at the far left end, Noleen was bearing down, her face blacker than her most cynical t-shirt slogan, her fists clenched, her feet making the walkway shudder as she pounded along.

"Kathi!" she bellowed.

"You push him on the swings, you buy him breakfast at the Red Raccoon . . ." said Della.

"Down here, Nolly," said a thin young man I had passed a time or two in the parking lot. "Room 106." Noleen wheeled around and made for the stairs to the ground floor.

"Two words," said one of the tourists as she passed them. "Trip. Advisor." He withdrew into his room and slammed the door. Roger rubbed his hands over his face and hurried after Noleen. I threw my eye mask through my open doorway and hurried after Roger.

The screaming had started up again. It

was a two-note scream, one voice providing a base line of quite lusty yells, lungfuls at a time with short breaks for breathing in, and the other voice adding percussive little squeaks over and over. I wasn't massively experienced in acute trauma and panic resolution, but it was the squeaker who worried me. The yeller was getting it out of their system and breathing deeply to do so. The squeaker would hyperventilate and keel over if they didn't calm down soon.

Noleen was picking over a bunch of keys when I got there.

"Kathi!" she barked as she jammed wrong key after wrong key into the lock and wrenched them out again. "Pipe down and open up. This is our business. This is our livelihood. You can't keep doing this."

"And you can put a sock in it too, Todd," Roger added in such a penetrating voice that, doctor or no doctor, I was sure he'd had some dramatic training somewhere along the line.

At last, Noleen found the right key and threw the door open. Inside, right at the back corner, beyond the bed, Todd and Kathi stood clutching each other, melded together, cheek to cheek to chest to hip to toes, and both were trembling.

"What the fuck?" said Noleen. I decided

she'd had even less (or at least worse) training in acute trauma counselling than I had, and I put a hand out to stay her.

"Bugs," said Todd, his voice cracking.

"Filth," said Kathi, her voice soft and guttural with disgust.

I turned to Roger and Noleen and said, "Leave this to me." Then I closed the door on them.

"I'll give you one Tiffany diamond for every bug you show me, Todd," Roger shouted through the gap as the door was closing.

"Okay," I said, in a calm, firm voice. "Where are the bugs?"

"And filth," said Kathi.

"And filth," I agreed. "Where are they?"

"Bathroom," said Todd, pointing a wavering finger.

I glanced at the bathroom door, which was just to my left side, then came past it towards them.

"Careful!" said Kathi.

"Stop and check yourself over," said Todd.

"Let's all sit down," I suggested.

Kathi looked at me as if I'd told her to drink from a toilet. "Sit down?" she said. "On the bed? On soft furnishings? In this den of squalor?"

"With lethal insects everywhere?" Todd added.

They didn't sound like the proprietor of said den and her best customer at all.

There was a little dinette set under the front window; a round table and two hard chairs with wooden seats and backs and so nowhere for beasties to hide. I took both chairs over to the back wall and set them down, then returned to the front and hopped up on the tabletop.

"Sit," I said.

Todd and Kathi inspected the chairs, paying close attention to where my (presumably plague-ridden) hands had grasped the back rails, then slowly and haltingly they broke out of their embrace and perched side-by-side. Kathi held her feet up off the ground, her thigh muscles quaking with the effort, and it melted my heart to see Todd take hold of them and rest them in his lap.

"Now then," I said. "What happened?"

"I couldn't sleep," said Kathi.

"I had to go potty," said Todd.

"And then what?" I said.

"I come to the clean room when I can't sleep, so I don't wake Nolly, cleaning our room."

"And I can't go in a dark bathroom," said Todd. "Obviously. So I come to the clean room where I can put the lights on and then in the morning I tell Kathi it's not clean anymore and she switches to a new one." He turned to Kathi. "I would have told you in the morning."

"I know. I trust you."

"You're good friends to each other," I said. "You take great care of each other. And show great kindness."

"But?" said Kathi. Todd laughed and squeezed her feet.

"But," I said, "you need to learn how to take care —"

"Of ourselves!" they said in chorus.

And it was a chorus of three, because of course they were right about what I'd been going to say.

"This ain't our first rodeo," said Kathi.

"But that's for another time," I went on. "For now, I'm going to open the bathroom door. Todd, you're going to see that there are no bugs in there and, Kathi, you're going to see a spotlessly clean bathroom sparkling from all your hard work."

"No deal," said Kathi. "You open that door and I will throw you out onto the street with my own two hands."

"Here's what's going to happen," said Todd. "You are going to go to my room and get a roll of extra-wide duct tape. You will bring it back here and seal all four edges of that bathroom door. And then Kathi and I are going to walk out. Kathi, I'm going to go somewhere else for the rest of the night, but you can come with me."

"We're not going anywhere!" came Roger's voice from outside. "There's nowhere else to go!"

"You can stay here if you like but . . ." Todd began. His voice shook and his cheeks had flushed.

"Roger," I called. "I'm in session here. Eavesdropping is not part of the process."

That was California-ese for *piss off out of it, sunshine* and I had delivered it perfectly. I heard Roger's bare feet slapping on the concrete as he schmopped off.

"You too," I called and heard the muffled thumps of Noleen's bunny slippers retreating too.

"What went wrong," I said, turning back to Todd and Kathi, "was that your expectations were confounded and that tipped you into crisis. Todd, you were expecting an empty room you could light up and check for bugs before using the bathroom and, Kathi, you were expecting a room untouched since you last left it. Am I right? But you met each other and lost your balances?"

"No," said Kathi. "We met each other and that was a bonus. I said I would check the bathroom and then Todd could use it."

I smiled at her. "You are a kind woman and a good friend," I said. "It's an act of love for you to project all your anxiety onto imagined dirt instead of onto your friend."

"And as for me, if Kathi hadn't been here, I might have had a stroke and died. Or a heart attack and died. Or an aneurysm and —"

"You can't have an aneurysm from shock," I said. "So you could only have died twice at the most. But you didn't. What *did* happen? After you found each other in here?"

"We opened the bathroom door," said Todd. "Duh."

"And then?"

"Armageddon."

"The seventh circle of hell."

"Catastrophising language doesn't help you," I said kindly but firmly. "Now how about this. We'll talk for just five minutes now, then we'll all go back to bed and back to sleep and we'll talk for ten more minutes tomorrow."

"Okay," said Kathi, but she was watching me closely for clues to the catch.

"What's the catch?" said Todd.

"First I open the bathroom door and we

all look at the pristine, bug-free emptiness."

Todd dropped Kathi's feet and they both sprang up to stand pressed against the back wall, once more clutching each other.

"Okay," I said. "You take any precautions you need to. You're not screaming now, so that's an improvement. Well done. Good work, both of you."

I slid down off the table, gave them a beaming smile, and opened the bathroom door.

My first thought was that the illegal insecticide Kathi got from her cousin in Costa Rica was strangely fragranced, like formic acid, or vinegar maybe. That was it. It smelled like a very old banana in a pickle jar.

I clicked the light on.

Legions upon legions of shiny red-brown insects skittered and scuttled over every surface. The folds of the shower curtain seethed with them. A helpless wriggling heap of them roiled in the bottom of the wash basin and the should-be-white lino was spattered all over with the reeking crumbs of their droppings.

I gulped and snatched at air, clawing for a breath to scream with but stuck like a gargoyle with my eyes bulging out and my voice turned to dust. Until, that was, one of the stinking little shitbags crawled onto my foot and bit me.

"JESUS FUCKING CHRIST, THEY'RE *REAL*!" I howled, kicking off my attacker and trying to squish him. He didn't squish. He crunched. I slammed the bathroom door shut, blatted the room door open, grabbed Todd and Kathi, one in each hand, and fell out into the safety of the big bad world.

"There's an in—" I screamed, but there were still half a dozen guests clustered around the walkway hoping for more action and *infestation* isn't a word hotel guests want to hear. "—teresting discussion to be had here," I finished, quite a lot quieter. "Where can we go to talk?"

Roger and Noleen were loitering over by the chain-link fence around the swimming pool, trying to look as if they just happened to have met and were passing the time of day, silk boxers and granny nightie with the ruffle neck and rosebuds notwithstanding

Funny thing was, Todd and Kathi came down larky and it was Noleen and Roger, after one peek round the bathroom door, who sat pale and shaking in the little private office behind reception, checking the corners and scratching now and then.

"Your face!" said Todd to me for the

fourth time. He caught Kathi's eye and they both snorted.

"Take a deep cleansing breath and feast your eyes on the pristine bug-free emptiness," said Kathi in a truly terrible Scottish accent.

"Sod off," I told her. "I've never said 'deep, cleansing breath' in my life."

"If you three could stop reliving happy memories," said Noleen, "what the hell are we going to do?"

"Getting that extra-wide duct tape and sealing round the door would be a good start," I said. "We wouldn't want them to swarm."

"It's bees that swarm," said Todd. "Not . . ."

"Right?" said Roger. "That's the thing. What the hell are they?"

"And where in God's name did they come from?" said Noleen.

"Do you think it's just that one room?" Kathi said, which sobered everyone.

"We'll know soon enough," said Noleen, twisting round in her chair to look at the wall clock. "Six forty-five. People will be getting up."

"But what in God's name are they?" I said.

"And," said Roger, "where the hell did they come from?"

The rest of us ran through these questions a few more times, while he made off to get the duct tape and start sealing, and we concluded we didn't know and hadn't a clue.

"Cindy Slagle," Roger said, returning after a few minutes and scrubbing his hands briskly at the utility sink. He made a proper job of it, what with being a surgeon and all, but still he had to shudder once when he was done. "She's an entomologist at the university. We had her in once at work to consult on —" He stopped. "I promised Todd I'd never tell him."

"Why an entomologist was called in to paediatrics?" I said. "I'm with Todd. I don't want to know."

"But she won't be able to tell us how they got in there, will she?" Todd said. "I mean, they didn't just look in the window and like what they saw."

"Someone —" said Kathi.

"Don't say it," said Noleen.

"Someone —"

"Kathi, don't say it."

"Let me speak! Someone put them in there."

"So we call the cops," I said.

"No," came a chorus of four voices.

Noleen and Kathi I could understand.

188

Police call-outs are public record in California. It makes for one of the more entertaining items in the *Cuento Voyager* each week. *Verbal domestic dispute: parties counseled* and *Failure to stop at a red light: warning issued* and the occasional *Texting while travelling by skateboard after dark against flow of traffic without lights: kids today.* I don't know which of the Cuento cops wrote up the blotter, but they had a sense of humour.

And Mike struck me as a straight dealer. I didn't understand why Todd and Roger would be against the notion.

"I'll text Cindy," Roger said. He patted his sides as though searching nonexistent pockets for his phone and only then seemed to realize how nearly naked he was. He stood, cleared his throat, and made to leave.

"And I'd better . . ." said Noleen, looking down at her nightie for the first time.

Well, none of us had stopped to put on a cocktail dress when we heard screaming, had we? As I had the thought I glanced at my own outfit and was surprised to see spaghetti straps and a groin-high split. I stood, holding the split together to mid-thigh.

"And I'll just . . ." I said, following the others.

"Can you stand to look them up on the

internet?" Kathi was saying, as we all trooped away through the front office.

"Could I trawl through pics of bugs?" said Todd. "That's no' verrrry kind and prrrotective." He was doing my voice again.

"What's the prob with the cops?" I asked Roger, trotting to catch up as he took the stairs three at a time towards our rooms.

He looked at me a while then, just as he opened his mouth to speak, the door of the Disneyland-to-Oregon tourists banged open and the husband one, even more disgruntled than before, skewered me with a glare and jabbed his finger at me.

"Your phone's ringing off the hook," he said. "This place is a joke. And we've been to *India*!"

"What did India do to des—" said Roger.

"Answer the goddam phone!" said the tourist and turned his back, stalking off, the glitter-paint of his magic castle winking.

TWELVE

I said goodbye to Roger and went to answer the goddam phone.

It was Visalia, with a very timely offer for someone who wanted to quiz experts about firework-lore. She was going to the factory to address the work force and wanted moral support.

"I think it's marvellous of you to go and I think it's very wise of you to take someone," I said. "But — I think I mentioned this, Vi — I'm not much of a one for fireworks. I don't actually think I'm the best choice. What about Father Adam?"

"But Lexy, there won't be any fireworks going off. Why, a firework factory is the last place on earth you'd ever hear fireworks or see them."

"Oh," I said. "Well, if you're sure . . ."

"You'd be more likely to get shot in a bullet factory."

She probably thought that would comfort me.

"In that case, I'd be delighted. Will I meet you there or can I pick you up at home and drive you?" Either way was fine by me. I could go early to the factory and schmooze the drones before she arrived or go early to The Oaks and find whatever Mike didn't want me to find.

"Oh, Lexy," she said. "I'd love you to come and get me. Oh! What would I do without you?"

Lean on her niece, nephew-in-law and, at a push, their cousins, I thought.

"Glad to help," I said. "I'll be there at ten."

"I'll be waiting for you," she said. "I've got an appointment at nine with Father Adam, as it happens. But that's something I need to do alone."

"Confession?" I said.

There was a long fluffy silence on the line, like tumbleweed in aural form, and a couple of crackles, like crickets.

"No," Visalia said at last. "Father Adam doesn't approve of my plans for Clovis's send-off and he is punishing me by withholding the sacraments."

"He is?" I thought of the flip-flops and whale-saving bangles and couldn't see it somehow. "Can he do that? Can't you report him to the Bishop or something?"

"He's got me," said Visalia. "We're not supposed to confess a sin we're planning to commit again."

"But don't you pretty much just confess the same stuff every week?" I asked.

"Planning to," said Visalia. "That's where you get the wiggle room. But Father Adam says Cousin Clovis spoke to him often about his horror of cremation and together they talked about the best kind of mausoleum. So he — Father Adam, this is — doesn't believe that I'm carrying out Clovis's wishes. Which is a sin. And I can't confess it unless I cancel the funeral plans. And I can't take Mass without confession. So I'm screwed."

"Sin?" I asked. "Did he tell you *what* sin? It sounds like a con."

"What? What sin do you *think* it is? Disobeying your husband, *cara.* An oldie but a goodie."

For a minute I couldn't speak. Then I couldn't stop. "Gimme a break! I mean, *donnez moi un* BREAK! That sanctimonious bachelor with a pedicure actually spouted this shit to you on a pastoral visit? When he was supposed to be comforting you? I hope you sent him packing with a foot up the Bermuda shorts, Vi. JESUS!"

"Calm down," Visalia said. "His hands are

tied, if you'll pardon the expression. Can't fight two saints and two Popes. It'll blow over."

"Wow," I said. "I mean . . . wow. Vi, I have my opinions about schools of thought and psychological models, but I will ditch every one of them before I'd use them against you. WOW!"

"You're a good girl, Lexy," Vi said. "I'll see you soon."

"I'll be there at ten," I said. *I'll be there at nine,* I thought. *Neighbours, beware!*

Here's the thing about America. Okay, *one* of the things, as well as the portions, the outlandish friendliness, the penchant for genealogy, and the renaissance fairs: It's huge. If you fly from coast to coast looking out the window you'll go cross-eyed and slack-jawed from the yawning impossible enormousness of it.

And yet all the houses around Casa Bombaro, each probably worth a cool few million, were jammed onto acre plots. Just room for an ostentatious drive, enough lawn to make it worth having the sprinklers rotate, a house ten times bigger than anyone needed, a garage for three times as many cars as they owned, and a swimming pool to accommodate the household plus enough guests to fill the garage for the weekend.

They called their acre plots "estates," even though you could see the boundary fence from every window in the house. There was no home farm, no grouse moor, no timber forests, and no row of cottages for rosy-cheeked yokels to sleep in after long hard days spent in servitude.

Anyway, the upshot of a huge house on a tiny lot was that I reckoned there were four sets of neighbours who could easily be engaged in a war with Clovis Bombaro and might have got fed up with attrition and decided to go into battle once and for all: the houses on either side, the house across the back fence, and the one over the road. There were two more who shared a corner of the back fence, but they had their own neighbours pressing in close on four sides of their million-dollar piles, so I shelved them.

I was feeling confident bordering smug about knocking on their doors too, because I had stopped off at the thrift store and invested in an old but unmarked Pyrex dish, the white kind with a motif of little blue flowers and a clear glass lid; the sort of thing that might have been a wedding present in the fifties. What Californians would call, quite without irony, an antique.

I marched up the path of the house opposite Casa Boom, put a bright smile on my face, remembered the context, toned it down a notch, and rang the bell.

It was answered by a woman so identical to Brandeee that I took a step back before a second glance clued me in. She actually had darker hair, bigger teeth, ropier biceps, and tighter work-out clothes.

"Yes?" she said, casting a scathing look at me.

"Is this yours?" I asked, holding out the empty casserole. "Mrs. Bombaro just said the neighbour sent it over and asked me to return it. She didn't say which neighbour and she's napping."

"Who?" said Not-Brandeee.

"Visalia Bombaro," I said. "Across the way there. Her husband died on the Fourth?"

"Oh, yeah? Well, no. A casserole? No, not me."

"So you weren't aware of the incident?"

"Not until the disturbance."

"You *heard* it?"

"And saw it. Two police cars, with lights flashing and engines running. I've sent an email."

"I'm sure you have," I said, and moved on to the neighbour on the east side.

"What kind of casserole?" said the not-quite-Brandeee I found there. She was in uniform — yoga pants, Lycra top, iPhone, and go-cup. It seemed a strange question and I couldn't muster an answer at first, since nobody with running shoes that matched her Fitbit ever made shepherd's pie, braised oxtail, or liver and onions.

"Coq au vin?" I said at last, which was basically spotted dick all over again, only with no teenaged boy to find it funny.

The woman blushed, frowned, then called over her shoulder. "Luisa? Did you bring a dish from home with a chicken braise for poor old Mrs. B?"

"No, Mrs. Mandeeee," came a voice from the innards of the house. Practically.

And so, since the *poor old* had seemed genuine enough, I left it there and moved on to the neighbour on the west side.

"Certainly not," said the third woman. I'll call her Kandeee. "That old thing? I use brushed steel and I'm vegan."

I believed her.

"And were you at home when Mr. Bombaro died? Visalia wants to know but can't bring herself to ask."

"On the Fourth of July?" Kandeee said. "Of course not. I was giving service to veterans."

I was pretty sure she didn't mean she was a hooker, but I checked anyway. "Service?"

"At the soup kitchen."

"Ah," I said. "Kind of warm for soup, though, isn't it?"

"Chilled eggplant gazpacho," she said.

"Ah," I said again and left quickly before I punched her.

I got back in the car to go round the block to the neighbour over the back fence, wondering just a bit if investigating was really this easy or if I was doing it wrong.

The fourth place was as big a spread as the Bombaro "estate" but built on different lines. To my eye, it looked more like a house and less like a medical centre. It was white, with symmetrical windows and a proper peaked roof on top. It had pillars on either side of its red door and a brick path lined with roses, pruned like lollipops.

When the doyenne answered the door, I twigged: this was plantation architecture and the woman standing before me with a meringue of pink-blonde hair and the strange, mottled-tuna look of a face-lift was a bona fide Southern Belle. She was about Visalia's age too, and I felt sure she'd have tales to tell me.

"That poor dear sweet soul," said the neighbour lady. She had told me her name was Dorabelle. "She and I have been friends for sixty years. We were living here already when Clovis and Visalia first came. When the little old house was there? They were beside themselves to be owners of property. It was the cutest thing! And here we still are, all these years later! They did so well for themselves and made a fine life. They threw some of the prettiest parties. Once poor Visalia learned how it was done."

I was nodding with a fixed grin plastered on my face. It was the best I could do. Dorabelle was a humungous snob. I only hoped (and felt pretty sure) that she'd be a gossip as well and that seeing poor sweet little Visalia suffer the social blow of a murder — my dear! — she'd relish the chance to chew it over, even with the likes of me. I was right; she invited me in for tea.

"Were you here the day he died?" I asked. "Did you see anything?"

"Well now," said Dorabelle. "I see nothing from spring to fall. Once the leaves are on the mimosa and the buckeye over there, why I'm just in a perfect bower! I'm in a forest *glade.* And sometimes it seems that sweet Visalia and poor dear Clovis . . . Well, they forget that I'm so close and hear so clearly. And of course, being Italian, they're so very . . . unguarded. Don't you always think so? I don't mean to say that I am a cold-hearted woman. Why no. The women of my family are as vivacious as anyone I ever met. But we place a high value on decorum."

I murmured, encouragingly. A small section of my brain was wondering if I could get her to say an actual *fiddle-di-dee*.

"Why, if I was of a mind," Dorabelle said, coyly, "I could tell you things about Clovis and Visalia that no one but no one should know."

I cast my mind back over the seven full seasons of *True Blood* I had watched in the post-Branston doldrums and everything I could dredge up from Whatshername in *The Golden Girls*.

"You don't say," I breathed for starters.

But that was plenty. Dorabelle set down her tea glass and scooted forward so that I was looking right down her powdery cleavage.

"Eighty-six years old and they still fought like newlyweds," she said. "Slamming doors, firing good dishes like cannonballs. Why, that woman doesn't have a single piece of her wedding china left to her name. And the language that flew through the air? My late husband could cuss up a blue storm like any Texas man. If the cards fell bad or the well went dry, he could shrivel a peach blossom. But not once in fifty-three years of wedded bliss did he raise his voice or use a foul word to me. Once — one time! — I had a little fender-bender in his Caddy and he told me I was careless. 'Well,' I told him, 'I won't be so careless as to share my bed with a man who talks to me that way.' I spoke very quietly and walked away very slowly. Six weeks later he gave me an emerald necklace and begged me to be friends again." She sighed and stroked her throat, remembering the necklace, or maybe the friendliness.

"I tried to teach Visalia to deal with Clovis in the same way — like my mother taught me — but even as late as this spring, when she caught him sending flowers to one of his lady friends, I heard her — all the windows wide open! — 'Filthy pig' she called him. 'I should turn the' — I can't say the next word, dear, my daddy would come back and haunt me but — 'turn the hm-hm hose on you, you pork-oh shi-foso!' I just can't imagine *what* that means. Can you?"

"Italian for filthy pig, I think," I said, which disappointed her greatly.

"And then lately," she went on, "and this will tickle you like a goose feather, they've been in counseling! Can you believe it? Counseling, at eighty-six! You could have rolled me in panko and called me a fishstick when Visalia told me."

"Fish!" I said. I was using a plain old ballpoint, not a Sharpie, but I drew an outline on my hand with it.

"Go to the Nugget," said Dorabelle. "Theirs is freshest."

"And did the counselling make a difference?"

"Oh, honey!" said Dorabelle. "It certainly did. Now instead of 'I'ma-gonna kill you, you bitch' and 'You should be spinning on a barbecue, you pig' it was 'You're revisiting past issues, you bitch' and 'Use eye statements, you pig.' Whatever in the world eye statements might be."

I didn't think it was worth explaining.

"One night, my Friends of the Library reading group discussed not one single word of *Pudd'nhead Wilson.* We were agog. Lined up on the terrace with our martinis — just agog."

"And on the last day?" I said. "Were they arguing then?"

"Oh, *honey!*" said Dorabelle. "That last day? I could have sold tickets and popcorn."

"Really?" I said. "They were at it right to the end?" I was feeling kind of sick. I had only come to the neighbours looking for disgruntled combatants in hedge wars. What I was finding out was that Visalia's story of truce and reconciliation, a second honeymoon in Sicily, a golden future in the lemon groves of home was so much . . .

". . . cornswaggle," Dorabelle was saying. I gathered my attention and gave it back to her. "There was no *end*. If they had stopped arguing, I might have worried about them. If they had stopped arguing, they might have been headed for the divorce court at last. But they were their same old selves. 'Stop seeing her, you pig!' and 'A man has needs, you bitch!' And then I heard the garage door and someone driving away and then . . ."

"And then?"

"And then the next thing I knew was police and ambulances and a news helicopter and those tacky reporters knocking on my door and asking their questions. Could I see into the house from my property and would I accept a thousand dollars to let them in with their zoom lenses. My grandmother LaFytte would spin in her coffin if I ever did anything so trashy."

"Plus you can't see a thing when the leaves are on," I reminded her.

"Honey, I know! I was up in my sewing nook, with my opera glasses, standing on a *chair* and I couldn't even see the blue lights flashing."

"Mizz Dorabelle?" I said. I had glanced at

my watch and I only had five minutes to get back round the block for Vi. "Who do you think killed him?"

She set her tea glass down and put a hand up to her neck. "Child," she said, "I am so glad you asked me that."

"Was it one of the neighbours?"

"What? No. Why? No. Who? No, of course not."

It seemed like a no on that one.

"I tried to tell the police, but they wouldn't listen to me," she said.

"*I'm* listening," I told her.

"Well, Clovis ran a very successful business," she said. "And running a business is not like running a day-care center. A good businessman has to make hard decisions and stick to them. A good businessman doesn't rise to the top without making enemies on the way." She sat back as if she had told me everything I could possibly want to know.

"Can you be any more specific?"

"I wish I could, honey," she said, "but unfortunately if you're looking around this once-great country of ours for someone too lazy to do an honest day's work for an honest day's pay, you don't need a spyglass."

"Umm?" I said.

"I think Clovis Bombaro was probably

killed by one of his former employer's, sacked for incompetence, laughed out of court when he tried to sue for wrongful dismissal, and determined to make Clovis pay somehow."

"Well . . ." I said.

"You see," said Dorabelle, "the trouble with these people is that they sit around their apartments watching their flatscreen TVs and letting their children run wild and they just get angrier and angrier. They think life owes them a living and they just won't take responsibility for their own poor decisions. And they *have* to resort to violence, oftentimes, to settle their differences because they don't speak English, you see."

I had lost my smile a while back and now I fought an eye roll. "Is there one in particular?" I asked her.

"Oh honey!" said Dorabelle. "That's what I'm trying to explain to you. They're all the same. But, like I said, the police didn't want to know. Politically incorrect, I suppose. So a cold-blooded murderer walks free."

I got out of there. I couldn't see a handy stick lying around anywhere in her immaculate gardens, so I didn't actually scrape her words off me with it. I contented myself with a thorough snort before I got back in my car.

Then, for the sake of the investigation, I tried to be objective. I would certainly ask Visalia about the state of labour relations at the firework factory. I had thought myself that the method suggested an insider. I shouldn't dismiss Dorabelle's intuitions out of hand just because she was a rancid old horror who made Scarlet O'Hara look like a hippie.

THIRTEEN

"Your neighbour over the back's a bit of a one, isn't she?" I said to Mizz Vi, minutes later. I had found her sitting in the foyer looking like she'd been sent to the headmaster's study for passing notes. The house was silent around her, no sign of any beloved relatives beyond a golf bag hooked over the finial at the bottom of the stairs. "I got lost in these winding streets," I said, "and she put me right. In more ways than one."

"Dorabelle?" said Vi. "She's lived there since before Cousin Clovis and I first arrived. Queen of the neighborhood. And then when Willard went to jail, she hung on by the skin of her teeth taking in paying guests and pretending they were relations."

"Wait, stop, what? Who's Willard?"

"Her husband. He did hard time for running a sweatshop."

"Ahhhh," I said. "Well, that explains a lot. She reckoned one of Clovis's employees probably killed him because he expected them to lift a finger for their salary."

"That sounds like Dora!"

"I take it you've got no suspicions in that quarter then?"

"Cousin Clovis ran a union shop," said Visalia. "Spons a lid a lee off a dendle, you name it. I never told Dorabelle because I didn't want to rub her nose in it, but those are the facts."

"A union shop," I said. "A lid, eh? Dendle." I had no idea what the hell she meant by any of it, but I didn't want to tell her. If she found out that I knew precisely fi-diddly-squit about factories, she might decide she'd be better off taking someone else along today.

"What are you talking about?" she said.

"Can I visit the powder room before we set off?" I asked, and once I was ensconced in a little grotto of onyx and jade with dolphin taps and a gold-lamé bog-seat cover, I phoned Todd.

"Translation, please," I said.

"Have you fallen down a well?" he said.

"I'm hiding in a bathroom and I haven't got all day. Listen, what does running a union shop mean? What would you be doing if you sponsed a lid and a lee off a dendle?"

208

"What? A union shop is a — what the hell are you asking me? A union shop is exactly what it says, where all the workers are in a labor union. But the rest of it is garbage."

"I'm just telling you what someone told me, Todd. Spons a lid, a lee, off a dendle. Is it like code that shop stewards would know?"

"Shop stewards?"

"The guys in charge of the union."

"Labor organizers. Spons a lid, spons a lee, offed a dend *OH MY GOD!*"

I took the phone away from my ears just in time to stop my eardrum exploding and spraying my blood all over the onyx and jade. Todd was whooping and shrieking so loud the line was cracking up.

"Todd? What is it? Is it the insects? Have they got out? Are you okay?"

When he calmed down to a moderate eleven from his initial hundred and fifty, I realized he was laughing. When I listened closely to the laughter I realized he was laughing at me.

"Is it possible that this person said 'sponsored little league and offered dental'? That would go with a labor union."

"It's possible," I said. "What does it mean?"

"What do you mean, what does it mean?

209

It means they sponsor little league and offer dental."

I waited.

"It means they put up the money for small children to play baseball competitively and they include dentistry in their healthcare plan. Wow, Lexy. I mean, wow."

"What? I'm not stupid. I just . . . listen, you're not stupid, but you didn't know what a shop steward was."

"I knew it was two words and that they were 'shop' and 'steward.' Do you want me to come help? Where are you anyway?"

"I'll manage, thank you," I said. And even to my own ears I sounded prissy. "I'll see you tonight."

"Wait, Lexy!" said Todd. "Before you go. Cindy Slagle came to look at the you-know-whats."

"That was quick."

"She's a big fan of Roger's. Whatever it was he called her in for that time, she got two papers and a conference in Cairo out of it.'

"And did she know what they are?'

"Were," said Todd. "They're dead."

"Costa Rican insecticide strikes again?"

"No need," he said. "They all just died. They were dead when Cindy went in. They couldn't survive without a host."

"What? What the hell were they?"

"*Anoplura*. Parasites. But here's the really interesting thing. Cindy was absolutely stumped about how they got there. There's no way in the world they could have gotten there. And yet there they were. She was like a kid in a candy store. Of course, I didn't see this, but Nolly reported back. Cindy took about a million photographs and then resealed the bathroom and asked if we'd leave it so she could bring back a couple of grad students."

"And can she?"

"Noleen said she would rather bake the dead *Anoplura* in a pie and eat it with booger ice-cream."

"How did Professor Slagle take that?"

"She's okay. She'll get another paper anyway with what she's got. Noleen went in and cleaned the place out. Good as new, she said."

I grimaced. "It'll still be a while before she can rent out the room, though."

"Hah!" said Todd. "There's a couple of kids on a budget honeymoon trip in there now. They asked in the office for extra bubble bath and an ice bucket too, so they're definitely making full use of the place."

I grimaced with a hard swallow. "God, I

hope the little shits really *are* dead. Look, Todd, I've got to go. I'll speak to you later, okay?"

"Tummy trouble?" said Mizz Vi, when I got back to the foyer. I had been gone a long time, I supposed.

"Time of the month," I said, rubbing my belly down low and grimacing.

"Oh, I don't miss all that," she said. "The menopause was the best thing that ever happened to me. The last thirty years have been the best years of my life."

I nodded, slowly, trying to make that little remark fit the overall picture of a marriage of flying plates and a sudden gruesome start to her widowhood. She was looking into one of the outsize mirrors, fussing with a chiffon scarf.

"Is this too much?" she said. "I don't want to look as if I'm enjoying it, but I want to look respectful."

She was wearing sleeveless lavender-grey crepe and Tahitian pearls. In other words, mother-of-the-bride, if the bride died on the way to the church and was getting buried instead of married.

"You look perfect," I said. "And there really won't be any fireworks?"

"None at all," said Mizz Vi. "Ready?"

I had been expecting something like the

toy factory from *Toys* or the chocolate factory from *Charlie,* but the firework factory, just off the causeway on the road to Sacramento, could have been manufacturing safety caps for medicine bottles or grip strips to join carpets together for all the pizzazz it showed on the outside. Not a single fountain, wrought iron starburst, or even exclamation mark hinted at what was going on inside. There was only a sober white sign proclaiming BOMBARO (LLC) MANUFACTURING *Please report at reception* and a gate in a chain link fence leading to a car park full of modest, middle-aged sedans in front of a modest, middle-aged breezeblock building with a black tissue-paper rosette affixed to the door. Long story short, it looked a lot more like a morgue than the morgue.

"Oh!" said Mizz Vi. "That's a nice touch, isn't it? I'll bet that was Lucinda. She's been Cousin Clovis's personal secretary for forty-five years. She had silver and then gold ribbons for the big anniversaries and a yellow ribbon up when he came back to work after his gallstones. She'll be destroyed! Absolutely destroyed."

She was. The woman who met us just inside the reception foyer doors was a walking wreck. Her eyes were sodden, her lips

213

swollen, her cheeks pale, her nose red. Her voice was a crow's croak and her walk a drunk's totter.

"Oh, Mrs. Bombaro!" she said and dissolved into a fresh flood of tears, sinking onto one of the chairs in the little waiting area and sobbing there.

"You shouldn't be here, Lucinda," said Vi. "Why not take the day off?"

Lucinda blew her nose, volcanically, and then dropped the tissue into a waste basket. We heard it hit the bottom. "Where else would I be?" she said. "How could I?" She sniffed, pretty much as if the nose-blow hadn't happened, and then shifted gears. "I've told the floor bosses and the office managers that you're coming in. I've had all the extra chairs set out in the cafeteria and the lunch staff have prepared iced tea and muff-muff-muff-"

"Cousin Clovis tasted the morning muffins personally every day," Mizz Vi explained.

"His favourite was pers-pers-pers-" said Lucinda.

"But they're out of season so what did you order?"

"I ordered frozen mashed persimmons, of course," Lucinda said. "Are you going to talk about the electronic initiative?"

"I'm only going to ask for ideas about the memorial cere— What?" said Visalia, saving me from looking crass by asking the same.

"Serpentina told us about it when she came yesterday," Lucinda said. "Now you know I don't like to cross the line between work and family, Mrs. Bombaro, but I didn't think it was the time. No one here was ready to listen to new ideas yesterday. Of course, it would be very different coming from you, but even today I wondered if perhaps it might be too early."

"Lucinda, my dear, you can't overstep the line between work and family; you *are* family," Visalia said. "What electronic initiative?"

"To replace factory jobs with machines?" I said. It was the only thing I could think of.

"To replace fireworks with lightbulbs," Lucinda said. "To replace gunpowder with electricity."

"What?" said Visalia. She sank down into the chair opposite Lucinda and looked her very steadily in the face. "You're telling me," she said, "that my niece was here yesterday talking about scrapping fireworks and making lightbulbs instead?"

"She touched on it," said Lucinda. "Amongst other things."

215

"Such as?"

"She told everyone not to pass idle gossip on to the police. She said we owed you our loyalty no matter how sad and angry we were and that Bombaro's needed continuity and containment if we were to weather this scandal and transition into our new form without the loss of any jobs."

I worked my jaw, trying to get back the power of speech, and I saw Vi doing the same. She looked like a carp who'd jumped out of its tank. *Fish!* I thought, fleetingly, but before I could find a pen to add a tiny ink fish friend for my regular-sized ink fish, Vi recovered.

"Serpentina said loyalty was key, because if I got nailed for Boom's murder everyone would lose their jobs while she did what she's dead set on doing?"

" 'At's about the size of it, Miss V," said a new voice. I looked up and saw a factory foreman. He might as well have being wearing a sign. He was a squat little barrel of a man, with the brawny forearms of someone who mended large machines mid-shift to keep the production line rolling, the thick misshapen fingers of someone who didn't always go about it the orthodox way, and the missing thumb of someone who, at least once, hadn't switched off the machine

216

before piling in. He had a pencil behind his ear and a red spotted handkerchief sticking out of his trouser pocket and when he sat down with a grunt on the fourth leatherette chair, he gave out a puff of perfume that was a cocktail of WD40, fried onions, and the sweat of honest toil.

"Now, I didn't stay married all these years by listening to womenfolk when they start in on all that pansy-ass nonsense," said the foreman. He spoke companionably, as if we might welcome his words. "But she got my attention, let me tell you."

"And how did it go down with the sparklers?" said Visalia. She turned to me. "We call the guys and gals who work the production line our sparklers. It started out it was just the softball team — the Scrapping Sparklers — but we were so small in the early days most everyone in the factory was on the team, or cheerleading, or doing snack duty . . . and it stuck. Or spread. It spread and then it stuck." It sounded gross. "Gather them, Lucinda," said Vi. "I'll be there in a few."

Lucinda went back into her office and after another monster nose-blow she announced over the kind of tannoy I hadn't seen since *Grease* that Mrs. Bombaro had arrived to say a few words and could everyone please gather in the cafeteria where Lana and Bertha (I think) were serving refreshments.

"I don't know what she was thinking!" said Vi, once the salt of the earth with no time for womenfolk and their nonsense had lumbered off cafeteria-wards. "How could she do that? Why would she?"

"I can think of one reason," I said. "It's a brilliant double-bluff."

Mizz Visalia gave me a quizzical look over the top of her powder compact — she was dusting her nose with the sort of pink powder you have to send away for these days.

"If Serpentina and the Dolshikov contingent killed Clovis," I said, "the dumbest next move would be for them to reveal they had a plan for after he was gone."

"You think his own niece killed him?"

"I think at least that she married his rival and she didn't want him to know."

"I always talked him out of sending someone down to Dallas to see what they were up to," she said. "I thought it would kill him. Now I think I helped kill him anyway. If he had known about Sparky and Jan, he would have been forewarned."

"Send someone down to . . . You mean like a spy?"

"We don't call them spies."

"But they're real?"

"We don't talk about it."

"Visalia, for God's sake. You do *want* this murder solved, don't you? If the firework business really has honest-to-God spies, the police should know."

"This she agrees they should know!" said Miss Vi to the ceiling. "They should know everything, Lexy. They should know about the Poggios, certainly."

I tried to smile instead of sighing, but the sigh came out anyway and whistled down the sides of my teeth like a Welsh curse.

"I'll tell them," I said. "I promise. There's something else I want to mention to Mike anyway. Nothing to do with this case, just something that came up in the place where I'm staying."

"Oh?" said Vi.

"And nothing for you to worry about either," I told her. "You've got enough on your plate. Are you sure you're up to this speech?"

Mizz Vi gave me a look of steely dignity, her eyes a lot more Bette Davis than Garfield now. "My family needs me, Lexy," she said. "It's the Bombaro way."

FOURTEEN

She was a marvel. There were about one hundred and fifty "sparklers" gathered in the cafeteria, half of them women in white coats and hairnets, a third of them men in blue overalls and work boots, the rest in shirts and ties or skirts and blouses, with either the slightly deranged smiles of sales staff or the absolutely deranged smiles of pyrotechnicians, who were the twitchiest bunch of misfits I have ever seen gathered together anywhere they might get their hands on matches. I sidled away from them and I didn't care if they saw me.

All of them, hairnets to twitchers, had been or were now crying, although no one else reached the heights of extravagant grief that Lucinda had scaled. But all of them rallied as Vi addressed them.

"We will go on," she said. "We will survive. But first we will give my dear husband the send-off he deserves. I will put a book of —

What's that? Of course. Lucinda has already put a book of condolence in each of the locker-rooms and the sales office and any messages you want to enter there will form part of the ceremony. Bubba and the boys will start working on a show for his funeral. I will take personal responsibility for clearance from the fire marshal. My dear Cousin Clovis knew very well that he would not be buried in a cemetery plot, since there was no way we could get permits for a pyrotechnic show worthy of his memory in a graveyard. It will be the last Bombaro family celebration at the Creek House. It is what he wanted and I agreed. And he will not just be the honoree of the display we design in his memory, he will be a part of the show. We must of course work to fulfill our orders, but when Bubba and the boys decide what they need, anyone who works overtime to build the stock will be paid double and will be in my prayers of thanks. I thank you all, my family, for being here to help me say goodbye and send our dearest Clovis on his final journey."

In other words, if I caught her drift, Clovis's ashes were going to be sprinkled into a bunch of fireworks like so much goldfish food (*FISH, Lexy!*) and he was going to be blasted into the sky. Shame I'd miss the funeral.

And the twitchy guys were under the command of someone called Bubba.

"Now," said Mizz Vi, after she had taken a sip of tea and a bite of muffin, and dabbed her lips, "does anyone have any questions?"

"What about the lightbulbs?" said a timid voice from somewhere in the middle of the crowd.

Visalia's face turned icy and her eyes flashed.

"I will be taking up that topic with my niece and her connections this very day," she said. "Be assured that Bombaro's will continue to be the biggest and best firework manufacturer and the most innovative and exciting provider of pyrotechnic displays in this country. No forty-watt bulb is going to change that."

There was a rousing cheer and even Lucinda managed a smile; watery and accompanied by a hiccup, but still a smile.

"Who did it, Mizz Visalia?" came another voice, just a bit bolder.

"Who would harm that man?" someone else chipped in.

"I will be taking up that topic too," said Mizz Vi. There was a rustle of shocked whispers as it sank home. *She suspected her niece!*

"Now before I go," Mizz Visalia said, "there's one more thing you can do for me. Cast your minds back and see if there's anything suspicious — anything at all — that you think the detectives should know. Anyone hanging around, anything Mr. Bombaro said, anything out of the ordinary. Anything you heard on the grapevine. Any little thing whatsoever that might possibly be useful information to the police — you march right down there and tell them. Now I know how busy you all are with your home lives and your families, so you have my permission to take time out of the working day if you need to go. You don't have to sign off. This, after all, is the greatest work you'll ever do for the Bombaro family."

The squat foreman rumbled a bit at that but everyone else in the room immediately got very concentrated looks on their faces. And who could blame them? They'd just been given a free pass by the boss to bunk off work and go swanning down to Cuento if they felt like it. I'm sure lots of them really wanted to tell the cops about shady characters lurking at the factory gates and veiled hints dropped by Clovis in his last days, but some of them — at least a few of them — would be thinking about pedicures and matinees.

"And," I said, stepping forward, "if anyone needs to talk, my name is Lexy, and I'm a qualified counsellor. I'll be here for the rest of the morning." Mizz Visalia turned and stared at me, but what was she going to do? She could hardly argue. "I'm going to sit right here and if anyone wants a quiet word or advice about techniques in dealing with grief, just come and see me."

I thought I saw a few of the women tear up and start to sniffle in preparation for spending the rest of their shift sitting on their behinds in the cafeteria chewing the fat with me instead of working.

"Thank you, Lexy," said Mizz Visalia as I helped her down from the makeshift podium of pallets where we'd both been standing. "I want them to feel part of this and I want them to know I'm thinking of their pain and loss as well as my own."

I nodded. Truly, California is nothing like Dundee. If a factory boss in Dundee died, the workers would wonder whether to send flowers or just a card. And if they sent flowers, it would be because that way there didn't have to be a poem.

"Anytime," I said.

"But once you're done," said Visalia, "will you come back to the house? I want someone there when I tackle Sparky. And Father

Adam has declined. He hasn't been the support I was expecting."

"I'd be happy to," I lied. "But can I just ask this? What makes you so sure it's Sparky and not Boing-Boing or the other Dolshikovs?"

"Bang-Bang," said Mizz Vi. "That's a very good question. I can't honestly say. It's no more than a hunch, I guess."

"Well, don't ignore it," I said. "I'm a firm believer in the power of the hunch. Don't let her get you alone."

Visalia had been girding herself for a dramatic exit, tweaking her scarf and shifting her hanky round to a clean bit, ready for waving, but that stopped her dead in her tracks. She stood gawping at me. "Do you think I'm in danger?"

"Do you think you're not?" I came back with. "If Sparky killed her uncle to get control of the company and run it into the ground, leaving the way clear for the Dolshikovs, aren't you in her way? Who inherits the business anyway?"

"Me," said Mizz Vi, in a breathless kind of voice. "But . . ."

"But nothing," I said. "You were surprised by how quick they got here, weren't you? Well, if they knew in advance he'd died, that would certainly give them a head start."

"I need a nap," said Vi, and she sounded as if she really did.

"Lock your door, punch in 911 to your phone, and leave it handy," I said.

"Oh dear," she whimpered. "Oh dear."

"Look, get Lucinda or that foreman guy to take you home, eh?" I said. I was beginning to feel like a bit of a brute for not offering, but I did so very much want to make the most of being here in the factory while I could.

Visalia nodded. But funny thing — as I was setting up my grief-counselling corner just a few minutes later, I caught a glimpse of her striding across the car park back towards the gates where a cab was waiting. She looked tip-top and raring to go.

I watched her until the cab was gone, then I went back to fiddling with the window catch, which was why I was standing there in the first place. It was one of the hardest things to get used to in my new life: shutting the windows when it was hot instead of opening them. It drove Branston nuts during our short bout of wedded bliss. I'd leave the bathroom window open to clear the steam and the bedroom window open to freshen the room and then I'd forget. It was the suburbs and, my whole life, the only reasons I'd ever closed a window was for security in a dodgy area and to stop horizontal rain coming in. In this neighbourhood, under a blazing blue sky, I was trying to change the habits of a lifetime and failing.

And anyway it wouldn't have been so bad in a house with a few bloody doors. As it was, we'd come through from the garage, and the heat would paff us in the face like a big fart. There was no mistaking it. Then Bran would groan and I would apologize and then he'd sigh and I'd tell him to get over it and remind him that the air-conditioning would have all four of our nipples on parade in ten minutes flat. And then he'd lecture me about carbon emissions. And I'd ask him whether ten minutes of air-conditioning was really worse than him changing every stitch he wore every day, trousers included, and taking two clean towels — one big, one wee — for his two daily showers and washing it all in a machine the size of my first flat and then tumble-drying it instead of hanging it in out in the sunshine that made him sweat enough for the clothes change and the two showers in the first place.

It was a failure of a marriage in most respects, but we really had managed to get in a full lifetime's worth of bickering.

I turned at a polite cough behind me.

There were two of the hairnet women standing there.

"Hi," I said. "Sit down. Can I get you a cup of tea?"

"What? Why?" said one.

"It's all right, Darla," said the other one. "She just means 'Hello.' " She turned to me. "I watch a lot of *Masterpiece Theatre*. I understand your ways."

"So," I said, "how can I help you?"

"It's the lightbulbs," said the TV fan. "It's gotten out of hand and we think you should know — we think Mrs. B should know — what really went on."

"And what was that?" I said.

"Sparky didn't mean to suggest she was shutting production or moving away from pyrotechnics," Darla said. "All she meant was that she had been developing a second string and she was determined to see it through even without his know-how and guiding hand. We thought it was a good idea, didn't we, CeeCee?"

CeeCee nodded. "Light shows, Sparky said. Drought-compliant light shows to get round the city, county, and state restrictions until it rains again. And — this is the real smart part — light shows could get permits for venues that firework shows would never be allowed in. National parks, residential neighborhoods, historic monuments . . ."

"What historic monuments?" I asked. About an hour's drive away there was a flat rock where native people used to grind acorns and they'd drawn some pictures on it with a sharpened stick. But no one would want to set off fireworks there, surely.

"Like the gardens at the Crutchley house on D street," said CeeCee. "It's a wedding venue but there are no fireworks there because it's historic."

"It is?"

"1870," she said, nodding.

"Of course," I said. "Well, that sounds pretty clever actually. I've seen one. There's one in a forest in Scotland every winter and it's pretty cool and a lot less alarming than a pyrotechnic show. Especially for the deer."

"Right, wildlife. That's another thing," CeeCee said.

"So . . . this is going to sound strange," I said, "but how come you understood it and everyone else has got the wrong end of the stick?"

"Oh," said Darla. "Well . . ." I looked around for eavesdroppers but the lunch ladies were busy behind the counter, a long way from where the three of us sat, and the cooling fans that were working against the heat of the ovens were basically great big white noise machines.

"Everything you say to me is in the strictest confidence," I said. "I've got client confidentiality that covers all counselling sessions."

"Is this a counseling session?" said Cee-Cee.

"How did you feel when you heard about the murder?" I asked.

"Awful!" said Darla.

"It is now." I smiled at them. "So?"

"Well, we overheard her practising what she was going to say to Chucky Cheese."

"Who?" I asked.

"Chuck who was with you at the front today," said CeeCee. "She practised her presentation in the executive washroom." She paused and looked at Darla.

"And we were in there at the time. In two stalls with our feet up, reading the new *People* and letting the white strips work on our teeth for a double date that night. Confidentiality, yeah?"

"Absolutely," I said. "The work ethic is responsible for more ill-health, mental and physical, than all the other ethics put together. Everyone at Bombaro's has been through a great shock and you all need to take care and take time. If you need to curl up in an armchair and read — or sit in a

230

toilet cubicle and whiten your teeth — you should listen to your bodies."

They drank it down. Of course they did. It was carte blanche to be a pair of lazy wee shites in the bosses' bathroom.

"So how exactly did the message get garbled?" I said. "It sounds pretty clear to me."

"It was Chuck," said CeeCee. "When Sparky finished up talking about Uncle Boom-Boom . . ."

Darla giggled.

"Isn't that a euphemism for . . . ?" I said.

Darla giggled again.

"Anyway, when she started in on plans for the future, Chuck was all 'step aside, little lady' that way he is, you know? And he managed to make it sound completely different. Then Sparky tried to come back with a clarification and Chucky just shut her down. Said his workforce was too upset to be asked to make decisions about pay and hours at a time like that."

"Pay and hours?" I said. "What was he on about?"

"No idea," said Darla. "But it worked like a dog whistle."

"I can imagine."

"The only thing we could think of was that we get hazard money for working with gunpowder, making fireworks, and we wouldn't get it if we were working in a light-bulb factory."

"But hang on," I said. "That doesn't make any sense. Sparky's idea was for light shows to get round the fire regs and stop — well, blimey — nearly a hundred and fifty whole years of architectural history being lost." They were nodding solemnly and that made me feel mean so I stopped. "That would be an add-on to the *display* bit of the business, surely. There would be more jobs. For designers. As well as those guys I wouldn't let on the forecourt of a petrol station."

Darla huffed a laugh. "The pyromaniacs? Yeah they're a bit weird, aren't they?"

"But surely" — I dug my phone out of my back pocket and started thumbing away — "surely, the people who put on the light shows just buy all the rigging, don't they? They don't manufacture all the fibre-optics and fairy lights and all that. Look." I handed over my phone, playing a film of the Enchanted Forest.

"Oh! Pretty!" said Darla.

"Man, that would be way cool if you'd had a smoke," said CeeCee.

"So how could it affect anyone who works here apart from making the whole business more secure? That was a wee bit of a low trick, wasn't it? Dropping hints about pay and conditions?"

"Sure was," said Darla. "There was no chance of anyone shutting up and listening to Sparky again after that."

"Huh," I said. "I wonder what he was up to. Chucky Cheese."

"Maybe," Darla said, "he wanted to throw suspicion on her."

"Why?"

"To throw it off him?"

"Was it on him?"

"To *keep* it off him?"

"Was it headed his way?"

"Who can say?" said CeeCee. "You think we should go down into Cuento and tell the detectives about this?" she added, looking hopeful.

"I honestly wouldn't," I said and saw her shoulders slump. "You see, once you tell the police, it's public record and if it gets out that there's trouble at Bombaro's you could lose orders and, worst case scenario, lose jobs."

That got their attention. Of course, I had no idea if it was true and I wasn't greatly concerned even if it was, but I wanted to contain the news until I had got a better handle on it. Dorabelle had been sure the workers loved Clovis. Would the foreman hate him for that? Nah. No factory boss would care enough about productivity to kill.

"Changing the subject just a bit," I said, "can I ask you a question? I mean, if you're the right ones to ask."

"Shoot," said Darla.

"How could you tell if a firework had been set off with a timer instead of just with a match?"

"A timer?" said CeeCee, with golf-ball eyes. "That is the worst idea I have ever heard in my life. A timer? No one would ever do that. That's a surefire fast track to a Darwin award."

"Okay, so not a timer," I said, desperately trying to remember what the other thing was that Sparky had talked about. "A remote match?"

"A what?"

"You'd have to ask the maniacs about that," said Darla. "We just make them. There's no matches anywhere near the production line. We're not allowed to have cigarette lighters or matchbooks in our pockets. We don't even take our phones onto the floor in case they short out. We don't even flirt . . ."

"Oh Darl!" said CeeCee and her eyes filled with tears. I quirked a look at them.

"That was one of Mr. B's sayings," she said. "No smoldering looks on the line. Flirt in the lunchroom."

"Right," I said. "And where would I find the . . . maniacs then?"

"The design office is right above Lucinda's room," said Darla. "There's a door to the right. You want one of us to come with?"

"No, that's okay," I said. "They might speak more freely if it's just me."

FIFTEEN

Behind the glass partition of Lucinda's domain, she was turning the pages of a commemorative volume and weeping copiously onto its gilt-edged pages. I didn't disturb her, just made my way to the narrow stairway off to the side that rose up between institutional green walls — the same green as the morgue basement, unless I was greatly mistaken. It ended at a door with a poster hiding the window. *Welcome to The Inferno* it said in hellacious letters with flames licking at their bottoms and smoke belching in billows from their tops. A figure stood staring out at me from his red eyes. Either he did a lot of glute-work in his exercise routine or he was a demon form, because his haunches were extremely equine, going nicely with the hair that tumbled over his glistening naked shoulders and could easily be a mane. I knocked on the door, avoiding rapping the poster-beast-guy anywhere too tender.

"Enter," came a voice.

I sidled in. He wasn't one of the twitchy ones I had seen downstairs and, at first glimpse, I couldn't help thinking of the Wizard of Oz behind his curtain, because the actual person behind horse-dude on the door was an inch taller than me, perhaps a hundred pounds soaking wet, with thinning ginger hair and a *Keep Calm* t-shirt. When he stood up from behind his monitor I saw that it was a *Keep Calm and Blow Stuff Up* t-shirt, but he had an elasticated belt holding up his cargo shorts and a band-aid on his shin just above his black socks.

"Are you the . . . ?" I said. But I could only think *pyromaniac* and *pantechnicon,* the actual word staying tantalisingly out of reach of my tongue. And I couldn't bring myself to say "Bubba" to his face.

"Bilbo," the guy said. Ahhhh. Not Bubba. "And you are?"

"Lexy," I said. "I didn't see you downstairs at the . . . when Mizz Visalia was addressing the ranks."

"No," he agreed. "I've got documentation. I don't do crowds."

"How do you do firework shows if you don't do crowds?" I asked, instantly intrigued. Every psychologist will tell you, on the record, that spot diagnoses are unhelp-ful and unprofessional and we never slip into them. They're lying; we do it all the time and I had this poor wee scone taped as a generalised social phobic with attendant anxiety disorder already. I was halfway there by the time I'd seen the scary monster covering up the window.

"The crowds are prevented from getting close to the fireworks by sturdy physical bar-riers," he said. "And I'm the designer anyhow. I'm not required at installations."

"I see," I said. "Hm, maybe you're not the one I need to talk to then, Bulb-Bilbo. Bilbo, eh?"

"My parents are geeks," he said, not even smiling. "My sister is called Nyota. They really hate Jackson and Abrams."

"Bilbo, I'm sorry," I said, "but I didn't understand anything after 'sister.' "

"Uh-huh," he said. "They named me after an obscure character in an obscure British work of literary fiction and my sister got the first name of a character from an old TV show that had only been used in a subse-quent tie-in novel. Then JJ Abrams made a movie and Peter Jackson made six and we're both uncomfortably prominent wherever we go. My sister says her name is Nina most days."

"That's awful," I said. "My geography teacher was called Harry Potter. But who was Nyota? What TV show is that?"

He looked at me like I'd asked if Sherlock had a flatmate. "Lieutenant Nyota Uhura was the communications officer on board the USS *Enterprise*," he said. "And what was it you wanted to know?"

"Well, since you missed the address downstairs," I began.

"I didn't miss it. I listened remotely."

"Ah," I said. That put a kink in me pretending that Vi had said any of the stuff I was going to pretend she had said, to get this interview going. "Well, anyway, what I wanted to ask was this: how could you tell if a firework had been lit . . . Ha! That's it. *Remotely*. A remote switch and an electric match. I remembered!"

"Is this the firework that killed Clovis?" he said. "The one the police were asking about too?"

"That's the one," I said.

"There isn't a way," he said, and he sounded very sure. "Assuming the remnants of the wire were removed, which the police confirmed they were."

"They did? How did you get them to do that? I kind of tricked them into nearly saying it, but they really just told you straight out?"

"I offered to look it over to see if I could tell anything about it and they said it was gone."

"Huh. Did they tell you how they knew about the remote switch?"

"They *didn't* know. They thought it might have been a timer, but I told them that was unlikely."

I sighed. He was just as obsessed as the rest of them. In my opinion, if you'd decided to blow up an old man, arse first, you were probably beyond worrying about some gopher or sparrow that might wander on-set and get caught in the action.

"But did they tell you what makes them think the perpetrator wasn't there when the firework went off?"

"No," he said, "I told them."

"You . . . what?" I said. *"What?"*

"They called me in the small hours of Monday morning to ask my opinion."

"And what did you tell them?"

"That it had been done by someone with at least a working knowledge of firework construction and behavior and that it had been triggered remotely."

"And how did you know?"

"I've been a pyrotechnician and display

designer since I graduated college with my PGI DOC. Fourteen years."

I took a deep breath to calm myself down. "I'm not disputing your qualifications, Bilbo, but I meant what were the clues in this instance."

"Oh," he said. "Well, the lift charge had been disabled. See, ordinarily, the lift charge in a full tube would have fired the rocket out of . . . harm's way . . . before the burst charge could do any damage. Someone who knew nothing about fireworks would have missed that. Or they might have taken a mortar out of the tube and used that. But they didn't. It was a full tube but it didn't lift off. It just exploded."

Just a few days before I had actually laughed about it. Now I couldn't imagine how I could ever have been so heartless.

"And . . ." I said.

"And so it was someone who knew enough to tamper with the lift and leave the burst."

I worked hard at suppressing another sigh. Bilbo was hard work.

"I meant, and how do you know that the person used a remote switch?"

"Because no one in their right mind would stay in a closed garage with a lit rocket after disabling the lift," he said. "Or 'duh' for short."

"Okay," I said. "So . . . it's a supposition rather than knowledge, is it?"

"It's a supposition I used to instruct the police in collecting evidence to cement the knowledge," he said.

"And what were the instructions?" I asked. I didn't add anything for short; not FFS or anything.

"I told them there would be residue on everything in the garage and if anyone else was in there, there'd be a body print, like a stencil. I told them that if the person lit the fuse and ran away to hide behind the door like a radiographer, then came back immediately after the explosion, the warm residue would stick to their shoe soles and clothing and they'd leave a trail. If it was later and the residue was cold the trail would be differe— Look, I can email you a link to a blog post instead. It would be much quicker."

"But," I said, "everything you've just said suggests that someone lit the firework and scarpered — no remote, no wire, no return to remove them. Right?"

"Yep," he said.

"I'm lost," I told him. "Where did the thing about a timer come from then?"

"Not a ti—"

"OH MY GOD!" I said, quite a lot louder

242

than I meant to. "Look at it this way: scenario A — strike a match and run. Scenario B — set it up, leave, and return. Okay? How did scenario B get traction when everything points the other way?"

"Ohhhhhh," said Bilbo. "I see. That's probably because they know someone came back after he was dead."

"And how do they know that?" I said, almost weeping.

"Because they took off the handcuffs and ankle-cuffs."

"The what's that?" I said. "How do you know there were handcuffs?"

"The police told me."

"The . . . police just . . . told you?" I said. "Why?"

"I don't know." He looked puzzled, remembering. "I really don't understand why. That woman —"

"Plainclothes Mike?" I said.

"I was talking to her about, well, this and that, pretty much the same stuff I've been talking to you about. Answering her questions and taking it all seriously, and she just got more and more weird. And then she just kind of exploded and told me all about it in one long sentence without taking a breath. I have no idea why. It doesn't seem like a very great habit for a cop, if you ask me."

Poor Mike, I thought. Briefly.

"So *what* did she tell you in the one big long sentence?" I said

"That he had marks on his wrists and ankles from being handcuffed and ankle-cuffed and that they'd been cut off post-mortem."

"How could she tell when they'd been removed?"

"Because there was a lot of blood and so on and it was drying by the time the hand-cuffs and ankle-cuffs came off. If they'd been taken off immediately — the handcuffs and ankle-cuffs — then the blood on his arms and legs would have smeared. But if they — the hand cu—"

"Got it!"

"If they were taken off once coagulation had begun, when the blood was gelid or tacky, it wouldn't smear. And it didn't."

"After Mike blurted all that," I said, "didn't she tell you not to tell anyone else?"

"Oh, yes," said Bilbo. "But that's not enforceable. There's no detective-witness covenant. Once she made the mistake of telling me, she lost control of the information's future dehiscence."

"She really did, didn't she?" I said. "Can I ask you one last question?"

"Is that it?"

"No, Bilbo, that's not it."

"Go ahead."

"And will you keep it quiet that I've been speaking to you?"

"Is that it?"

"No. Will you?"

"Is that —"

"Bilbo!"

"Yes, I will. I will uphold a voluntary covenant of secrecy with you, Lexy. I don't want Visalia to know the upsetting details about what happened to Clovis just before he died."

"Why do you call them Visalia and Clovis?" I said. "That isn't it," I added.

"What *is* it? Waiting's beginning to make me anxious."

"Did Mike really say the cuffs had been cut off?"

"Yes!" he said. "Clearly. She said he was handcuffed and ankle-cuffed and they were cut off. That suggests that the person who put them on — presumably the person who set up the wire and switch and perhaps also the person who disabled the lift charge, although that's less certain — wasn't the person who took them off. Because that person would have the key. That clearly follows from what I've told you."

"But how could you tell that they'd been

cut?" I said.

"The handcuffs and ankle-cuffs?" said Bilbo. "I have no idea how you would tell something like that. If it was done soon after death, the cutters might have made a characteristic trail through the blood on his skin, but since it was done when the blood was drying . . . I have no idea."

"Well, thank you, Bilbo," I said, standing. "You have given me no end of help. And thank you for saying you'd keep quiet. I will too. I agree that Mizz Vi should never know." I smiled at him. "Stay safe," I added. It was one of those strange American things people said to each other all the time. They said it before all the holidays and I could never work out what dangers they had in mind. If it was just Thanksgiving, Christmas, and New Year it might have been snowy roads and drunk drivers that was worrying everyone. And Independence and Memorial Days had the threat of salmonella from bad barbecuing, but they even said it at Easter when the biggest worry was a chocolate coma. And they said it before every trip: "Stay safe!" And sometimes just at the end of random phone calls. Life certainly did seem to be pretty scary.

"Wait," said Bilbo and he leapt to his feet. "We haven't finished our conversation!"

"Oh?" I said. "Go on then."

"I use their first names because I'm a Quaker. Goodbye." He sat down and spun away to look at his laptop. At the first mouse-jiggle he was lost to me.

"Right," I said and left him.

I talked myself in and out of going to report to Mike seven times on the drive back to Cuento and happened to be passing the entrance to the police station car park while I was talked in. Another five hundred yards and I'd have talked myself out for the eight time, but I decided not to question the universe. I pulled in, parked, and went to ask the dispatcher if she would page her.

There was no need. I met her in the foyer. The fact that she was carrying a Dora the Explorer skateboard and — I looked closer — a block of Crisco, hardly even registered.

"I've got to tell you something," I said. "I had an anonymous phone call, from a woman. I didn't recognise the voice."

"Oh?" she said. She put the skateboard down and we both pretended not to notice as it rolled slowly away across the floor. She held out her hand.

"What?" I said, frowning at her hand.

"Show me your phone, so I can see the number," she said. Boy, she was good at this.

"It was on the landline at the motel," I said.

"Okay-doke," she said. She sounded so jaunty, it was obvious she had busted me. It just wasn't obvious how. "I'll get the records. What did she say?"

"She told me she had the handcuff key. Does that mean anything to you?"

"What handcuff key?"

"That's all she said."

Mike put her foot out wide and brought the skateboard back towards her. She flipped it and caught hold of it in her hand.

" 'I've got the handcuff key,' " I said. "Those were her exact words."

"Was she British?"

"No!" I said. "I mean, no." I, on the other hand, was shit at this.

"So she'd have said 'I *have* the handcuff key' not 'I've got.' What are you up to, Lexy?"

"Okay!" I said. "Bilbo didn't keep his promise about keeping his mouth shut."

"What?" she said. "Are you high?"

"Bilbo, the pyrotechnician at Bombaro's," I said.

"Ah. Yes," she said. "Well, I've met his sort before. I'm surprised he hasn't written a blog yet. No biggie. Free speech. What handcuffs, though?"

"Right," I said. "An ongoing investigation. No way you're going to share the details with me." I turned away, but she put a hand out and touched my arm.

"Seriously," she said. "What handcuffs are you talking about?"

I frowned at her. "The handcuffs and ankle-cuffs used to —"

"Oh!" she said. "I see. Great!"

"I don't understand," I said.

"I know." She smiled at me. "I like that."

"I suppose you would," I said. She gave me a puzzled look and God help me I sank to her level. I showed off. But oh so subtly. Not.

"Any time they're asked," I told her, "law enforcement professionals tend to say they joined the service to protect and serve, or out of a concern for justice, or even because of that time they fell down a well and a big cop saved them, but I've never bought it. It doesn't surprise me at all that you take pleasure in knowing more than me and feel happier that way."

The smile was gone. Totally gone. Simultaneous strokes on both sides of the brain gone.

"Be careful, Ms. Campbell," she said.

"Yeah, see, that was definitely a flex of your professional muscles, wasn't it?" I said.

"That wasn't protection, service, or justice calling the shots there."

"Be very careful," said Mike. "You don't want to get on the wrong side of your local police force."

I considered saying more. I half considered saying a lot more, but in the end I just nudged her with my elbow and said, "Only kidding."

"This is your lucky day," she said to me. "It's not often you get to assault an officer and walk out of here."

"Assault?" I said. "You mean that right there when I nudged you?"

"Be careful," she said, "and don't say I didn't warn you."

SIXTEEN

I walked back out into the car park trembling, almost swooning as the peak of the day's high-bake-setting hit me. I had got this seriously wrong. I had watched too many Inspectors — between Morse, Frost, and Lewis — and not nearly enough of *The Wire*. I had genuinely thought she didn't mind me poking my nose in and I had even wondered if maybe we might be friends one day, Plainclothes Mike and me. I remembered Roger's knee-jerk plea to leave the cops out of it and his flat look when I asked him why. I didn't know if he'd been picked on for being gay or picked on for being black, but I felt stupid for not guessing, at least, that he'd been picked on.

I chirped open the Jeep then jumped at a voice behind me.

"Is that your vehicle, madam?" It was Soft Cop.

"It belongs to a friend of mine."

"And do you have written permission confirming your right to be in possession of it?"

"Aw, come on!" I said. "Did Mike send you out here to hassle me?"

"If you don't have proof that you're in legal possession, you'd better leave it here until you get some."

"It's bloody boiling!" I said. "I'll get sunstroke walking in this and I'll sue the city."

The cop looked up at the sky. "Pfft," he said. "It ain't even close to hot yet. Mid-nineties. Start moving. No loitering on police property."

I was beginning to get how this worked. No one — not Noleen, not Della, not this guy — would entertain the notion that it was even warm until it hit a hundred. And they were all as wrong as they were crazy. It was *melting.* Even in the shade under the tunnel, I sweltered.

All of a sudden, I wished with all my heart I was in Dundee, even with the drizzle and the roadworks and the only thing stopping the kebab wrappers blowing along the streets on a Sunday morning being the puddles of vomit. I looked at the ground here in the darkest part of the tunnel. No litter, no puke, not even a dogshit. It wasn't natural. Then a car coming up behind me slowed and I heard the window going down. My gloom deepened. A kerb crawler. Perfect.

"You look really unhappy!" came a familiar voice, and I turned to see Father Adam hanging out of the driver's window of a Mini Cooper and grinning at me. Grinning for all the world as if he was really what he dressed as: a laidback, anything goes, California priest who would surf to work if we lived near the beach.

"You'd know all about that," I said. "Sorry to snatch away your chance to ruin my day. It's ruined already."

"Huh?" he said. "Can I give you a ride?"

"Much as I'd love to sit beside you and tell you what I think of you on a long road-trip," I said, "I'm just up here." I pointed to the motel. "So it's not worth fiddling with the seatbelt."

Huh?" he said. He checked in his rearview mirror, such a conscientious driver, not wanting to be holding anyone up. But no one was coming. Where was he going anyway? There was nothing this way except the motel and the Skweeky Kleen, a self-storage facility, and then a back road to the next one-horse town. "Lexy, have I done something to upset you?"

"Ha!" I said. "No, but you've done something to piss me off and make me despise you and everything you stand for." Partly I just wanted to enjoy talking to someone who wouldn't threaten me. Mike had seriously given me the willies. But partly it was true. "Visalia needs love and support and a listening ear right now. She doesn't need you standing there with your rolling pin and she doesn't need saints and popes giving her what for."

"What are you talking about?"

I rubbed my eyes with my knuckles. This felt like the fiftieth conversation today where I couldn't make myself understood or understand what was being said to me and it was exhausting.

"She blew your cover, Holy Boy."

"What the hell does that mean?" he said, jerking his chin into his neck and staring at me.

"Visalia told me you won't give her communion because she won't agree to a church funeral."

"What?" said Father Adam. "She . . . what? Oh my God! I *knew* she wasn't listening. I think she was drunk."

"Two daiquiris," I said, "but she hadn't slept well." I took a deep breath and tried to sound a bit more friendly. "What really happened then?"

"I offered confession and communion. She refused. It's quite common to be angry at God when something terrible happens. And of course we're having Clovis's celebration of life in the church. Of course we are. No internment, because of his last wishes. Have you heard what he wanted done with his bodily remains?"

"I heard what's *being* done," I said. "Visalia thinks you think she's doing it against Clovis's wishes and thereby disobeying her husband. Which, as you know, is a big fat sin."

"What?" said Father Adam, again. He put the car in neutral and pulled on the handbrake. Then he just sat there gaping up at me.

"And it's not as if he's here to see it."

"Although I would say he's looking down with interest," Father Adam said. "But can you back up a bit there to the sin of disobedience?"

"Was she not supposed to tell me? Was it hush-hush? Understandable."

"Hush-hush?" he said. "It's bullshit."

"Vi said two saints and two popes —"

"Oh, yeah, yeah, they sure did. Peter and Paul. Big fans of docile wives. And slavery. Every family has a couple of crazy uncles."

I laughed out loud. I couldn't wait to tell Visalia how firm a grasp she'd taken of the wrong end of this stick. I gave Father Adam my best smile, hoping he'd forgive me for calling him names and telling him I despised him.

Then I kind of ruined it, mocking his beliefs. "So," I said, "you really believe Clovis is up there watching all this?"

"I really do. Fluffy cloud, harp, the whole enchilada." Then he laughed at me and I let him.

"Even if he died in a state of . . . whatever it is? Because of almost running off with Barb?"

"God is love," he said.

" 'Kay," was all I could dredge up in answer.

Father Adam leaned out of the open window and twisted until he was facing the roof of the tunnel. "Who killed you, Clovis?" he yelled, his voice booming in the echo chamber.

I glanced up at the dome of cobwebby brickwork above my head.

"Made ya look!" said Father Adam. Then, seeing a car coming up behind him, he pulled his head in and drove away waving. I noticed that his licence plate was JESUS FTW and I was grinning as I waved back.

The Mini Cooper and the car coming up behind it both turned in at the Last Ditch. Father Adam stopped in front of the launderette and hauled a huge sack of laundry out of the little boot. The other one, a Land Rover, stopped at the fifteen-minute space at reception and a tall woman jumped down. She didn't look like the Last Ditch's typical client: too prosperous to be staying here by choice and not knackered enough to be stopping because she couldn't find the strength to drive another yard. She gave me a friendly nod and threw open the back doors. When I got closer I saw the refrigerated cases and the selection of butterfly nets and binoculars, so I took a guess.

"Are you Cindy Slagle?"

"At your service," she said.

"Is there more trouble?" I said. "I saw the . . ."

"Anoplura," she said. "It was quite remarkable, wasn't it?"

"It was disgusting," I said. "Are they really all dead?"

"Of course they're dead," she said. "They were parasites with no host."

I knew it was irrational, but I started to itch. I willed myself not to scratch my head but I failed. At least it made Professor Slagle happy, laughing at me.

"Do they carry disease?" I asked.

"Well," she said, which wasn't a great start. "Of course, there's pediculosis, but it's nothing to worry about."

"Thanks," I said. "So, it's none of my business of course, but if the nanopurples —"

"Anoplura."

"Yes. If they're dead, why are you back?"

"I put one in Plexiglas as a souvenir," she said, opening one of the cases in the back of the Land Rover and drawing out a little bubble of clear plastic. She held it on the palm of her hand as if it was a golden goose egg.

"Ahhh," I said. "You might not want to be waving that around here." But just then I saw Kathi coming out of the Skweeky Kleen to say goodbye to Father Adam. "Well, actually, if you give it to Noleen right now you'll be okay."

I even kind of wanted to follow her in and see what Noleen made of the gift, even just see what Noleen had selected as a t-shirt message that day, but I was exhausted and hungry and I'd sweated through my posh undies and t-shirt walking from the cop shop, so I left them to it and climbed the stairs to the walkway and my room, not touching the metal rail. I was half sure I could see it pulsing with heat.

Surprisingly, there was no sign of Todd and no evidence that he'd been in my room. I made for the bathroom, already stripping my damp t-shirt off. The door seemed sticky and in the extra two seconds it took me to shove it open I had time to think *he's been in and put a fluffy carpet down* then *that sounds like duct tape letting go* then *why would my door be duct-taped shut from the inside* then *what's that funny noise.* Then a pall of stink so thick and strong that I thought I could see it (it was yellow) rolled over me and a cloud of enormous oily-green insects rose like a tiny tornado from where they had been feasting, in my bath, on a raccoon, deader than any roadkill I had ever seen or smelled or dreamed of after French cheese for supper.

I took a breath to scream and inhaled one of them. Coughing and gagging, I reeled out and across the room. I pelted along the walkway and down the stairs. The Land Rover was still there. I burst into reception, hacking and whimpering, and shot straight through to the office, where Cindy and Noleen were sitting with cans of Coke.

"CRGHK!" I said.

Noleen leapt to her feet, got into position behind me, and wrapped her arms around my bare midriff. It was only then I twigged I was running about in my bra. Noleen jerked her elbows in and then, like the pro she was, Professor Slagle caught the insect in her baseball cap.

"Oh, Noleen!" I said and threw my arms round her.

"Chew your food," Noleen said, patting me once on the back and then extricating herself firmly.

"Hmm," said Professor Slagle. "*Protophormia terranovae*. Rather pedestrian after last night's adventures."

"Pedestrian?!" I said. "Are you kidding me?"

"It's a Northern Blowfly," Professor Slagle said. "Or bluebottle."

"Come with me," I said to her. "You too, Noleen, please."

I was hurrying because I thought, now the door was open, the bluebottles would soon be gone. I hadn't reckoned on the attractions of a very dead raccoon, bloated and stinking, though. When we got back to the bathroom, most of them were still there, resettled on their treat, so that the grey fur rippled and hummed with life as if a breeze was blowing through it.

Noleen dropped down onto the closed toilet lid. Her t-shirt today read *Loan me a damn and I'll give it* but it was lying now. She gave a damn about this.

"Entomologically speaking," said Professor Slagle, "this is of no interest, compared with the *Anoplura,* but in other respects, it raises questions."

"Questions like how did a dead raccoon get into my bathroom and close the window behind itself and tape round the door?" I said.

The prof stepped up onto the rim of the bath and opened the small window there.

"Cindy," said Noleen, with a break in her voice, "I swear to God, if you slip and put your foot through that critter, I will kill you. Once I've stopped throwing up, I will kill you with these two clammy hands."

"It must have been someone pretty small and agile," Cindy was saying. "I wouldn't fit through here, although I could easily get up the tree. I do a lot of tree climbing on my collecting trips. Entomology is pretty much a licensed lifelong childhood in a way."

"That's great," I said. "But how could someone climb the tree and get in the window carrying a dead raccoon?"

Cindy looked over her shoulder at me with a look doing its best to tell me I was an idiot.

"You're an idiot," Noleen said.

I opened my mouth to disagree but just

then I heard footsteps on the metal stairs and went to shut and lock my door.

"Thank you," Noleen said when I was back again.

"I am an idiot, though, aren't I?" I said. "He would have brought the raccoon in through the door, sealed *this* door, and then *left* through the window."

"Probably releasing the *Protophormiae* just before closing it," Cindy said.

"Do you have security cameras?" I asked Noleen. She nodded. "So how about you and I sit and look through the tapes?" I said. I left a big outrageous pause.

"I need to clean all this up first," said Noleen, leaving another one.

"Actually," said Cindy, "if it's all the same to you, I'd like to take this with me."

"The raccoon?"

"And the *Protophormiae*. Don't look at me like that. I've got a student doing a thesis on larval distrib—"

"Be my guest," said Noleen. "Can you move it without anyone knowing what it is?"

"It'll be in something as innocent as a cooler," Cindy said. "It'll look like a picnic."

Noleen gave her a sickly grin, and I managed one too.

"It's okay," Cindy said. "I know I should be grossed out and it grosses you out that

262

I'm not, but it's just like being an eye surgeon, you know?"

It was a good analogy, but when your stomach's turning somersaults from putrefying raccoons and bluebottles laying eggs on them, thinking about surgeons slicing eyeballs doesn't really help much. We left her to it, stopping to pick up a t-shirt, and went back to the office.

Noleen's face was as grey as her hair when she flumped down into her Barcalounger.

"What's going on, Lexy?" she said. "Is it Todd? You understand more about these things than I do. What do you think? Is it Todd and Kathi?"

"Kathi?"

"If we look at this video, will we see one of them going into your room with a garbage sack?"

"I have no idea what would make you think that," I said.

"It doesn't seem too big a leap to me," said Noleen.

I knew where she was pointing. Pathological cleanliness and cleptoparasitosis seem so disordered to anyone who doesn't suffer from them. Why not sprinkle a little Münchausen dust on top and have Kathi douse a bathroom in mysterious ketchup to *prove* that life is crazy and the world is

263

filthy, like she's been saying? Why not have Todd lure a thousand bluebottles with a dead raccoon, and a million *Anoplura* with whatever nasty little treat *they'd* been lured by? I took a deep breath and prepared to explain why it couldn't happen in a hundred years and I was personally willing to guarantee that it hadn't happened here.

"I know you argue about dirt," I said. "And I know Todd and Roger argue about bugs, and it must seem as if they've won a round with all this happening. But the thing is, their problems are their problems — all the time, twenty-four-seven, whether you're arguing or not, whether you're there or not. They could no more do those things than you could . . . what? I know you don't have a pathology like Kathi, but there must be something you hate. Cotton wool, nails on blackboards?"

"Worms," said Noleen. "Bait worms. I used to have to bait my daddy's fishing line, sitting in that little boat, heaving up and down on the swell, sick as a dog. It's one of the house rules here: no bait in the rooms. I didn't tell you because I didn't have you pegged as the fishing sort, but if I see a man in the right kind of hat, I tell him straight away."

"Okay," I said, "so worms. You wouldn't

go and get a bucket of them just to win an argument, would you?"

Noleen shuddered. "I need a drink," she said. She leaned over sideways and got a bottle of Jack Daniels and two glasses out of a low drawer. She held it up to me enquiringly.

Now I shuddered. "Whisky is my worms," I said. "First time I ever got drunk was on whisky at a school disco. I'll never forget it and I've never drunk it again. I'd die for a cup of tea, though."

I did my best with the microwave, Lipton's, and powdered creamer while Noleen found the file we needed from the security camera.

"Funny how we still say 'tape' when it's not even a disc anymore," I said, settling down beside her. "Okay, you're in charge. You'll know who belongs and who doesn't."

God, it was dull. We sat there looking at a grainy picture of a car park, a fence, half a dumpster, and the bottom of a metal stairway. The most excitement was when I left, then when Todd left, then when three sets of tourists left. And that was exactly as exciting as it sounds.

Kathi crossed the frame a few times, once going upstairs wiping the banister rail with her cloth and once coming down, wiping the underneath of the banister rail with a different cloth. Then nothing. A blue jay sat on the dumpster lid for a while but flew off again.

"Aren't these usually motion-sensitive?" I asked.

"The expensive ones are," Noleen said. "This just loops. And the loop's going to run out pretty soon. We're at lunchtime already."

We sat, stupefied — her by whisky and me by the truly godawful cup of tea — and kept watching. I started glancing at the little sidey-ways egg-timer that showed how much tape was left to play. It was getting tight.

"If it runs out, we can always ask around the other rooms," I said.

Noleen shook her head firmly. "I'm trying to run a business here," she said. "How would you feel about a place where you were asked if you'd seen strangers running around with bloated animal corpses? Would you book for same time next year?"

"I'll make something up," I said. "I'll say . . ." I stared up at the ceiling, hoping for inspiration.

"That you'd ordered take-out and they swore they'd delivered and charged your credit card, so they must have gone to the wrong room?"

"Kind of a big take-out order," I said. I looked back at the monitor but Noleen was rewinding, the screen a Missoni scramble. "Have you seen something?"

"Watch," she said grimly.

The grainy car park, fence, half-dumpster, and stair-bottom sat there for a moment or two and then from the right we saw a small figure with a logo on the back of his striped shirt that matched the logo on the front of his baseball cap and the logo on the top one of five pizza boxes he carried. He bustled to the bottom of the stairs and took them two at a time without pausing or raising his head.

"That's a lot of pizza," I said.

"That's five fake pizza boxes with a dead raccoon inside," said Noleen firmly. "I know every pizza joint in Cuento, and that ain't any of them."

"Did you recognise the guy?" I said.

"Sure I did. He's the guy small enough to fit through the bathroom window and he's a pro. I recognize that much."

"How do you know he's a pro?"

Noleen rewound the tape again and this time, as she let it play, she hunched forward and pointed to the clues. "He knows where the camera is. Look at the angle of his hat!

And then when he turns at the bottom of the stairs, he twists his head away. He's not looking where he's putting his feet and he's not looking up at where he's going. He knows where he's going, because he scoped it out. He's done this plenty." She sat back. "Now let's wait for him coming back down."

It was only five minutes later, right at the end of the loop. With his head bowed even lower and the cap pulled down like a Fedora, he came skipping down the stairs and, face turned away, he disappeared from view. And he was still carrying the boxes.

"But they look lighter," Noleen said. "They look one big-ass decomposing raccoon lighter to me. How 'bout you?"

"Why didn't he take the boxes out the window?"

"Huh," said Noleen. "Would they fit?"

"Oh, right. No. Or not without folding them."

"And they tell you not to do that at pizza-delivering school, don't they?"

"Play it again," I said. "I know we can't see his face but let's look at his ears and hands and feet. There must be something somewhere."

Noleen gave me a look. "You think we're going to zoom in and see his irises reflected in the shine on the pizza label?" she said. "I couldn't afford motion sensors, Lexy; this is not high-def."

"Just humour me," I said. "I'll look at the head and you look at the outline. Look at the walk. See if this is anyone you've ever seen before."

"Me?"

"You. Because this is a vendetta, Nolly," I said. "This is no prank. This is a message. And it's your motel. Who else are they sending it to?"

"Todd? It's bugs, isn't it?"

"Or Kathi?" I said. "Because it's not the height of hygiene."

"But if it was Kathi, it would be in the laundromat. And if it was Todd it would be in his room or in his car. Wouldn't it?"

"How would they get in? Mind you, how *did* he get in?"

"Like I said, he's a pro."

We stared at one another for a bit. And then Noleen smacked her hands together and said we had nothing to lose from trying. She played the footage five more times. I saw that the guy had no visible tattoos, jewelry, piercings, bruises, scars, or unusual brand of cigarette tucked handily behind his ear.

"Well?" I said to Noleen, when she froze the frame for the last time. "What's your gut reaction?"

"Never seen him before in my life," Noleen said.

"Describe him in three words."

"Pizza. Delivery. Guy."

I sighed. "Time to call the cops," I said. I didn't add that I had offended the formerly friendly Detective Mike. I'd fade away in the background and hope that if she didn't see me, I wouldn't occur to her.

But Noleen wasn't having it. "You've got to be kidding," she said. "They would shut us down in a hot minute. And even if they didn't, the report in the *Voyager* would do it for them."

And it was while we were sitting there, clueless, that Kathi suddenly spoke behind us.

"What the hell's *he* doing here?" she said. When I spun round she was staring at the monitor screen with angry blots of colour rising up from the open neck of her overall towards her jaw.

"You know this guy?" said Noleen.

Kathi came forward and peered closer at the screen. Then she straightened up and laughed. "Jeez, flashback!" she said. "He looks like someone I *used* to know. But it's not him. No way the guy I'm thinking of would be delivering pizzas."

"Kathi," I said, "who did you think it was? It's really important."

"Why?" said Kathi, looking from one to the other of us. "What's happened?"

"Nothing," said Noleen.

"Oh sure, it looks like nothing. You drinking in the daytime and watching the security feed."

"Okay," I said. I held out a hand to quell Noleen before she could stop me. "It's not nothing. He broke into my room and left a dead raccoon in the bath."

Kathi looked over her shoulder and up towards where my room sat, as if she had X-ray eyes. "How dead?" she said. "Decomposing? Sloughing off on the floor and seeping down the cracks in the tile?"

"In the tub," I said. "Right in the tub."

"Hey, hey, hey," came a voice from the front office. It was Todd. He appeared with a cardboard tray of coffee cups. "I took a chance and here you all are," he said. "Thank you, universe! Lexy, your large English breakfast tea, with whole milk. Triple latte, Nolly. Kathi, a salted caramel iced macchiato with extra sprinkles and a shot of insulin. And for *moi* . . . What is it?"

"Someone put a dead raccoon in Lexy's bath," Kathi said.

"How dead?" said Todd. "Dead enough to

attract egg-layers? Because those larvae hatch *quick.*" He put the tray down and went to stand beside Kathi.

Noleen gave me a look that spoke. *It was your bright idea to share the news,* the look said, *it's your problem to contain it, sweet cheeks.*

"Not very dead at all," I said. "Fresh, fresh, fresh. Practically still alive. No decomposing, no egg-laying, and definitely no sloughing. And it's gone."

Then Cindy joined us and ruined it all.

"I got most of the bluebottles and almost all of the putrefying host material," she said. "Just one tiny spill and not on the carpet."

Todd and Kathi shrank back against the filing cabinet, faces white and eyes wide.

"Great," I said. "Cindy, this is Todd, who suffers from cleptoparasitosis, and Kathi, who suffers from severe germaphobia. They both *live here.*" *You clueless freak,* I chose not to say.

Cindy nodded slowly a few times. When she opened her mouth to speak I cast my eyes about, wondering whether to ring a fire alarm to drown out the sound or just hit her with the whisky bottle. But she surprised me.

"I'm afraid of kneecaps," she said. "Genuphobia. I'm truly sorry to have caused you

272

distress."

"Is that why you went into entomology?" said Kathi. It seemed a silly question to me, but what did I know?

"It took me into the sciences, certainly," Cindy said.

I blinked. Nothing, that's what I knew.

"Everyone has to wear long pants in the lab and in the field. It's the only way I can live in a warm climate. I take my vacations in the Dakotas. In February. Again, I'm very sorry."

It was a moment of peace and fellow-feeling, like a little oasis in the middle of chaos.

"Excuse me," said Todd, wrecking it. "I happen to have had a run of bad luck with infestations, but I don't *suffer* from anything except being married to a dork."

"And I happen to like things tidy," said Kathi. "I'm a psychobabble-phobe, but that's all."

"Let me make it up to you both," I said. "Come to the pet shop with me and help me choose fish for Diego, then I'll take you for ice cream."

"But not Pet Planet out at the strip mall," said Todd, "because those filthy freaks have stick insects. In a pet store!"

"And let's go in my car," said Kathi. "No

offence, Todd, but your Jeep hasn't been cleaned for days."

I thought of the pristine Jeep — which was still sitting at the police station, damn it! — and had to bite my tongue down on a torrent of scorn, but I managed to say only, "See you out front in five."

SEVENTEEN

"Is it okay to leave the launderette unattended?" I asked as I buckled myself into the back seat of Kathi's SUV and sank back waiting for the a/c to kick in.

"It's self-serve," Kathi said. "And there's a drop-off for the dry cleaning. You'd know if you'd been in there." I wasn't sure if she was chiding me for being slovenly about washing my clothes or just for being unfriendly and not dropping in to chat. I caught her eye in the side mirror and couldn't get any clues. She was hard to read. Hard to warm to. Fierce as Noleen was, I felt closer to her after our few action-packed days than I did to this enigmatic woman who was staring back at me.

I smiled at her and she snapped her eyes away.

"So," said Todd, "you've got a new job, huh?"

It wasn't until he twisted round in his seat

that I realized he was talking to me.

"What? I'm on my way to the airport as soon as I'm finished with Mizz Visalia," I said. "Where'd you hear I'd got a job?"

"You said you were at an interview and you'd excused yourself to go to the bathroom," Todd said, speaking a bit too loud. "You said the company was community-minded with great benefits. Have you ever considered an MRI, Lexy? Just to be on the safe side?"

"Oh that! I was listening to Mizz Visalia's summary of her late husband's business practices," I said. "Have you ever considered reality as a location, Todd?"

"Some therapist you are," he said.

"You declined my services," I reminded him.

"Don't make me pull over," said Kathi, and we both laughed.

"So was it one of his employees who killed him?" Todd said. "In spite of him being such a great boss?"

"I have no idea who killed him," I said. "And I'll tell you this for nothing: it doesn't look good for Mizz Vi. She was his wife and she inherits. She's got an alibi, but it doesn't clear her because they think it was done on a tim— I mean, remotely. *And* he was cheating on her. But then it doesn't look good for his girlfriend either. Barb Truman. Because he was getting ready to dump her. But she swears she didn't know that. And she's got an alibi too. But it's not a good one. She was sitting alone in a busy airport but she hadn't checked in for her flight or gone through security. But she was wearing quite distinctive clothes. And speaking of flights, Clovis's niece got here from Texas licketier-splitlier than seems reasonable. And she's been acting dead weird ever since she arrived. And she's just married his arch rival and they're plotting to run down Clovis's business until the Dolshikovs control everything, coast-to-coast. Which sounds mad, but she has brought two Dolshikov cousins with her for no apparent reason and these guys could walk on as Henchman 1 and Henchman 2 without make-up. But then maybe she's not plotting against the business at all and it's just that the firework factory foreman made it sound as if she was and freaked everyone out. And that might be because he was trying to point to her to mask his own guilt. But it might just be because he's got a problem with powerful women. Or maybe just women in general. And Mizz Vi just keeps on and on about going back to Sicily, despite a blood feud back in the old country with some people called Poggio."

I paused, pretty impressed with myself for the clarity of my roundup. I waited, but neither Kathi nor Todd said anything.

"I suppose I just need to leave it up to the cops to straighten it out. They've taken a wheen of stuff out of her safe: his will and plane tickets and house deeds. Between those three things they could clean the whole thing right up. Because if the plane tickets are for the Caymans, Barb's in the clear. If the will leaves the whole shebang to Visalia, Serpentina's good. And if the house deed is for Sicily, then Mizz Vi can breathe easy. It's frustrating, because I know there's a receipt in the safe in her bedroom that would reveal all, but she's forgotten the combo. Poor old soul. So. Let the cops do their job and I'll do mine, I suppose."

I paused again. Still, they said nothing.

"Not that I'm the biggest fan of the cops."

Nothing.

"By any means."

I leaned forward and looked at Todd. "I was a bit of a plank to Roger, actually. I don't know if he told you. Acted like a proper straight white doofus. I need to say sorry."

"I was born in Cuento," said Todd. "Did I tell you that?"

"No," I said slowly. I hadn't wondered where he came from because, in Dundee, most of the people who're there have always been there, and most of the people who're ever going to be there are there already. Me upping sticks for California was just about big enough news to get in the *Courier*. My best friend Alison had been my best friend since I helped her pick out the edge bits of a forty-piece jigsaw puzzle first day of primary school. And once I got back into my groove after this little swerve, she'd be my best friend till both of us were racing our electric wheelchairs round the nursing home with our catheter bags walloping off the tight turns. In short, Dundonians might as well be plants as people, really. I was like a sunflower seed that had been eaten as a last-minute snack by a snow goose in Tayside and shat out as it banked north for Vancouver.

"Yep," said Todd. "Born here. Single mom, Caesar Chavez Elementary, MLK High, West Sac CC, transferred in on a full ride to UC."

"I have no idea what any of that means," I said, "or even why you're telling me."

"Barb Truman," said Todd, "is my mother."

"What?" I said. "Barb's your . . . *what*?"

"I knew she had a boyfriend and I knew she was headed out on vacation somewhere," Todd said. "But I didn't know his name and I haven't been in touch. Well, of course I haven't. I thought she was sitting on a beach with 'my new daddy.' "

"Kathi," I said, "can you take us to Gerbera Drive, please?"

"I already am," said Kathi. "And after that I'm going to wherever your 'sweet Mizz Vi' lives. Because I don't know much, Lexy, but you know *nothing*. That name you're throwing around is a mob name. This is serious trouble you've got yourself into here."

"And I don't suppose there's the slightest chance that 'mob name' is a cute little California expression for something harmless, is it?"

"Nope," said Kathi.

"Okay, but what good will it do to go round there?" I asked. "We'll be lucky to get her alone. It would be better to call, really."

"I don't want to get her alone," Kathi said. "I want you and me to sit and visit and drink mimosas while Todd cracks the safe and reads that evidence receipt."

It was my turn to sit like a dumb lump and say nothing. It lasted a good long while too. But I got my voice back eventually.

"What makes you think Todd can crack a safe?" I said. "It's got a keypad that counts your attempts and sends a message to a security firm if you go over."

"Oh, my sainted aunt!" said Todd, getting a chuckle out of Kathi. "How could I ever outwit such sophistication? Why, the very thought of it is just making my little head spin!" He turned and gave me a look that dripped scorn and pity like a mop drips soapy water. "You really are new here, aren't you? Chavez E, King High, and a transfer in don't mean nuttin' to you." His voice was changing.

"Not much," I admitted.

"I don run with them these days," Todd said, "but cut me through and Norteños is still writ there."

"I feel like I've turned over two pages at once," I said. "You're an anesthetist called Todd Truman. Who's Norteños?"

"I'm an anesthesiologist called Todd *Kroger,*" he said. "I took Roger's name. Cos no hospital board in Sac would open the medication locker to a brown guy called Teodor Mendez." He held up a finger. "Teodor Mendez Jr. I was named for my daddy."

"Huh," I said. "I thought it was a tan."

Before they recovered the power of speech,

I turned to Kathi. "And you! You know about the mob how exactly? What's *your* real name?"

"Katherine Mary Muntz," said Kathi. "*I* changed it too."

"Changed it to Muntz?" I said. "Does Nolly have any idea how much you love her?" For the first time since we'd met, I saw warmth in Kathi's eyes as she laughed back at me. "Okay," I said, clapping my hands. "Let's go visiting. It'll be daiquiris at Casa Bombaro, by the way. Not mimosas."

"But it'll be bourbon at Barb's," said Todd. "Unless she's changed a lot since Mother's Day."

The neighbour lady at 355 Gerbera Drive was pushing cucumbers today, on her little wooden market stall at the end of the drive. We parked in front of it and then Kathi edged forward so we weren't blocking the merchandise from passing trade. That brought us right in front of Barb's happy home. The curtains were closed. There was another newspaper yellowing on the drive and a black bin bag, tied shut at the top but ripped open by squirrels, had been added to the dead plants on the porch.

"Oh, Mom," said Todd. He took a deep breath and climbed down.

"Will we go in right now or give them a minute?" I said to Kathi.

Todd turned round and peered in at us through the tinted windows. "Get your asses out of the car and flank me."

Kathi and I scrambled down and we marched up the drive in lockstep.

Once again, Barb answered our knock after a pause just long enough to let her put down her whisky, close her bathrobe, and stagger to the door. But when she opened it, she was dressed in an overshirt and leggings with her hair up in a scarf and she was wiping paint off her hands onto a cloth.

"Teo!" she said. Then she looked at me. "I know you from somewhere," she said. Then she looked at Kathi. "And you're from the Skweeky Kleen." She shook her head. "Picked the wrong day to stop drinking. What the hell's going on?"

"Where's your garbage can, Mom?" said Todd. Barb leaned out and looked at the bin bag, then screwed her face up.

"Dammit," she said. "That looks tacky. Let me get that. Go around and in the slider, honey. There's dustsheets down in the living room." She gave us all a huge smile as she picked up the leaking bin bag and walked down the drive with it. "I decided to paint that man right outta my life!" she sang. "And send him on his wa-ay." She opened the wheeliebin of her next door neighbour and dumped the bag inside, then she scuffed her bare feet over the trail of — I'm guessing — whisky she had left on their shared drive. We heard someone knock on the front window just before we turned the corner and, looking back, I saw Barb lift a finger and give a perfect raspberry accompaniment. There was nothing about this woman I didn't love.

She set a dumpy bottle of ginger beer down in front of Todd without asking and then offered Coke, Tropicana, or Fiji to Kathi and me.

"I can't run to so much as a glass of white wine spritzer," she said. "This is a dry house now, Teo. And no bumming cigarettes either. I've quit."

"I quit when I was eleven, Mom," said Todd, which wasn't quite a classic testament to clean living but was pretty impressive. Any kid who could pack up fags at puberty, when looking cool never mattered more, was exactly the kid who could dig his way out of Norteños (they had explained on the drive over) and end up where Todd had ended up. Before the mental illness and the Last Ditch anyway.

"And how's my lovely son-in-law?" Barb

said. "You should have brought him."

"You know why that's not going to happen," said Todd.

"Oh honestly!" said Barb. She turned to Kathi and me and spread her hands. "I make one harmless little remark . . . anyone else would have seen it as the gift it was."

"What did you say, Barb?" I asked.

"Who are you now?" she said, squinting at me. "Did we meet down at the airport on Sunday?"

"No," I said.

"Sure? I could have sworn I remember you complimenting me on my playsuit."

"Playsuit, Mom?" said Todd. "Seriously? You're fifty-five years old."

"Well, don't take out an ad!" Barb said. She rolled her eyes and turned away from him. "Do you have kids?"

"Not so far," I said. Kathi said nothing.

"Well, don't count on grandkids," Barb said. "I made one harmless suggestion and Dr. Pretty walked out and won't come back."

"Mother," said Todd. "You offered us an egg and a womb if we kicked in Roger's sperm."

Kathi inhaled a mouthful of Coke and started cough-laughing, then blew her nose and said, "Ow. Fizzy."

"It was a very practical suggestion, given your circumstances," said Barb. "And plus I was hammered. So you tell Dr. Pretty to take the stick out of his butt and get round here for my steak dinner one night while he still can. If there's one thing the last week has taught me, it's that life is short and precious and we need to make every day count."

"It would help if you didn't call him Dr. Pretty," said Todd.

"I'm willing to forget what I overheard him call me," said Barb. Kathi and I both looked at Todd with longing in our eyes. He shook his head very slightly and snapped his fingers.

"Okay," he said. "Mom, we need to straighten out your alibi for your boyfriend's murder. And it wouldn't hurt to prove that you knew he wasn't going to leave you any money too. What have you got? Emails, letters, texts? Notarized pre-nup?"

"I *did* see you at the airport!" said Barb to me. "I *clearly* remember you admiring my playsuit. And — just for your information, Teo — I am fifty-four and I have the legs I had when I was twenty-four. The only bit of me that's headed south is my rack and that's from feeding you until you were a year old so you should thank me."

"If you really want Roger to come round and eat your good home cooking, Mom, you could maybe lay off the rack talk too."

"He's a pediatrician!" said Barb. "He must have mommies sleeping over with their little babies all the time and feeding them like nature intended. Does he gag like a fag at work?"

"Wow," I said. "Barb, I wasn't at the airport. I was here on Tuesday. I suggested that your playsuit was so 'memorable' that someone must be able to alibi you. And then I took you to the police station. Tuesday."

"Which was yesterday," said Kathi.

I rolled the can of Tropicana across my forehead and tried to believe her.

"I've been to the police station?" said Barb. Suddenly I could believe she was only fifty-four. I could see the girl she'd been at fourteen. She looked so completely lost gazing at us.

"Ho-kay," said Kathi. "Barb, do you have a family doctor? A primary care physician? Todd, does she?"

Todd was nodding and rootling in his back pocket for his phone. "I'll call Roger," he said. "Mom, you need to do a pee test and get your blood alcohol logged. We'll get everything you said at the cop shop struck down." He stared into space as the phone rang and then turned away. "Hey, babe," he said. "You busy?"

"Cop shop," Kathi said. "He learned that from you, Lexy."

Funny how the world turns, isn't it? That was the first moment in California that I truly felt I belonged.

Kathi took Barb to the hospital in her truck. Todd said, "I can't. I'll strangle her. I'll kill her with my bare hands. And anyway, it's time Roger manned up. When you marry you get a family, right?"

Instead, he found the keys to Barb's car and we set off together to Casa B.

"So," I said, after a few moments silence, "what did he call her?"

"What? Oh. Empress of Hagistan. He loves her, really. *I* love her, really."

"Hey," I said, "you're preaching to the choir. I loved her as soon as I met her and that was with her triple bourbon dripping off my chin."

"Oh yes," said Todd. "She's always been a big drink thrower. She taught me and I was awesome in my day."

"Well, you're going to school now," I said. "Mizz Vi will put you both to shame." I cleared my throat and then did my best Dorabelle voice. *"Do you know, she doesn't have a single piece of her wedding china left to her name!"*

And so, despite the mission we were on, and the mess his mother was in, and the mob and the bugs and the dead raccoon, when we got to the gate we were laughing.

"I'm so glad to see you, Lexy," Visalia said. "And your handsome companion." She batted her clogged, stumpy lashes at Todd and he winked, making her trill with girlish laughter. "Come in, come in. Can I fix you something to eat?"

"Actually," I said, "I'm famished. That would be great."

"Not for me," said Todd.

We sat in the breakfast bulge while she warmed up chicken noodle soup (comfort food cares not for heat waves) and grated cheese onto bread to make toasted sandwiches. She put out a bowl of crisps and a tub of onion dip to keep us going in the meantime.

"So, how did you get on at the factory?" she said.

I boggled. I hadn't officially told Vi I was investigating. I boggled again as I thought that; I hadn't officially admitted to *myself* I was investigating. Then, just in time, I remembered my cover story. "A couple of girls from packing came to talk to me —

289

DeeDee and Carla? — and I spoke to Bilbo in the design office too. He seemed kind of overwrought, but I don't know how he is normally."

"Bilbo?" said Mizz Vi. "Hm, strange boy. But a whizz with all that fancy stuff he does for us. He once designed the Governor's inaugural ball finale and our orders doubled for weddings and races. He's working on Cousin Clovis's send-off already, you know."

"You're having a firework show for your husband?" said Todd.

"*Of* her husband," I muttered. "So, Vi — you don't mind speaking in front of Todd, do you? Can I ask —"

"I don't mind at all!" said Mizz Vi, fluttering again. "As long as you don't mind an old woman satisfying her curiosity: how did you meet and when, and how will you cope long-distance when Lexy goes back?"

"Not at all," said Todd. "Although, actually, how rude when I've just met you, but can I ask where your little boys' room is, Mrs. Bombaro? I need to go tinkle."

"Of course! It's just along the hall and on the left there."

"And . . . is there anyone else in the house?" Todd said. "You'll think I'm a silly old thing but I have a horror of a locked door and I wouldn't want anyone to walk in on me."

"Oh no, no one will," said Vi. "My niece and nephew are golfing and the boys have gone for a massage. They won't be back for hours."

It was neatly done. Todd excused himself and hurried out with a hand lightly cupped over his lower abdomen, explaining the refusal of food, suggesting the "tinkle" was a lie, and assuring himself a good stretch at the safe with no chance of Visalia coming near him.

"Poor boy," said Vi. "What have you been feeding him?"

I gazed at her. Not everyone has strong intuition — I know that — but Todd couldn't look any gayer if he burst out of a cake in a gingham leotard.

"So," I said, "it's good in a way that Sparky and Jan are out, because I want to ask about them."

"About what about them?" said Vi. She set a bowl of soup down before me and slid a sizzling grilled sandwich onto a side plate.

"How well do you know the Dolshikovs?"

She served herself a tiny cup of soup and picked some of the crusted cheese shreds off the bottom of the frying pan. "I've been hearing about them for the last twenty years since they started expanding westwards," she said. "When they were only in Jersey, Cousin Clovis used to joke about them. He said they'd done him a favour, taking New Jersey off his hands. Said it saved him having to go back there. Then they were in Pittsburgh. He kept joking. Who wants to go to Pittsburgh? And Boston, and Miami. Miami was the first time I saw him worried. Like he had bit down on a sore tooth? But we were the only show in town all the way from Denver to Hawaii." She drank a few spoonfuls of her soup, pushing her lips out and sucking noisily.

"Then came Dallas," she went on. "And Clovis just wouldn't see reason. He was only months from retirement."

"But he must have wanted to hand the business on in good shape," I said. "My dad had a carpet shop and fitting business and he worked harder the year before he retired than any other. He gave it to my brother and dropped onto the couch to eat biscuits and watch soaps for a year. Drove my mum nuts."

"If he had known about Sparky and Bang-Bang, he might have worried less. He might have retired a bit earlier. We could be in Trapani right now, sipping cocktails." She looked down at her soup and pushed it away. "Assuming he could swallow a Dolshikov in the family. But chances are he'd have suspected a coup."

"Or worse."

"How 'worse'?" she asked.

"You don't think Clovis would maybe have been . . . right . . . to suspect the Dol-shikovs of bad intentions? I mean, you don't think Jan and his cousins are maybe . . ."

"Killers?" said Sparky. I jolted and sent a long splat of soup over the breakfast table.

EIGHTEEN

"I thought you were golfing!" I said. Or maybe shrieked. Certainly the lamp above us rang a little in a sympathetic echo.

"I couldn't stand thinking of you sitting here all alone, Auntie Fizz," she said. The nickname was news to me, but it made sense along with Boom, Bang, and Sparky. "I know you need time on your own to process things, but I need to be near you."

Mizz Visalia looked sourer than I had ever seen her, except maybe when I tried to make her say Barbara's name. Barbara! The mother of Todd, who was right now upstairs trying to break into a safe.

"Did your husband bring you home?" I asked, slightly keen to reassure myself that someone with a "mob name" hadn't just heard me slandering him.

"Are you kidding? And miss the end of his round?" said Sparky. It was then that I realised that she wasn't angry with *me*. She was seething, it was true. But none of it was headed my way. I reckoned I could call her bridegroom a lot worse than "killer" without it troubling her today.

She served herself some soup, wiped my splat with a wad of kitchen roll, and sat down. "I wish I had told Uncle Boom-Boom about the wedding and all our plans," she said. "He would have . . . ."

"Well, Sparky, like I was just saying to Lexy here, your uncle was a proud man."

"I told myself it was because I was so busy. A busy executive that doesn't have time to call her only uncle and tell him she's getting married and she's had a Eureka moment about California fire codes."

"I know, dear," said Visalia. "Cousin Clovis was just the same. No time for anything."

I would have turned and stared at her with my mouth hanging open — Clovis had "time" for a racetrack habit, a weekday afternoon poker game, and, well, marriage guidance counselling — but I was too busy following the path of what Sparky was saying.

"He would have what?" I asked her. "Your uncle — if he had known about your wedding and all your plans — he would have what?"

Sparky put down her soup spoon and sniffed. "He would have been a third opinion on it all," she said.

There was more going on there than triangulating business opinions, I knew. That sniff was the start of a crying jag, not just hot soup after a sweaty golf round. I would have asked more, but *now* I was too busy working out how to warn Todd there was someone else in the house. Someone who, judging by the dark patches on her golf clothes, would definitely want a shower quite soon. Especially after a bowl of chicken soup and some pretty snottery tears as a chaser.

"Vi," I said, "if you don't mind, I might just go and see if Todd's okay. Take him a glass of water."

"Who?" said Sparky.

"My boyfriend," I said. "He wasn't feeling very well and he just popped to the powder room."

"He's not in there now," Sparky said. "I threw my cleats in on the way past."

"He must have gone upstairs," I said. "Well, if you're feeling volcanic, you do want to step away, don't you?" I ran a glass of water and started edging towards the door.

"Don't take that nasty Cuento tap," Visalia

296

said. "I'll get a bottle from the refrigerator in the pantry."

"Oh, this'll be fine," I said and sidled a bit more.

"But it's probably the tap water that made him sick," Sparky said. "Is he over from Ireland?"

"Scotland," I said, before I could help it. I'd been trying to stop being so picky. "No. He's Cuento born and bred. He was raised on this." I lifted the glass and looked at the cloudy swirl with specks of God knows what.

"Bring him a Tums," said Vi, standing and rummaging through that same junk drawer with the cable ties and stumps of candle.

"Oh, I think I hear him calling for me," I said. "You won't come and embarrass him, will you?" Then I turned and scooted along the passage, across the foyer, up the stairs, and in past the urns and columns as fast as my legs would carry me without slopping the water.

"Todd!" I whispered as soon as the door was closed at my back. "Abort! Serpentina's back." My voice died to a croak and the words sank back down into me.

Todd was standing frozen in the middle of the floor in one of Visalia's dresses, with one of Visalia's handbags hooked over his arm and with his feet jammed into a pair of Visalia's peep-toe slingbacks.

I worked my mouth but nothing came out.

"Are you alone?" he hissed.

I managed a nod.

"Phe-ew," he said. Then, quick as a whip, he shucked off the dress and fired the shoes straight off his feet into the open closet. He lobbed the bag in after them and turned to where his shorts and t-shirt were puddled on the rug beside him.

He threw the dress at me and I caught it. On my face. I batted it out of the way. Todd was hopping about getting his shorts on and chasing his flip-flops at the same time.

"Shake it, Lexy," he said. "Hang that up and tidy the purse and pumps. C'mon, c'mon."

"I . . ." I said. Quite an achievement.

"Oh, for fuck sake!" said Todd. He pulled his t-shirt on, grabbed the dress back again, and disappeared into the closet. When he came back out he yanked me after him and we exited the room together. He dodged into a door three along, which was a bathroom. He flushed the toilet, took a great bale of toilet paper and stuffed it into the back of his waistband. Then he sprayed the air freshener that sat on the cistern, walked through it as though it was perfume, and yanked me back out onto the landing again.

"Jesus, Lexy," he muttered as we trotted down the stairs. "It's Snoopers' 101. Put on a dress and you've got an out for when they come and find you. It's so goddam embarrassing no one ever questions you and they can't get you out fast enough."

"Oh," I said. *Oh!* We were almost at the kitchen corridor, but I just had time to ask, "Did you get into the safe?"

"Duh," said Todd. We turned the last corner. "Mizz Visalia, I am just beside myself. I just want to die. I need to go. I have to stop at CVS and pick up some . . . Well, let's not be nasty. But I'm *mortified*! I — Oh God!" He pretended to see Serpentina for the first time. "Hi," he said. "I won't shake hands. I'm pretty sure it was my breakfast burrito, but just in case it's the stomach flu."

"You're Lexy's boyfriend," said Serpentina. She took in every inch of him from his perfect, half-inch ruffle cut, through his manscaped stubble, his sculpted biceps, his dull pink citi-shorts, his Adonis-esque calves, his diamonds (ear studs, nose stud, and wedding ring) and — oh yes — his Stonewall t-shirt. "As in . . . for a green card?"

"You know," said Todd, "I get that a lot

299

from straight women. Never from gay men. *They* see the lipstick on the pig."

"What are you talking about?" said Visalia.

"Nothing, Auntie," Sparky said. "I think I've been in Texas too long, is all."

We said our goodbyes and scuttled out of there like roaches when the lights come on.

Once we were back in the car, Todd started laughing. "Your face!" he said. "And then when I threw the dress and you just stood there and let it smother you!"

"Ha ha," I said. "Yes, I'm a comedy turn. Partly it was because you look better in a dress than I do. You look much better *out* of a dress than I do. When I get back to Dundee, I'm going to join a gym."

"Oh please!" Todd said. "Honey, you know what they say: you spend enough time in a barbershop, you're gonna get a haircut. How long did it take California to make you hate your body?"

"A week," I said. "Yeah, okay, I thought you were a creeper. After what Roger said about boundaries and all that, you know. So what did you find in the safe?"

"What did I find in the safe?" said Todd. He was giddy with it, teasing me. "What did I find? In the safe? Where are we going, by the way? Where should I take you?"

"Golf course to try to meet Bang-Bang

Dolshikov. He's beginning to change his tune about things. I couldn't get much out of Serpentina, but I'd love to know more."

"Are we going to go out on the course and track him down?"

"Why?"

Todd tapped the dashboard thermometer. "Cos it's ninety-nine now. It's gonna get warm."

"We'll play it by ear," I said. "Hey, Todd?"

"Ma'am?"

"What did you find in the fucking safe?"

"Receipts for airline tickets to the Caymans," he said. "Airline tickets for Rome with a connection to Palermo."

"Hedging his bets," I said. "Wait. You found the Rome *tickets*? Or a receipt."

"Tickets," said Todd. "Well, you know — a print-out of the confirmation number. And what else? Oh, yes. Receipt for a rental agreement on a beach cottage." He had joined what passes for a main road through Cuento and he scooted across all three lanes in one go. "Quick way to the golf club if you don't mind coming at it from the dumpsters," he said. "I worked there one summer of middle school until they fired me for knocking over the clubhouse. Now, where was I? House deeds for the gilded monstrosity we've just left. Ancient old house deeds for something called the Creek House."

"But no house deeds for Sicily?"

"Oh yes," he said. "I mean, no. The cops took the house deeds for Sicily, but left a receipt. There was a realtor's brochure. What a slice of heaven! Did you ever see that old Merchant Ivory movie with all the naked men?"

"I saw *A Room with a View* with two minutes of naked men and two hours of Edwardian fashion."

"Yeah, well the house in Trapani makes that look like . . ."

"*Trainspotting?*" I said. "Mizz Vi gave me the impression that the place they bought in Trapani was a condo."

"This was no condo," said Todd.

"Huh. So the cops took the paperwork — flight and house — for the Caymans trip and they took the house paperwork for the Sicily trip. But they left the Sicily plane tickets? Is it me or is that weird?"

"They left a lo-ho-hot of financial papers too. I photographed them. I'll ask Nolly what they are and what they say about the Bombaros' net worth. But I can tell you this: that old gal is not going to end her days on a corner with a cup out."

We were rattling along a gravel track that

looked like a dead end, but at the last minute Todd swerved left and found an opening between two industrial dumpsters. "Jesus, memories," he said, peering out of the side window. "I lost my virginity in these shrubs."

"While you were in middle school?" I asked him. "How old are kids in middle school here?"

"Old enough," he said. "And he taught me a lot. He was a doctor and now *I'm* a doctor. And he put me off golf clothes for life."

"I'm going to get you on the couch one day if it kills me," I said. "Gangs, creepy doctors at the golf club, and cleptopar—"

"I do not have that ridiculous fictitious so-called disease," said Todd.

"It's a disorder, not a disease," I said.

"It's a crock," he snapped, as we swung around the last corner into a parking lot. "And here we are," said Todd. "Playground of the great and the g— Je-*sus*! There he is." He ducked down in his seat.

"Dolshikov?" I said, scrunching down too.

"My first doctor!" said Todd. "Well, of *course*. It's Wednesday afternoon. It's twenty years later but it's still Wednesday afternoon and there he is."

Strolling across the car park, dragging a

wheeled golf trolley, was one of those American Men. I had been familiar with them for years before I ever came here, because they're the men who take cruises on the North Sea. They've got moustaches but never beards, they've never met a V-neck they didn't love, and when roughing it through St. Andrews or Virginia Water they wear their worldly goods lashed to their bellies in bumbags that they lock to their belt loops with security chains.

This one was a doozy. He had bright brown hair combed carefully over his ruddy scalp and wore a V-neck argyle sweater in a coral pink that clashed with his boozer's tan, over eau-de-nil slacks and white golf shoes with yellow laces.

"At least he's learned to dress a little better," Todd said, peering over the dashboard.

But I couldn't laugh, because I had just noticed his golfing buddy.

It was Branston.

Of course it was.

"Todd," I said, "you know how you lot always call vets and dentists doctors as well as real doctors? What was your shrubbery guy?"

"Hm?" said Todd. "He's a dermatologist. Why?"

"Cos that fine specimen in the mustard

Ralph Lauren is my ex-husband."

"Really?" said Todd, sitting bolt upright and lifting his sunglasses for a better look. "Real-ly?" His voice was getting sepulchral. "Well, well, well. Wanna have some fun?"

"I want to find Bang-Bang," I said. "Officially. But yes. If you do too."

We climbed down and Todd draped a casual arm around my shoulders before we sauntered over to where Bran and the pink sensation were standing, braying at one another like bull walruses.

"Yo!" said Todd, his voice had dropped an octave. Out of the corner of his mouth he added, "Put your shades on and pout, Lexy."

Bran was thunderstruck. I gave him the Oliver Hardy fingertip wave.

"Well, well, well," said Todd again, as we drew close. "Look at this, Lexy. Your old squeeze meets your new one. Are you tempted? Am I gonna lose you?"

"Teodor?" said the dermatologist. As the recognition took hold, his ruddy face drained to a colour that clashed with his coral sweater worse than ever.

"That's me," Todd said. "And my best girl. What a small world. One ex-husband and one ex- . . . ."

"Dermatologist!" spluttered the dermatologist.

"I've heard so much about you, Doctor," I said to him.

"I never mentioned Carl's name," said Bran.

"Not from you," I said. "From Toddles here."

"Me 'n' Carl go way back, Bran," Todd said. "Way, way back into the rough. Huh, Carlos?"

Carl was silent for a long, strained moment and then he put his hand to his hip. "Pager," he said hoarsely.

"Never figured you for a vibrate kinda guy," said Todd.

Bran looked from one to the other of us, outfoxed as ever. His golf buddy put his phone to his ear and bustled off, having one half of the lamest fake phone conversation I had ever heard.

"I thought you'd gone, Lexy," Bran said.

"Oh, she has," said Todd. "She's good and gone. So don't start getting any ideas, dude. You let her go and she is *gone*." He pulled me closer to him and gave Bran a look that could freeze a wart off.

Bran tried to sneer but spoiled it by taking a shaky step back when Todd took one forward. He knew he was beaten and left, walking so fast over to his Acura that his golf trolley overtook him on the slight slope and he had to run to catch it.

"Oh, that was good," I said, looking up into Todd's eyes. "Will you be my real boyfriend, please? I'm sure Roger wouldn't mind. And if he does, I think I can take him."

Todd laughed and let me go. I was surprised to find that my shoulder was damp where I'd been tucked under his arm.

"Take him?" he said. "Honey! You think *I've* got a checkered past. You don't want to see Roger when he channels his roots. He's got a wormhole to Stockton he can snap open like *that*." He clicked his fingers in my face.

"I don't know what that means, but I believe you," I said. "Can I ask you one last question before we finally start thinking about Bang-Bang?"

"Shoot."

"How come you don't know that guy? Socially? I mean if he's a doctor and you and Roger are too, how come you don't run into each other at benefits and things?"

"Benefits?" said Todd.

"Friends of the Library," I said, thinking of Dorabelle.

"Because the kind of benefits Zit-boy and

Mrs. Zit-boy go to don't invite brothers and Chicanos who work at public hospitals."

"Even in California?" I said. "I mean, I knew about Louisiana and all that down there, but —"

"You know what?" said Todd. "You're so right. I forgot we were in lovely liberal California! I just feel so dumb now. Thank you, Lexy. I'm going to call Roger this minute and tell him the good news."

"And I'm going to kill myself," I said. "Sorry."

Todd just smirked at me and rolled his eyes. "Now, for God's sake, focus!" he said. "Being a sleuth is not all cross-dressing and fucking with old flames. It's a hundred degrees out here, Lexy. It's too hot to dick around."

We squared up and faced the clubhouse. Then, without any clue as to how we were going to blag our way in, we started walking, because the tarmac was beginning to burn our feet right through our flip-flops.

"Oh wait, though," said Todd, stopping. "There's just one thing. Never call me Toddles again."

NINETEEN

God almighty, it was hot. I had thought they were all crazy, but I got it now: if you start whining at ninety there's nowhere to go when a hundred draws its fist back and socks you. A hundred degrees is just too damn hot. As we toiled across the car park of the Cuento Golf Club, I felt the sweat begin to gather between my shoulder blades. I felt my thighs begin to slip and slide inside my shorts and my hair soften and darken on my head. I felt drips begin to form along my jawline and my feet begin to squish from side to side on my rubber soles. I felt my lubricated buttocks begin to work independently instead of as a team and start to chew my knickers up into a sodden wad in between them.

"God, it's hot," said Todd.

I pulled open the door to the clubhouse foyer and felt the much-more-delicious-than-it-sounds sensation of my puddle of back sweat cooling in the frigid air, the rivulets coursing down my arms and legs, evaporating into no more than little stinky trails through the dust on my skin. I also felt my hair frizz. Nothing's free in this life. I plucked the wad of wet knickers out of my bum crack in as ladylike a way as I could manage and headed for the hostess desk cum cloakroom.

"Are you members, sir? Madam?" said the child, one of those spending the summer, as Todd had once, earning peanuts and losing cherries to lecherous doctors in vomit-themed golf attire.

"We're not," I said. "We've come to meet someone who's playing a guest round to-day." I could feel Todd start to gather steam to take over. I had just pegged us at the lowest rung of the clubhouse pecking order. Hangers-on of fly-by-nights. "Mr. Dolshikov. His wife left him here about an hour ago and set off on her own. I'm afraid we've got some very bad news for him."

The child scratched a badly covered spot at the side of her mouth and pondered all of this. "I can send a cart out to find him," she said. "It's too hot for you to walk."

I looked at Todd and managed to squeeze out a tear. It was easy. I'd sweated cheap sun block into my lashes crossing the car park and my eyes were stinging.

"I think we should just let him finish his round. It's the last round he's ever going to play before we tell him the news." Todd nodded and winked with the eye furthest from the hostess. I turned back to her. "If we could just wait. There's . . . nothing to rush for."

"Is everyone okay?" she said. "In his family?"

"I'm afraid not," I said.

"Oh my God," said the child. She licked the gloss right off her lips. Maybe it wasn't a zit after all. Maybe this was a nervous habit and she'd licked herself raw. "Did his wife make it home okay? It didn't happen near here, did it?"

"She did not make it home," I said. She hadn't; she lived in Texas. "But the death happened off the golf club property." It had; Clovis died at Casa Bombaro.

"Oh my God!" said the child. She put up her hand and picked at the sore. Maybe she'd get through the summer without any of the lecherous doctors bothering her after all. "Please sit down. Can I bring you a cold drink? It's so hot."

"Just a glass of white wine," said Todd. It sounded so much like *just a glass of water* until so near the end that the child was unfooted and only nodded and scurried away. She brought one for me too.

Todd raised his glass to me before he drank. "Masterful," he said. "And since you were trying to be a total porn-star Pinocchio with the twelve-inch nose and *yet* tell no actual lies . . . I'm assuming we've got some real bad news to deliver."

"Ew," I said. I swore I'd never say that. Like I swore I'd never use the drive-through postbox, eat raw kale in a salad, or download an app to help me count sit-ups. But in the end, California got me.

Jan "Bang-Bang" Dolshikov emerged into the foyer of the clubhouse from its nether regions about twenty minutes later, with a towel round his neck and rubber mob-caps over his golf shoes to stop them spiking the parquet.

"Wait," said Todd, watching him approach. "*That's* the husband of that dumpy chick in the bad shorts? No way."

"Poor Sparky," I said. I stood up. "Jan? Lexy. We met at Visalia's the other day?"

"If you're looking for my wife," he said, biting the word off and narrowing his eyes, "she flaked out on me and went running home."

Wow. What a prick.

I didn't say the words but, from the look he gave me, I think they might have been printed on my face. He turned away and stalked out, the rubber bundles on his shoes making the kind of squeaky clumping noise that could ruin a much grander exit.

"So your golf game was ruined, eh?" I said as I caught him up halfway down the steps.

"I had to ask to join the couple ahead of us, like a fifth wheel," he said.

"Third, surely," said Todd. "But never mind that, we need to talk to you. Should we get into your car and turn the air on?"

"I have nothing to say to you," he told us, "I don't know who killed my uncle-in-law and I don't much care. He was a stubborn old fool who didn't know when to step aside. My wife spent her life tiptoeing round him and expected me to do the same. I didn't get where I am today by letting old men, labor unions, or family slow me down."

"Now," said Todd, "was it Gandhi or Mother Teresa who said that?"

"It's good of you to be here supporting her," I said, "given that you feel that way."

"I'm here to make sure the factory keeps running smoothly," said Jan.

"Oh, come off it," I said. "I mean, yeah I get it — alpha male, blood on the boardroom floor, yeah, yeah. But keep it real."

Jan regarded me steadily. "Did you have something you wanted to ask?" he said.

"Yes. How did Serpentina get here so quickly?" I thought if I accused his wife, even obliquely, he'd spring to her defence. "Visalia can't understand how she made such good time unless she knew in advance she'd be needed."

"Well, of course she knew in advance," Jan said.

That was easy, I thought.

"We were coming to lay out the new business plan. Post-merger."

"Right," I said. "Boomshik-a!"

"Bullshit-a! I already said to you I'd never let family sentiment get in the way of business, and the Dolshikov name is a bigger brand."

"What about your cousins?" I asked. "Are *they* 'building the brand'?"

"Exactly," Jan said. "Their Bill and Melinda routine gives me cover for smarter business dealings than I'd have otherwise, in Dallas *or* in Jersey. But now I have a wife to take care of all that crap, I can let them get back to doing what they're best at. They'll be taking over in California."

"How did you meet your wife, Mr. Dolshikov?" said Todd suddenly.

314

"I flew to New York to a dinner I knew she'd been attending and wooed her."

"And was the marriage your idea," I added, "or did the whole board have to vote?" His eyes had narrowed to Voldemort-nostril dimensions. He didn't answer me. "And what makes you think Visalia will just 'step aside'?"

He made a sound I didn't immediately recognize as a laugh. "Whether she's headed to Sicily or solitary, she's out." He opened his SUV, kicked the booties off his shoes, dropped the towel from around his neck, and, leaving all of it lying on the hot tarmac, he climbed in and drove away.

"Wow. That guy is a prick," said Todd, my twin soul.

"Yep, he only wanted Sparky so he could get his mitts on the West Coast. And Sparky's just wising up to it now."

"Did she never look in a mirror and wonder?" Todd said, beeping open Kathi's SUV. "The open dating market doesn't make mistakes like that."

I grimaced. That little pearl of wisdom was quite a bit too close to home. "He definitely thinks Visalia bumped Clovis off, doesn't he?" I said.

"Or he's pretending to so we don't suspect it was *him*," Todd said. "Oh God, it's too hot. Let's go back, have cool showers and naps, and get together later over a jug of margaritas. Try to think this through."

I lifted my bum up off the seat, hoping to get the cold draft a bit further up my shorts. Maybe even out at the waistband if I was lucky. "If anyone in the factory got wind of the Dolshikov takeover, it puts the kibosh on them harming Clovis, doesn't it?"

"Does that help my mom?"

"Not really," I said. "The more suspects the merrier, in that regard."

"That's what I thought," said Todd. "Would you stop dry-humping the a/c and put your seatbelt on, please?"

I let my bum drop onto the seat again.

"Unless they thought the Dolshikov take-over was Clovis's idea. No, listen! If anyone at the factory heard about the Sicily retreat and the Dolshikov offensive and thought they were two halves of the same coin, they'd want to stick a spanner in it, wouldn't they?"

"Stick a what? And that's a lot of big *if*s, Lexy."

"Just sayin'."

"Well, how about this then?" Todd said, as we rumbled under the bridge, in sight of the motel. "What if Sparky knew deep down that Jan only wanted her for her merger

316

potential. Wouldn't she have a great motive to make sure nothing got in the way of it? If she knew her uncle would disapprove of the marriage and never agree to her plans, maybe *she* killed him."

"She was on a plane from Dallas."

"But *whoever* it is we're blaming," said Todd, "we know they must have had an accomplice. There was one to set it up and one to cut him loose."

"I've got two problems with that," I said. "Why wouldn't accomplices coordinate at least enough to make sure the right one had the handcuff keys? And also, how do the cops know that the handcuffs weren't opened by keys? And three, why didn't Mike the cop know what handcuffs I was talking about? I watched her face and she had no idea. But that's what she told Bilbo — handcuffs and ankle-cuffs."

We had arrived and parked in the shade of the balcony.

"So we've achieved absolutely nothing today at all, have we?" said Todd.

Just then Della's door opened and little Diego came bounding out, clapping his hands in anticipatory glee.

"Oh, Jesus," I said. "We've achieved *this*."

"I got it," said Todd. "I'll tell him there's three fishies coming tomorrow."

"I owe you," I said. "Interior design, lingerie, car hire — Oh! Your car's parked at the cop shop, by the way."

"Roger drove it home."

"So yeah. Car hire, food and drink, pet procurement, companionship . . ."

"Fucking with your louse of an ex-husband . . ."

"Invaluable," I told him. "Can't put a price on that."

For some reason, once I was out of my tepid shower and had the first half-pint of frosty pinot grigio down me, I phoned my mum. Maybe it was seeing Todd with Barb; maybe it was listening to the icy blast of Jan talking about his marriage; maybe it was the thought of Dorabelle sitting all alone in that ridiculous house with her edited memories. Part of it was saying to Todd I'd be at the airport headed east as soon as this case was closed and I was off the hook for Visalia's bail. Not having a job or a flat to go back to was bothering me. Funny. Never bothered me before.

Who knows. I dialled the number and it was only when my mum answered, groggy and strained after one ring, that I remembered the time difference. It was three o'clock in the morning.

"Mum, I'm sorry. I zoned out and forgot. I didn't mean to wake you."

"Didn't mean to wake me? What did you think I'd be doing at this time of day? Of course, you woke me."

"I forgot the time," I said.

"Lexy," I heard her say over her shoulder. "She's fine. Just felt like phoning and so she just phoned. Sleep be damned."

"It was a mistake," I said. "I'm sorry. It's been a long day."

"Oh? Another hard day charging fifty pounds an hour for a chat and taking your poor husband's credit card for walkies?"

If she knew how much I really charged an hour, she'd never sleep again.

"I don't have a husband, Mum."

"You've a stubborn streak a mile wide, Lexy. You were the same when you were a wee girl. Buying your own treats. Teaching yourself to read."

"I sound like a nightmare," I said. "Anyway, I'll call back at a more civilised hour. Give Dad my love."

"Is that it?" she said. "Half a minute when we haven't heard from you for weeks?"

"Since Sunday."

"Call that a phone call? That was even shorter than this one."

"You cuddle down again and go back to

sleep, Mum," I said. "I'll talk to you in the morning. Teatime, I mean."

She snorted. "Putting it off already."

"Or, here's a thought: You call me."

"In America?"

"Probably best if you want to catch me."

"I can't go calling America. There's a special code you have to know and heaven knows how expensive it is."

"So I'll speak to you tomorrow morning my time. Teatime your time. Sleep tight. Sweet dreams."

I put the phone down and stared at the bottle of wine. Or rather, at the wine bottle. Because it was empty.

TWENTY

I woke up to the pink light of a California dawn, the pulsing heat of a July day that meant business, and the familiar morning sounds of the Last Ditch Motel. Screams, banging doors, pounding feet, and angry voices firing threats of health inspectors and Yelp.com.

I couldn't face it. I pulled the sheet, slightly damp with sweat, over my head and lay in the dove-grey tent, running my tongue over my teeth and deciding that a bottle of wine before bed wasn't the perfect mouthwash. I even asked myself if living in the Beige Barn, charging by the hour for chats, and taking long walks through the mall with Branston's credit card would really have been so bad. I thought of how I could have filled every evening: yoga night, book club, midweek mani-pedi, movie night, Spanish evening class. And that would only have left two long empty days every weekend to co-exist with a philandering dentist in mustard golf trousers. I dozed off, thanking my stars I'd never have to.

Then someone a foot away cleared their throat.

I snapped my eyes open.

Todd, Kathi, and Noleen were gathered around my bed like the Magi.

"What, was Roger busy?" I said. I saw a ghost of a smile hitch up Kathi's mouth on one side before she brought the shutters down. Noleen's face had the shutters nailed down and the nail heads soldered over. And Todd looked close to tears. He had a cup of tea for me, but he couldn't meet my eye as he handed it over.

"I missed the margaritas," I said. "Sorry. I was just so tired." Unfortunately, as I sat up, the edge of the bedsheet caught the empty wine bottle and it toppled, hit the floor and rolled away. It didn't even hit the wall. It found the half-open bathroom door and bumped down onto the tiles to roll a bit further.

"Why didn't you come out when you heard the commotion?" said Todd.

"Tired," I said again. "Too tired to walk in a straight line. What happened?"

"What's your greatest fear, Lexy?" said Kathi.

I took a sip of the tea. Todd had hit his mark, as ever. It was hot, strong, milky, and sweet. Add a bacon and egg sandwich made with doorstep slices from an unsliced loaf and my hangover was history. I glanced at him but he was staring dolefully at me. Not a chirp, not a twinkle. Even his diamond ear studs looked murky.

"Oh, you know. The icecaps melting, dying alone. The usual."

Kathi nodded grimly. "Not raccoons," she said. "Dead or alive."

I took another big jolting step back to full consciousness. I had showered the night before in the bathtub of death and it hadn't even crossed my mind.

"Why?" I said. "What's happened."

"Is someone paying you?" said Todd.

"I have no idea what you're talking about," I said.

Noleen startled me when she suddenly grabbed my bedsheet and twitched it right off the bed, exposing me and making me slop a huge slick of tea over my silk teddy. "Up!" she said. "Come on. Come and look me in the eye while we're both standing right there and ask me again *what happened* in that bogus accent."

She grabbed me hard round my upper arm and yanked me to my feet.

323

"Steady," said Kathi. "She's just the sort to report you for assault. She's in deep with the cops, remember."

"I'm sorry, Lexy," Todd said. "But it does seem kind of hard to swallow. The bugs and now this."

"Now what?" I asked. Pleaded maybe. But I didn't have to wait long. Noleen was hustling me along the balcony to the far end.

"They were trying to get to Ashland, but they couldn't drive any farther, so they pulled off and checked in here. Just to sleep a few hours and be on their way. A sweet couple. Retired from the dispatch office in the Kern County sheriff's office. Not easy people to rattle. But how would *you* like to flop down into this bed?" Here she broke off to open the door of Room 216 and shove me across the threshold. "Look in that bed," she said. Then she went to the door and stood behind Kathi.

"And don't worry," Kathi said. "It's not a melting ice cap or a lonely death under there."

I took hold of the edge of the blanket and lifted it an inch or two, peered in, saw nothing. Noleen took another step backwards. I lifted the blanket up a little higher. There were a few dark spots on the top sheet below it. With my other hand I took hold with my fingernails and peeked underneath.

In the last week, I had seen a dead client, a dead raccoon, a swarm of disgusting red insects whose hobby was shitting, a swarm of disgusting blue insects whose hobby was egg-laying, a sociopathic golfer, a child-molesting golfer, and Bran. Anyone would think I'd be past caring what was under that sheet.

Anyone would be wrong.

It made me think of rosti, called hash browns in these parts. Thin strands of grated potato, tangled together to make a little cake, crisp on the outside and moist within.

Except this was a massive cake, four feet across, and dark brown, and the individual strands, matted and woven together, drying at the edges but still wet in the middle, were not grated potato but . . .

"Worms," I said. And my stomach detached itself from its usual foundations and rolled forward, over, and back up again, finishing at the base of my throat with a sour little gust of air.

"And what did Noleen tell you yesterday?" said Kathi. "Just you. No one else in earshot."

I swung round and hurried over to where Noleen was standing out on the balcony, feet planted wide apart, arms folded, face pale.

"Don't hold your breath," I said. "I know it feels like it'll help, but it's better to breathe deep. And turn round and look a long way into the distance. Look at that tree over there that's been trimmed to miss the power lines. It looks like Popeye."

"How could you?" said Noleen. "We took you in."

"I couldn't and I didn't," I said. "Cross my heart and hope to get married to Bran again. I would never do something so terrible to my worst enemy, and you are the nearest thing I've got to a friend in five thousand miles."

"Me?" said Noleen.

"All of you."

"You didn't do this?" said Noleen. I shook my head. "It's just that I told you yesterday and then Blammo! — here they are. It seemed pretty undeniable. Why else would there be worms all of a sudden? And after the bugs and the raccoon . . . it all happened after you got here."

"Well, yes but . . ." I said. I scraped around my brain for a kind way to say *creepy, yucky stuff happens here all the time* and, unsurprisingly, I failed. And actually, while I thought about it, the beetroot-related (possibly ketchup) plumbing fail had been after my first night in 213.

"So you think it's a coincidence?" Noleen said. "All these worms suddenly, out of the blue?"

I stared at her. Then I turned and stared out across the flat dusty fields that stretched away to the south of Cuento beyond the slough. Something was glimmering deep in the puddle of pinot grigio that passed for my brain this morning. Dusty fields full of crops and the daily gross-out in Last Ditch bedrooms and . . . Diego's fish, three and counting, were in there and even, somehow, my fantasy bacon and egg butty.

"No," I said. "Not a coincidence. But I can't see what the link is. It's close but it's . . ." I screwed my face up and concentrated really hard. From the combination of the hangover, the stomach roll when I saw the worms, and the long day of nothing much to eat the day before, as I wound up every fibre of my being in an effort to catch the thread, the inevitable happened.

Reader, I farted.

"And in a Zak Posen teddy too," said Todd.

"Don't worry, Stinker," said Noleen, throwing an arm around me and squeezing me fit to pop my collarbone. "You've found your people. Wait till chili taco night. I'll show you gas."

"Stand back, Lexy. She's all mine," Kathi said. She shut the door on room 216 and we went to Todd's, where this morning's coffee, he told us, was vanilla and there were *pains au chocolat* warming.

"Who wants to come with me to view a days-old corpse and see if we can tell that it had handcuffs cut off it?" I said twenty minutes later, dabbing chocolate off my lips with a checked napkin, for all the world as if I didn't have sweet milky tea drying down the length of my fart-contaminated teddy.

"I'm manning the office," said Noleen. "I should be there now."

"I'm in the Skweek," said Kathi.

"I'm going into work to have an interview with HR," said Todd.

"I could come to that with you," I said, "if you do my thing with me."

"You'd be such a help!" said Todd. "With your deep knowledge of California employment law, hospital policy, and my confidential file. Dream on."

So I went on my own. I was sure it was a good idea. Well, I was half sure it was the best way forward from where we'd run aground. That is to say, I couldn't see any

328

major disaster that seemed absolutely guaranteed.

Mizz Visalia took some persuading. She was in bed when I got there, which wasn't a great sign. Serpentina showed me into the bedroom and then went to fetch me an entirely unwanted cup of café con leche. It seemed like it would take the longest out of what she offered me and I wanted a good crack at Visalia on her own. Jan, she told me, was golfing.

"It's the . . . secondary actions," I said. "I don't know why the police think two people were involved in the . . . operation. The only thing I can think of is that there's some kind of mark on Clovis's body. And there's no way anyone's going to let me in to see Clovis's body, is there? But if you want to visit him, and you need someone to be with you for support . . . Do you see?"

"But I *don't* want to visit him," Visalia said. "I find all of that quite morbid. That's why I was so keen to have him cremated."

"You were?"

"Well, what I mean is, that's why I was agreeable to his wishes when they strike so many as quite heathenish and outlandish."

"Yeah, but that's the fireworks, isn't it?"

"No, Lexy, it isn't," Visalia said. "The destruction of his earthly remains is what worries Father Adam. How will Clovis rise up, on the Day of Judgment, to sit at God's right hand, if he's a pile of ash?"

"How will he if he's a pile of compost?" I said. "If Judgment Day takes a while, I mean. And anyway, you've got Father Adam completely wrong. He said to me yesterday that he believes — truly believes — Clovis is up there right now, looking down and smiling."

"That's not at all what the Church teaches," Visalia said.

"Well, you don't have to look," I said. She blinked a bit until she caught up with the switch back then she shook her head, as if she had water in her ear.

"If I don't look, who's going to believe I'm there to see him?"

It was a good point.

"Wear dark glasses," I said. "Like Jackie O. Say your eyes are strained from weeping and lack of sleep." I looked closely at her. If anything, her eyes were clearer and brighter than they had been in the last few months of thrashing out the end of the marriage with Clovis. And when I took a really close look, her cheeks looked a bit plumper too and her colour was good and the tremor had gone from her hands and her jaw. Her hair was soft and shining as well. But it was also a different shade of mauve, so I could put that down to the hairdresser's visit rather than whatever black magic had made an octogenarian bloom with dewy health after what she'd been through.

"I don't even know where he is," she said. "He's not at the funeral director's yet anyway."

"My guess is he'll still be in the morgue," I said. "While they wait for all the test results to come back. In case they need more samples of anything. You know, for the chain of evidence."

Mizz Visalia twitched her bed jacket sleeves into place. I loved that she wore a bed jacket. "My, my," she said. "*You* seem awfully well informed all of a sudden. You told me you didn't follow any of those dreadful shows."

I had told her that and it was the truth. But Noleen and Kathi had never met a *CSI* they didn't TiVo and they had shared the benefit over the vanilla coffee and pastries.

"Vi," I said, "I'm trying to help you. Do you remember three days ago, in court, in a shade of orange that, I'm sorry, did nothing for you? You were released on my signature —"

"Cosignature," she said. "So you see, you *have* helped me, Lexy. And you gave me an alibi. Where would I be without you?"

"Well, no, I didn't," I said. "Three burly firefighters gave you an alibi, Vi, if you remember."

"Not everything goes the way it's supposed to," she said.

I felt my chin pull back into my neck without my doing a thing to make it. *The way it's supposed to?* I mouthed the words over to myself. Like . . . I was supposed to give her an alibi but she got a flat tire and so the firemen did the job for me?

"What the hell does that mean?" I said.

Vi was retying the neck ribbon of her bed jacket. "Hm?" she said, mildly. Then, "Oh! I mean, they save the burly beauties for the calendar and fundraisers and the weedy little runts get to run around the back roads changing tires. Those men were nothing to break out a fire-ax over." She clucked at the memory of her disappointment. "Why? What did you think I meant?"

"Not important," I said. I waited for my insides to sit down and stop dancing the Macarena. A few more shocks like the worms and that little bomb she'd just dropped and I'd be necking Pepto like the rest of this troubled nation. I don't know if it's the portions, the stock market, or some kind of collective colitis, but indigestion is huge here. Turn the corner of a mid-sized chemist's shop and the tablets, powders, effervescents, and chalky solutions stretch to a vanishing point in the distance, like the *Matrix* weapon store. In fact, it's not just the stomach. There's not an inch of tubing from the face to the anus that Americans — wait, I can only really speak to Californians — don't think they can get closer to and improve. From snorting saltwater up one nostril and down the other if they catch a cold to the Zen balance of senna and Imodium they're always on the hunt for. Not to mention the yoghurts and yakults and yomilks, and of course the associated soyomilks and goyomilks and alyomilks (because cows are just the almonds, goats, and soybeans of the past and their days are numbered!). I don't know how they do it, because I certainly could not start every day with a product whose serving suggestion was basically *eat before shitting,* but Californians don't seem to mind. I'm convinced if someone marketed a yuk-blurk called I Can't Believe It's Not Faeces Already, they'd retire to the Caymans with a yacht.

The Caymans!

I blinked myself back to Visalia's bedside, ready to double down and persuade her if it killed me.

But she had changed her mind all on her own.

"I'll do it," she said. "Forgive me, Lexy. I'm not myself and I'm not thinking very smart thoughts. I never meant for you to get mixed up in all this sordidness." She smiled. "But I'm very glad you are. I couldn't do this without you."

"Well, that's kind of you," I said. I wasn't thinking very smart thoughts either, of course. Vi wasn't herself after sudden widowhood and incarceration, but what was *my* excuse? "I'm glad you're beginning to think of me as a friend," I said, "because I can't be your counsellor again after this. We've lost every trace of our professional relationship."

It didn't help that, at that moment, Visalia was climbing out of bed and heading towards her bathroom to ready herself for another trying day. "Really?" she said as she shrugged out of her bed jacket. "You think we've blurred the line? I've been keeping note of your hours to settle up when it's all over."

"There's no charge for friendship," I called after her.

"I don't agree," she called back. The shower went on. "I will reward you for this somehow, Lexy. What do you want most in the world? What's your heart's desire?"

"Um," I shouted. The sink taps were running too. "I'm pretty easy really. Nothing much I'm pining for."

"I'll surprise you then," she shouted. "Even though we might be thousands of miles apart, I won't forget you."

"Seeing you free and at peace and Clovis's killer brought to justice will be plenty reward," I yelled over the sound of the toilet flushing.

She put her head round the door, probably thinking I couldn't see her, forgetting the mirror behind her. "Well, will you please tell that nice detective about the Poggios, in that case?" she said. "Because I'm more convinced than ever that one of those *stronzi* is responsible for this."

"I'll try," I said. "I kind of burned a bridge there, but I'll try. And you know what? We might not be thousands of miles apart."

I had no idea where that had come from. Part of it was the sight of Visalia's old lady body, her skinny legs and her droopy bottom and the long curved line of her back with her bird bones and the swags of skin. Life, it told me, was short. So maybe it was a good idea to go through it saying "wheeeeee!" Maybe I shouldn't assume that I'd be back in Dundee before my next haircut. I'd never seen the redwoods yet. Or the desert. Or —

"Well, no," said Vi. "Not thousands. You'll be in Scotland and I'll be in Sicily."

"You'd really defy the Poggios even after this? Don't they frighten you?"

"You wouldn't understand if I told you," she said. Then she looked over her shoulder as a plume of steam spread around her. "Water's wasting. Ima go make myself purty for Cousin Clovis."

I stared at the space where she'd been. You'd be looking at this morning's mission a long time before you thought of a hot date, but there was no other way to take what Visalia had just said. I shrugged. Like the internal workings of a blood feud, this was just one more thing I didn't understand.

TWENTY-ONE

"He looks," I began an hour later, in the viewing room at the morgue. I knew what I was *supposed* to say: so peaceful.

"Dead," said Visalia, and it was hard to argue. Cousin Clovis on Monday had been dead beyond a shadow of a doubt. Cold, stiff, and pale. But looking at him then I could see how Mary Shelley might have got the idea for *Frankenstein,* one night after a good dinner in that villa in Italy, as the mints went round and the candles burned down. Looking at him now, four days later . . . I could only imagine her out for lunch with her editor in London, giving the two-minute pitch, and the editor saying, "I dunno, Mary. What else you got for me?"

That same orderly was standing off to the side, scrolling through his texts. Hard to believe there was a signal down here, but he was certainly engrossed in something.

I had tried to strategise on the drive over,

suggesting that Mizz Visalia throw a wobbler and have to be taken away, leaving me alone with the body. She pointed out that anyone falling ill on county property would be whisked into the ER in case of litigation and she'd had a "potful of county facilities at the jail and could do without the hospital chaser." Then I suggested she faint and grab hold of the sheet on her way down, uncovering the body and letting me take a quick couple of photos while the attention was on her. "ER for me again," she said, "and jail for you when they hear the camera click." I suggested the application of some *more* dead guys — presidents, to be specific. Visalia pointed out that the staff member would gladly pocket the money and then keep coming back for more until we were both destitute.

"I'll take care of it, Lexy," she said. "Leave it to me."

She sighed and smiled at the orderly. He scrolled. She cleared her throat. He scrolled. She said, "Pardon me." Maybe he thought she was excusing a burp, but in any case, he scrolled.

"Sir?" I said. "I think Mrs. Bombaro would like to ask something."

The orderly raised his eyes. They were deader than Clovis's in their way, since

Clovis at least had that residual look of surprise he was taking into the hereafter. My heart sank. This guy had no spark of humanity about him anywhere. Whatever Visalia had in mind, he'd snort and go back to scrolling.

I was wrong.

"Can I look at him?" Visalia said. The orderly glanced at the table and poked his head forward, just once, about six inches. I had no idea what he meant to convey but Visalia, for all she was (Bakersfield) Italian, did better with the minimal gesture than me.

"Oh, yes of course," she said, "It's wonderful to see his sweet face, but can I look at . . . more of him? Can I look at . . . all of him? He was such a passionate man and marriage is such an intimate relationship and we've been married so long . . ."

It was a masterstroke. There was no way for the orderly to refuse her request without implying that he was repulsed. And repulsion takes investment. Repulsion is a shit that must be given.

To prove he didn't have the fixings, the orderly shrugged and went back to scrolling again.

Visalia looked pointedly at me. I had nothing to prove, possessed several shits, and gave them all: repulsion, trepidation, regret, nausea, light-headedness, and — oddly — a clear memory of Clovis's brown slip-on shoes and long cream-coloured silk socks. But this had been my idea, so I stepped forward and folded back the white sheet, uncovering his pale, hairless chest with its badly-stitched seam, his white belly, concave now after the removal of so many organs and samples, and . . . Hallelujah, a pair of paper drawers the same cement-grey as the staff scrubs. I kept unrolling the sheet, past his purple, bruised wrists, his doughy thighs, scraped knees, spindly shins, purple, bruised ankles, and long yellow feet.

"Underwear off?" said the orderly in a lazy drawl. Visalia gasped and he finally betrayed an emotion. A smile-like lift struck one side of his mouth very briefly.

"Underwear *on*," I said. I had never been more grateful for the wide streak of Puritan-ism that still ran through American society, even all the way over here on the wacky West Coast, three thousand miles and a can-nibalistic Christmas picnic from the pil-grims' landing. Breastfeeding under a tar-paulin and trying to give smear tests by touch alone was never going to seem any more normal to me than inside cats and lunch at eleven, but I was a big fan of morgue shorts. Big fan.

If I ever needed to tell someone what I did for a living but didn't want to end up offering therapy — on a plane, for instance, with a chatty neighbour — I was going to say I worked for a company that manufactured paper underwear for cadavers. That would stop a conversation like rolling a marble into a cowpat.

I turned my attention (at last, perhaps) to the bruises on his wrists and ankles. I happen to know that handcuffs come in different sizes. And Clovis was not a big guy. Yet the marks of his restraints were enough to make me wince and want to rub them with balm. His wrists had been badly pinched and mashed together. I looked down at his ankles and saw the same story there. And something else. There was a rectangular dent about the size of the smallest Lego brick, the one with two bumps, except without bumps.

At my side, Visalia let go of a long low breath. "Goodbye, my dear old friend," she said. "Goodbye, love of my long life. Goodbye."

I pulled the sheet back up to his chin, said, "Goodbye, Clovis," and then let it drop over his face. "We'll see ourselves out," I said to Scroller Boy and, hand-in-hand, Visalia and

341

I made our weary way up to the ground floor and out of the formaldehyde chill into the fetid breath of the day.

"I loved him," Visalia said.

"I know."

"He made me want to take off my shoe and beat him to death sometimes."

"Of course."

"But if I had my time all over again, I wouldn't change a thing."

I decided she meant *up to but not including Sunday* and just patted her hand gently.

"Did you recognise the pattern the restraints left on his skin?" I asked, once we were underway again. "They didn't look like handcuffs to me."

Visalia gasped. "Handcuffs?" she said.

"That's definitely what Bilbo said the police told him."

Visalia took a huge breath. I was convinced she was going to say something momentous. But in the end all it was, was: "I'm an old woman and I want to rest. It's so damn hot."

It was a sharp drop after the way she had bounded out of bed so recently. I even wondered if she meant *rest* in the Clovis sense. As in, rest side by side in the morgue and have a double funeral. I wondered briefly if they made grey paper bras for lady

342

corpses, then I wrested my mind away and told her I'd drop her at home and would she just phone the factory and tell them I was coming back. If anyone wanted counselling, they should wait for me in the cafeteria.

And what a shower of lazy wee toe rags! The lunchroom was packed solid when I peered round the corner and in through the glass doors. I did a Pink-Panther tiptoe past and then scuttled up Bilbo's stairs and burst in without knocking.

"You didn't knock," he said.

I didn't say *duh.* I'm very mature sometimes. "Sorry to disturb you again," I said. "I've got a question."

"About fireworks?"

"No. About Clovis and the handcuffs."

"Cable ties," Bilbo said.

And a choir of angels sang a chorus above my head as the clouds parted and sunbeams shone through. "Cable ties!" I said. "That's what that square shape was. That's it. Cable t— How did you find out?"

"I *told* you," said Bilbo. "That lady detective said it."

"No, no, no," I said. "Categorically not. You said she said handcuffs."

"Yes, I did. Well, she didn't. She said cable ties."

I waited.

Bilbo's eyes strayed to his screen. "Well, if that was all, I've got a funeral display to design."

"No, that's not all," I said, drily. "Of course it's not." I waited. In vain. "Why did you say handcuffs?"

"Because Mrs. Bombaro asked me to. She asked me not to say it was cable ties."

"So why did you say it was cable ties?"

"I didn't," said Bilbo. "I said it was hand-cuffs."

I sighed. "I now understand why you *initially* said handcuffs. Mrs. Bombaro told you to."

"Correct. But I blew it saying 'cut off.' I should have extended the deception and said 'unlocked.'"

"That certainly would have helped," I said, as dry as if I'd sprinkled salt on my earlier dryness, left it overnight, and then wrung it out in a towel. "But anyway, now that that's all straightened out, why did you stop saying handcuffs and start saying cable ties just now?"

"Because Mrs. Bombaro asked me to," he said. "She asked me not to say it was hand-cuffs."

"You just told me she asked you not to say it was cable ties!"

"It's pretty straightforward," he said. I

didn't beat him around his head with a computer keyboard. I'm proud of that. "Mrs. Bombaro told me that she didn't mean you to be told the handcuff lie."

"What?" I said, and I had to grab a breath to say it with.

"She told me she hadn't ever meant *you* to be included in the audience for the handcuff lie. That was just for factory workers so that they didn't feel suspected or even start to suspect one another. Because we use exactly those cable ties for packing and on the mounting boards. Everyone who works in this factory has got some at home too. Clovis was never strict about that. But Visalia never meant *you* to be told that version. You don't work in the factory and there was no need to protect you."

"Right," I said. "That makes a lot of sense. That's very clear."

"It didn't cause you any trouble, did it?" he said.

"What?" I said, and I flapped a hand at him. "Of course not. No trouble at all. Can I ask you one last question?"

"Is that —"

"Bilbo!"

"Yes, you can."

"When did Mrs. Bombaro tell you to stop saying handcuffs to me and start saying cable ties?"

"About twenty minutes ago," said Bilbo. "Lucky timing."

I sneaked back past the gaggle of traumatised employees in the canteen and back across the baking car park to phone Todd from his own car.

"The plot splits like bad mayo and turns to a watery mess," I said, and then went on to tell him what Bilbo had told me.

"Sheesh," said Todd, "those people are going to get the shock of their lives if Bang-Bang really does take over and fires their asses. She wanted to protect them? She's a sweetheart, isn't she? But you know the only thing that worries me?"

"Shoot."

"What did Visalia think you were going to the morgue for, if she already knew he had marks on his body from cable ties?"

"Oh," I said. "That's because . . . . Hang on. That's a good question. Why didn't she tell me this morning in the bedroom instead of me having to go into that viewing room and see things that made me want to bleach my eyeballs? That's a very good question."

"How about a very good answer?" said Todd.

"Got it!" I said. "I'm an idiot." The car was starting to warm up, so I fired up the

346

engine and cranked the a/c round to cryogenic. "I was trying not to speak too plainly. I think I maybe didn't actually cough up any of the sordid details. I think I just said that the cops reckon two different people were involved and I wanted to find out how they knew."

"But they don't, right?" said Todd. "That was just Bilbo getting his story pretzeled."

"Yeah," I said. "So . . . hey! You know what that means?"

"Vi's in the clear?"

"Vi's in the clear!" I grinned at myself in the driving mirror. "Yay!"

"Only . . ."

"Only . . . Why did she pretend not to recognise the marks? Why didn't she tell me that the killer used cable ties? Why did she tell Bilbo to tell me?"

"Because . . . she was . . . ashamed of having told him to lie in the first place and she didn't want to come clean to your face?" Todd offered.

"Huh," I said. "I was going with because she knew I'd go straight back to the factory to ask him and she wanted to get rid of me for some reason."

"But it can't be that, if she's in the clear."

"And she's in the clear!" I said. "Yay."

"Yay," Todd agreed. "Who did it?"

"I don't care," I said. "Someone with access to cable ties and knowledge of fireworks. Sparky, Chucky, Jan, a workers' uprising? Not Vi and not Barb. That's good enough for me."

"This is a good day all round."

"Oh? No more worms? No bugs?"

"More than that," Todd said. "Something really truly good is happening. Noleen and Kathi have got guys in to clean the pool and get the filtration system going again. The Last Ditch is gentrifying."

"That's your fault," I said. "First the gays move in and soon there's no yolks in the omelettes and all the daycare's for dogs."

He blew a raspberry at me, like a real chip off the old Barb. I hung up and headed . . . back to the Last Ditch, which some bit of me not under the jurisdiction of my conscious mind seemed to be telling me was my . . .

Well, I went back anyway.

And standing looking through the chain-link fence surrounding the pool when I got there were . . . the people that same bit of me was calling my . . .

Well, I was glad to see them anyway.

"How's it going?" I asked as I joined them. Inside the fence two guys in the white t-shirts and work boots I'd come to know so well when I was an up-suburb girl were watching the pool fill from a gushing hose that led from a water tanker parked at the far side. One of the guys couldn't have been knocked over by a wrecking ball. He made Fred Flintstone look willowy, but the other one was five-ten with broad shoulders and slim hips and . . .

"You're drooling," said Todd.

"Fuck off," I said. It's the Scottish version of a raspberry. It made Bran cry once.

"Fuck off yourself," said Todd. "I've already ascertained that he's straight and single and if Noleen agrees, he'll be here twice a week. I've looked online for swimwear half a size too small for you and we'll get you a gym membership."

"Half a size too small?"

"Trust me."

"And *does* Noleen agree?" I said.

Noleen looked at the guy's bum in his jeans and then at me and screwed her face up. "I'm happy to have this windfall," she said, "but pools cost money and I can just as easy do it myself."

"What windfall?" I said vaguely. My guy had bent over.

"We won a pool rehab," Kathi said. "One of those big bowls you toss your business cards into on service desks? A pool company bought the list this month and they offered either a pool rehab or patio landscaping."

"Call me a bitter old cynic," Noleen said, "but I thought I knew how it would go. I reckoned they'd come do the pool and tell us — surprise, surprise — it needed a ton of extra work not covered in the small print and could they go ahead and bill us on thirty-day terms. But they've restored my faith in humanity. They said the pool's fine and they gave us two planters and a cabana they can't be bothered to cart back."

Then she said some more, but my guy took his t-shirt off and stretched his shoulder muscles out and I didn't hear her.

"I'm outta here," Kathi said, fanning her t-shirt. "It's too hot."

"I'm willing to stay and get heatstroke," said Todd. "Lexy, you with me?"

Todd lasted twenty minutes, which was fifteen minutes more than me. I went to stand under the shower and fantasize about swimming every morning again. That is my story of what I fantasized about in my shower and I'm sticking to it.

Moving on. I heard Todd come upstairs when I was sorting out a load of sweaty laundry for Kathi and I called him in.

"Your Adonis has gone to sit in his truck," Todd said. "Thank God because I was beginning to get red spots in front of my eyes."

They were prophetic words, as we were to know before the sun rose again.

TWENTY-TWO

It was a quiet night at the Last Ditch Motel. Thursday after a holiday, it seemed everyone who'd been on the move was home again and no one was planning a long weekend away. The regulars were there, of course, and one of them needed to be assured that Nemo, Gill, and Dory would be there the very next day with their *other* friend, who just couldn't bear to be left behind but needed one more night to pack and say goodbye.

"A seahorse?" Diego said, his eyes now taking up about half his face. "A real seahorse?"

"And the tank it needs and the filter for the tank and the lights and some spare lightbulbs?" said Della.

"Absolutely," I said, thinking I'd need to go to Sacramento for it. Or down to Monterey and break into the aquarium.

The pool helped. Diego splashed around

on an inflatable in a Little Mermaid scuba mask and flippers until he was too tired to scream when Della fished him out and crammed him into his jammies. She sat on a lounger and rocked him to sleep while the rest of us had a little pool-warming ceremony.

Noleen and Kathi went first. Noleen wore a black bathing dress with a long history and a pair of yellow goggles. Kathi wore a polka dot bikini that had me humming for the rest of the night. They held hands and jumped in the deep end and then Todd, in a tiny white Speedo and a ton of oil, walked sedately down the steps at the shallow end with a tray of mint mojitos and served them. Roger shed his robe and dived in with barely a splash. Then it was my turn.

"Oh my GOD!" I said, pointing at the sky and then making a run for it. I fooled everyone except Todd, who pretended to retch and told me my first gym visit was in the morning.

We floated, drank, tried (and failed) to get Della to join us, then when Diego had gone to his bed and wasn't around to be traumatised, we talked of murder.

"I like the Dolshikovs," I said. "One of them or both of them or add the cousins and it's all of them."

"Families!" Kathi said. "Do you *have* to keep digging?"

"I promised Mizz Vi I'd present her crackpot theory to the cops, so I should really keep my word. Dob in the olive growers. But I don't know how to say it in a way that doesn't sound totally barmy."

"Blame the language divide," said Todd. "Dob them barmy."

"And the other question," I said, "is whether it should actually be me who goes at all. Detective Mike's gone off me."

"Really?" said Noleen. "What did you do?"

"I gave her the benefit of my psychological insight," I said.

"About whom?" said Roger.

"Cops," I said. "So . . . yeah."

"Well, I can't go," said Todd. "And Roger can't go."

"Jesus Christ," said Roger. "Todd, you are thirty-five years old and the 'adorable' routine is getting tired. You can't just blab my business like you blab your own." Then he lifted himself up like a dolphin and swam away underwater to the far end of the pool.

"Come back, you big dork," Todd shouted, when he resurfaced. "Lexy's met my *mom*. She knows I married up. She's not judging you."

"I'm really not," I called. "I don't even know what I'm not judging you for. That's how much I'm not judging you."

Roger swam back. "I ran with a gang," he said when he was close enough to speak quietly but still have me hear him. "As you would know if you could read tattoos. I did bad things and hurt good people."

"And got some piss-poor therapy," I told him. "I know learned routines when I hear them. Okay, so not Todd and not Roger. Noleen?"

"Too many parking tickets," she said, and sent a playful splash Roger's way. "You're not the only desperado around here."

"So that leaves Kathi," I said. And the silence went on long enough for all the waves from Roger's swim and Noreen's splash to die down to ripples around us.

"No deal," Kathi said. "And not just because cops play the stereotypes either. I'm not a good witness. I imagine things. I make mistakes." She was floating on her back not looking at any of us. Noleen reached over, grabbed her toe, and pulled her close.

"What things do you imagine?" I said.

"Like that guy on the security feed the other day," said Kathi. "I had a flashback. All the way back to Queens."

355

"Queens College, Cambridge?" I said. Probably the dumbest thing I've ever said. And that, as Americans say, is a deep bench.

"Queens, New York," said Kathi. "Where my family lives and works and disowns aberrations like me."

"Assholes," Noleen growled.

"I think you won that war," I said. "You followed the sun and here you are in your own swimming pool with your loving wife and your good friends."

This time even the ripples from Kathi's little four-foot journey to Noleen's side were gone before anyone spoke again.

"Via the old country and a forced marriage," Kathi said. "Noleen isn't my wife, Lexy, because I'm married already."

"What old country is that?" I said. "Katherine Mary doesn't sound like a forced marriage kind of name. Sorry if that's racist."

"It's not Italy's fault," said Kathi. "This is a Poggio specialty."

I drank a good slug of pool water before I came up spluttering. *"Poggio?"*

"Lex," said Todd with eerie calm. "Isn't that the name of those Sicilians Mrs. Bombaro keeps on about?"

"It is," I said, just as calm as him. "Kathi, why didn't you say something?"

"What?" said Kathi. "I did. I told you it

356

was a mafia name and you should be careful."

"I thought you meant Dolshikov," I said. "Wait. Let me think. Shoosh a minute."

"No one else is speaking," Roger said.

My brain was sparking like a funereal firework show. "Your name is Poggio?" I said.

"Her name is Muntz," said Noleen. "But carry on."

"And you think you recognised a Poggio carrying the fake pizza box with the raccoon in it up the stairs?"

"Not just a Poggio," said Kathi. "*The* Poggio. Marco Poggio. He's not active in the family. He's too dumb for that. But he is my husband."

"Wow," I said. "I mean *wow.* I truly thought Visalia was havering with all this."

"All of what?" said Kathi. "You said there was a feud and I said 'that sounds about right.' "

"Visalia thinks one of the Poggios came over here and killed Clovis. Now, wouldn't you agree that sounds a lot less far-fetched if someone else saw a Poggio here up to absolutely no bloody good whatsoever?"

"You can't tell the cops about the raccoon," Noleen said.

"But a man died," I insisted.

"And a hotel with bluebottles and worms and whatever the hell those red shitting things were will die too and it won't bring him back." Noleen had never looked sterner. There wasn't a slogan t-shirt in print in the world that could have expressed it better than her stony face.

"And if they send the Health Inspectors they'll take away Diego's fish before he's had a chance to name them," said Kathi.

"And we won't be allowed so much as a loaf of bread to make toast in the morning," Kathi said. "We'll have to take 'Continental Breakfast' off the sign by the freeway."

"But someone has got away with murder!" I said.

All four of them stared back at me.

"Mizz Visalia and my mom are in the clear, Lex," said Todd. "Isn't that the main thing?"

"But how can you just wait for him to come back? What do you think the next thing is going to be?" I felt it again. The faint glimmer somewhere, like a dream of a memory, or a memory of a dream.

"I think it's over," Noleen said. She lifted her mojito glass and drained it. "Our luck has turned. This pool is the start of good times."

"Can I at least talk to Mizz Vi?" I said. "Now that I'm taking her seriously? God, what a nerve I had. Dismissing her like that! But now that I'm taking her seriously, can I ask her again for anything else she might know so I can talk to Mike and leave the Last Ditch out of it?"

Noleen gave me a curt nod. "Bombaro understands business," she said. "You might think she's some kind of mother hen — keeping the little tidbit about the cable ties from the workers — but if you were a boss, you'd know it's all about productivity. She's no fool."

"Okay then," I said. I paddled to the edge and hauled myself out. "I'm going to go and call her right now."

I felt marvellous, climbing the stairs. My skin was tingling all over and even my mouth felt fresh enough to fizz. *If that's what a mouthful of pool water did,* I thought, *I might gargle with it every morning.*

Inside my room, I wrapped myself in a towel and settled down for a nice chat. Except for the subject matter and the late hour and the fact that I had been told not to say the very things that would be most helpful, I was looking forward to it.

"It's pretty late," Sparky said when she answered the landline.

"I think I've thought of something relating to your uncle's death," I said. "Something that will exonerate your aunt. And everyone associated with her," I added hastily.

"Is anyone associated with my aunt under suspicion?" said Serpentina coldly.

I prickled with either annoyance or embarrassment, hard to say. But this woman literally rubbed me the wrong way. I chafed the goose bumps off my arms and tried again.

"I'm not being very diplomatic," I said. "I had no idea I needed to be. But I'll try to step more gently around this area now I know it's a sore spot for you."

"I have no idea what you're talking about!" Serpentina said. "I'll transfer you up to Auntie's room."

People are so easy to manipulate, it's a blessing I only use my powers for good.

"Hi, Vi," I said a minute later. "The day ends as it began, I'm afraid."

"We're not going back to the morgue!" said Visalia. I heard the television sound go down and then a lot of fluffy rustling as she sat up. I could imagine her rearranging her bed jacket. I needed to tread carefully. I needed to make this easy on her. I needed to stick to the spirit of what Noleen had said rather than the letter.

"I think one of the Poggios is in Cuento," I said.

"Not still," said Mizz Vi. "But yes, of course. That's what I've been trying to tell you. One of them was here on Sunday. To kill Clovis. Did you tell the police? Did that nice detective convince you I'm not just a crazy old lady after all?"

"I'm going to talk to the police in the morning," I said. "And he was still here yesterday, you know."

"How do *you* know if you haven't been to the police yet?" Vi said. "Do you have contacts at the airline?"

"No," I said. "What airline?"

"Oh!" said Vi, and there was more rustling as she fiddled with her neck ribbons. "I'm such a creature of habit. I still think only Alitalia flies to Rome. Of course, these days everyone with a pilot's licence and a big box of peanuts flies just everywhere. So what makes you think there was a Poggio in town yesterday?"

"He was caught on video," I said. "Although, actually, that was before."

There was a long long long silence. No rustling; no bed jacket work going on.

"Before," said Vi, at last. "Do you mean to tell me that you have a videotape of my husband's murder?"

"No," I said, "I'm saying I've got a video-tape of someone recognised as a member of the Poggio family, on Wednesday, pretending to be a pizza delivery boy and putting a dead raccoon in a hotel bathroom."

It wasn't the sort of sentence a sleepy eighty-six-year-old needs to parse every day and I was ready to have to tell her a few more times before it went in. What she said next floored me.

"For the flies." It wasn't a question.

"Well," I said. "There certainly *were* flies." My skin prickled again and all of a sudden I had a sour taste in my mouth too.

"And there have been other . . . disturbances too?" Vi said. She might have been taking lessons from Noleen, her voice was so cold.

"There have been," I said. "Several."

"*Figlio de puttana!*" she said. "*Stupido figlio de —*"

"What?" I said.

"They never change, those Poggios," she said. "This is very bad, Lexy. This is terrible."

I hadn't *enjoyed* the raccoon so I wasn't going to argue, but my private opinion was that neither it, those nanowhatsits, nor the worms, were in the same league as Clovis and the firework.

362

"Should I go to the cops tonight?" I said. "I was planning it for first thing but I can easily bob down there. Tell whoever's on duty."

Mizz Vi took her time and then said, "No, you're right, *cara*. Better to tell the horse's mouth in the morning. Let's get our beauty sleep."

Which was ironic, given what happened next.

I made myself a cup of chamomile tea, snuggled down as best you *can* snuggle under a thin sheet in a hot room, and drifted off. The dreams that visited me weren't my usuals (teeth falling out, stuck in a tunnel, still married to Branston) and I kept struggling up out of them, almost to waking, only to sink back again. I was in a church, listening to Father Adam preach in Italian and asking my mother "What's he saying? What's he saying?" and then I was in a doctor's waiting room at a renaissance fair waiting for it to be my turn and hoping my prescription wasn't leeches. I could see them in a jar behind the doctor's desk, jumping and landing like Mexican beans. They weren't leeches. The name was on the tip of my tongue and I couldn't say it. I turned to my neighbour in the queue to ask them and it was Barb, trying to open a take-out pizza. But, when she finally raised the lid, a jack-in-the-box bounced out, its eyes wide and its mouth a perfect O. I turned and ran, my feet leaden and my voice a plug of glue in my throat. And then they started screaming. I felt myself begin to surface. My feet were freed, the fair was gone, and I was awake.

But people were still screaming and my throat was still closed.

I opened my eyes and what faced me was worse than the Clovis-death-head-jack by far.

I tried to scream for real, failed for real, and thrashed my way out of the tangle of bedsheets. Two zombies were leering at me. My whole body crawled with terror and I spun away to see Todd, wrapped in a bath sheet, tears pouring down his face. And another zombie behind him.

Except of course they weren't zombies. They were Roger, Kathi, and Noleen, red-eyed and raw-skinned, angry pustules erupting all over their faces.

"Mmrhmhm," I moaned.

"Open your mouth!" said Todd then, when I did, he took a step back. He looked round at Roger. Rather, at the Quasimodo wreck of Roger's beautiful face. "Saline gargle?" Todd said. Roger nodded.

"It's going to sting, Lexy," Todd said. "But you've got it in your mouth for some reason, as well as all over your body." He went over to my little kitchenette and started mixing.

"How come you're okay?" I tried to ask Todd. "Huh hm mmuuu ayy?" was what came out, but he understood me and opened the bedsheet to reveal the horrors from his neck down.

"I have no idea," he said. "What *is* it?"

"It's Poggio," said Kathi. "It must be. I just don't know how he did it."

"An allergic reaction?" said Roger. "Something in the mojitos? Are you sure it was mint, Nolly?"

"But why does Lexy have it worse than us?" Noleen said. "And how come Todd's head is okay? Lexy, are you allergic to anything that looks like mint leaves?"

I thought back to the night before. We all drank the mojitos. It couldn't be that. We all floated around and . . . Suddenly, I could see it clearly. Kathi and Noleen jumping in; Roger swimming under water; me sinking and gulping. And Todd, his vanity keeping his beautiful face up out of the chlorine like an old lady doing laps in a flowered skull cap.

"Fuh-ing hulll!" I said.

"Telling me," said Roger. "Let's all get

365

our asses over to the ER."

"Ih wa hu wooooo!" I said, grabbing him with my scabby hands and making him yelp. "HEYHO!"

He blinked at me just once. Then he got it. "It was the *pool*!" he said. "DIEGO!" He wheeled round, but Todd, finished with my salt draught, caught his other arm and made him yelp again.

"Baby," he said, "you can't knock on Della's door looking like that. Let me go."

"I'm a pediatric—" Roger got out, then he deflated. "Yeah. Yeah, you're right. Hurry, though."

We all crowded onto the balcony to listen.

"Do you know what time it is?" came Della's muffled voice after his knock. Then, "What the hell are you wearing?"

"Is Diego okay?" Todd asked.

Then Diego's voice, rough with sleep, piped up: "Are my fishies here?"

We heard his scampering feet and then Todd spoke again.

"Hey, little guy! Later today, I promise. Not long now. Ontday etlay imhay in the oolpay, Della. Got it?"

"What?" she said. "What the hell is wrong with you?"

"It's locked," Noleen shouted down and Della came out from under the balcony and squinted up at us. She paled, turned, and ordered Diego to go inside in a stream of staccato Spanish and then looked up at us again.

"What in the name of the Holy Mother is that?" she said.

I had swirled and spat three mouthfuls of Todd's saline solution. He was right: it did sting. But it worked too and I could speak again.

"Boils," I said. "It's a plague of boils."

TWENTY-THREE

We didn't have to wait long at the ER.

I'll take a second run at that. Once we had got past the receptionists, filled out a total of thirty-five pages of paperwork, paid four deductibles varying between fifty and two hundred dollars, and they had run Branston's credit card for the uninsured subhuman who had the nerve to be cluttering up their waiting room for a few blemishes without even having the wit to invent a time machine, go back, get coverage, and *then* need medical attention, and was ungrateful enough to do a big fake "Ennn-aitch-esss!" sneeze while she was at it . . . we didn't have to wait long at the ER. For one thing, the nurses wanted us out of sight and for another, two of us were doctors and nepotism rules. Thankfully.

I only just had time in the waiting room to lay the theory out before them. "I kept thinking about Diego's pets and sandwiches," I said. "And I couldn't work out why. I even dreamed about it last night."

"What are you talking about?" said Todd. "Sandwiches?"

"Loaves and fishes," I said. "And flies, and boils, and I bet if we phone Cindy Slagle we'll find that the common name for those . . ."

"*Anoplura?*" said Kathi.

". . . is lice. Whose fingers aren't too sore to Google the plagues of Egypt?"

Noleen did it, with a few ouches and one mother*fucker* that made the receptionist look up and scowl. "Gimme a break," Noleen said and the woman nodded, winced, and then looked away.

"Yep," she said, reading from her phone. "Lice, flies, worms, boils."

"The raccoon was a red herring," I said. "It was just the host." I wondered why that bothered me.

"So what's next?" said Roger.

"Hail, locusts, darkness, and . . ." Noleen said.

"Death of the firstborn child," said Todd. "Don't even say it. Don't say his name."

No one said it, but we were all thinking the same thing: those little feet and that croaky voice saying, "Are my fishies here?"

"Call Mike and tell her to come," Kathi

said to me. "Nolly, you dial and hold the phone to her head."

"At least we dodged the blood and frogs," Noleen said, still reading. Then she smacked her head with her hand, making both weep with watery blood. "No we didn't, though, did we? I wiped the mess up with my own two hands and we put the frogs back in the slough." She looked round at us all. "Okay, I'm dialling."

"You can't use cell phones in here," said an approaching nurse. Then she took a second look at us. "You do what you gotta do," she said. A third look. At Roger. "Doc Kroger, is that you? What happened? Jeez Louise!" A fourth look, taking in Todd. "Doc Kroger II? What happened to them?"

Todd slipped his bath sheet off one shoulder. "It happened to me too," he said.

"Holy crap! Get back here!" the nurse shouted, fishing a mask out of her scrubs pocket and slapping it on. "Cubicles A through E."

With that, our ER wait was over. Wincing and bleeding, we shuffled away.

I got seen first, since my mouth was affected, but it didn't get me much of an advantage in the end because, once the word got out, every doctor on duty was on deck, dabbing, swabbing, looking stuff up,

370

and calling their old medical-school roommates to send pictures of us and ask for help.

"The dermatologist is on his way in," one of the ER docs told me after ten minutes.

"Wait?," I said. "The guy with the beergut and the orange hair?"

The ER doc had a great poker face, but his eyes twinkled. "It's the other dermatologist who's on call today," he said

"Bingo!" a cry went up from two cubicles along. "I know what it is." Then he let out a string of gobbledygook worse than lawyers, judges, and Professor Slagle combined. A low whistle went up from the cubicle on the other side of me.

"Can we just open the curtains and do this together?" I said.

Once the cubicles were combined, the winning doctor resumed. He was holding his phone on his shoulder and twirling swab sticks through the worst of Roger's lesions. "Contaminated water and did you consume alcohol? You did. Well, you're going to be okay. I mean, you're not going to be pretty for a while, but you're all going to be fine. *You* should see a good dentist in a week or two, League-Said."

"Lexy," I told him. "I don't know any good dentists. I only know Branston

Lancer."

"That fucker?" said one of the younger doctors, then blushed. "Excuse me. I'm sleep-deprived and last night was a rough one."

"Plus it's a fair comment," I said. No one disagreed.

"It's a fungus," the doc with the phone went on, relaying the news from his friend. "Found in the hills of northern . . . where? You broke up."

"Sicily," said Kathi. The doctor clicked and winked.

"Found in the hills of northern Sicily — good guess." He plugged his free ear with a finger and listened. "Rare and easy to mistake for . . . yeah, I have no idea what you just said . . . easy to mistake for some other fungus. Harmless if ingested or applied externally unless you add alcohol. And then . . . Quasimodo. Instant Dermageddon. Short-lived but epic. Thanks, man. I owe you. Give my love to Laurel and the rugrats." The doc holstered his phone with a flourish.

"And what's the treatment?" said Noleen. "Because I run a service business and this is not a good face for customer relations."

"Uhhhhhhh, Clearasil?" said the doctor. "Jamie?" He turned to a colleague. "Cleara-

372

sil, right? You got any better suggestions?"

"Can I take a group photo for our newsletter?" Jamie said.

And so we were almost happy to hear Mike arrive. She had Soft Cop with her and made a nice contrast to him, since she looked as hard as a granite puck studded with hobnails.

The sight of us unbent her a little. Kathi had a boil in the corner of each eye and tears streaming unstoppably down her face making tracks in the lotion the nurses had dabbed on. Roger had one nostril almost closed and one ear so lavishly be-pustuled that he had just slathered a poultice over the whole thing and was trying to ignore the melting ointment dripping down his neck. And then there was me. The only way I felt even halfway comfortable was to keep my tongue hanging out whenever I wasn't using it, and my eyes were half shut because I had a boil in the crease of one that itched if I opened them. It wasn't a great look.

Mike subjected the four of us to close study and swallowed hard. She flicked a glance at Todd and opened her notebook.

Todd cleared his throat. "I know I look as if I got off lightly," he said. "But that's only because you can't see my bathing suit area."

"Oh, tell me your worries!" Noleen said.

"Me, Lex, and Kathi have got nooks and crannies you can't imagine, Todd. And I've got belly folds too."

"For your information," said Todd, "I am intact in my lower regions and, while I'm usually thankful that my mother was a hippy . . . not today."

"Okay," said Mike. "So who wants to tell me what's going on? We can leave the bathing suit areas out of it if it's all right with all of you."

"First, I need to apologise," I said. "I was unfair. I took what I believed about some members of the entire class of cops and judged you on the strength of it. Basically, I profiled you."

"Wow," said Mike. "You just can't stop that mouth."

"Anyway," said Roger. "We need to report a crime. Someone added an irritant fungus to the guest pool at the Last Ditch Motel and the results are before you."

"Well," said Kathi, "it's more accurate to say someone contaminated a tanker of water and pumped the water into the pool. But yes, the results are before you."

"And we know who it was," said Noleen.

"Kind of," I amended.

"It was a member of the Poggio crime family, from Sicily, Italy," said Roger. "We have him on video and we have a witness who can ID him."

"And," I said, "we have a motive for him to murder Clovis Bombaro."

Mike sent Soft Cop for coffees and sat down on one of the examination tables to listen to the whole story.

"So," she said, once we were done, "you've experienced an escalating series of harassment. Do you have the logs of your reports to the city environmental protection inspector to corroborate any of them? Any case numbers from any agencies?"

Kathi and Noleen looked down at their feet.

"We've got an expert who'll testify," I said. "Professor Slagle."

"The bug lady?" said Mike.

"And we've got five people right here who're telling you what happened," said Roger.

Mike nodded slowly. Her eyes were travelling over Roger's arms, where a few of his tattoos were partially visible in between the dressings. "You're a resident at the motel, aren't you?" she said. "Can you give me a list of your other addresses since you left . . ."

"Stockton," said Roger. "Yeah, I moved around a bit."

"Doesn't have to be today, Mr. . . . Kroger, wasn't it? Compile a list of addresses and bring it in to the office. If you need someone to help you, you can dictate it to one of the dispatchers. Mornings are quietest."

"Wait, what?" I said. "Are you trying to imply that maybe he can't write? And it's *Doctor* Kroger, by the way."

"And he lives at the Last Ditch because of me," said Todd. "I have a psychological disorder, currently under treatment, that has forced us to leave our home on Cardinal Way and sublet it."

"Cardinal Way?" said Mike. "You left Stockton with a pretty decent chunka change then."

"He's. A. Doctor," I said again. "Do you need someone to help you with the hearing?"

"You're all very close and cooperative," said Mike. "Any witness outside this tight little crew?"

"I met them all for the first time on Sunday," I said. But it did no good.

"Quick work," she said. "Anyone else?"

"There's Della and Diego," I said.

Mike missed the quick headshake Kathi gave me. "Who's Della and Diego?" she said.

"Transients," Noleen said. "They were

staying on Monday night and Lexy got talking in the laundromat. But they paid in cash and moved on in the morning."

"I thought they might have," Mike said. "Well, that's unfortunate."

"Look," I said, "do you think we did this to ourselves? Would *you*?"

"I'm not here to answer your questions," Mike said. Soft Cop came back with the coffees and settled down to enjoy his. I suppose after what came seeping out of the omni-spout machine in the cop shop, hospital slop was a holiday.

"But what the hell is it you suspect us of?" I said.

"Absolutely nothing," Mike said. "Why would you sit on the identity of a suspect in a murder until you all got your stories straight so you can peg him for whatever this is too?"

I had to run this through a few times before it made any sense at all. The strange thing was that the others didn't seem to have any trouble with it. They sat, stone-faced and dead-eyed, as if she'd hypnotised them.

"So . . . you think we know who did this and, instead of having him caught and having the trouble stop, we're pretending it was someone else? And I am obstructing the investigation into my client's murder by adding this fictitious crap to help people I didn't even know a week ago?"

I thought Mike's face clouded briefly, but she got hold of her expression again before she spoke. "There are faster ways to stop trouble than having the police build a case," she said. "Ain't that so, *mi amigo*?" She smiled at Todd.

"Will you at least talk to Visalia and try to see if any of the Poggios is in town?" I said.

"I've told you before, I don't need your help," Mike said. I couldn't believe I had thought this woman and I might be friends one day. She looked down at her notebook. "Anything to add?"

"A question," I said. "Are there any public servants it's illegal to insult or does free speech cover that?"

"Lex," said Roger.

"What sort of thing did you have in mind?" said Mike.

"Hypothetically, I was interested in calling a certain official a myopic, egotistical joke," I said. "But I don't want to be arrested. You know, if 'he' called the cops on me."

"First amendment's your best friend," said Mike. She stood, snapped her notebook back together and left with Soft Cop ambling after her.

"Smart move," said Roger. "The city of Cuento's going to get rich off your traffic citations, you know."

"I'm leaving," I said. "As soon as I look like someone they'd let on a plane, I'm on a plane." But I was surprised at the slump in my chest when I said it. "At least that was the plan."

"It's a good plan," said Roger. "You've made an enemy for life in Mike."

"I dunno," I said. "There's a story there and I'd love to get to the bottom of it. There's more to Miss Mike than meets the eye. And don't trade looks about me. I can *see* you." I blinked my swollen eyes. "Kind of."

TWENTY-FOUR

The next few days, for the five of us, were a haze of Neosporin and acetaminophen. I wanted calamine lotion and Paracetamol but I'd have had to go to Mexico and run them back up across the border, so I dealt with it as best I could: bitching and whining and bugging everyone.

We kept a careful eye on the place, but there were no more visits from the scion of the Poggios. Roger coughed up to have the pool drained and cleaned and Diego was so inconsolable that on the third day, I finally knocked the crust off the worst of my facial boils and set off, with Todd, to the pet shop. We had parked outside when my phone rang. My blood ran cold when I heard the voice on the other end of the line.

"Beteo County courthouse, clerk of courts here, for Lee—k—seth Campbell?"

I cleared my throat. "This is she."

"This is she," said Todd in a Monty

Python voice, and rolled his eyes.

"There are papers in the mail, Ms. Campbell," the voice said, "but the judge wanted to make sure you got this immediately."

"Oh?" I said. Here it was then. The start of the citations that would line the Cuento coffers and empty Bran's bank account.

"I'm calling in connection with case number —"

"Wait, wait!" I said, scrabbling for a pen as he reeled off a string of digits.

"— and to inform you that your undertaking is complete."

"I don't know what that means," I said. I waved a hand at Todd to try to stop him mouthing *What? What?* at me.

"You are the Lee—k—seth Campbell who cosigned a bail bond for Mrs. Visalia Bombaro in the matter of —"

"Oh!" I said. "Yes!"

"Some people would remember a thing like that," the clerk said. "Well, anyway, the case against Mrs. Bombaro has been dropped and she has been released without prejudice from her bail conditions."

I clutched Todd's arm. He wriggled out of my grasp and smacked me. His main aim was to get through the boils without any permanent scars. Remembering how he looked in the tiny white Speedos, I agreed it was a worthwhile goal. Me? I'd seen my body in enough swimsuits to know it was no biggie.

"They've caught the real killer?"

"I'm just passing on a message. Mrs. Bombaro was insistent that you be told immediately."

"Well, that was nice of her," I said. "She could just have phoned me though. Is that all?"

The clerk huffed. "Some people would think that was plenty."

I killed the call and turned to Todd with tears in my eyes. "Vi has been released from her bail," I said. "She wanted me to be told straightaway."

"Why didn't she tell you herself?"

"I don't know," I said. "I hope she's okay. Could you . . . ?"

"On it," said Todd, already taking a late corner and heading for The Oaks. "I know it's not likely, but will you call . . . ?"

"On it," I said, already dialling. "Barb? Lexy. Just checking in. You're okay, are you? Nothing going on?"

"Lexy!" Barb sounded sober, cheerful, and entirely un-arrested for murder. "Nothing's going on here except me getting tormented every day by the neighbor from hell over a few small lapses in cleanup during my remodeling project."

"Oh?"

"Her kids used my paint cans as helmets and might have got a tiny little bit of paint in their hair. An improvement, if you ask me. Dishwater blond and not a single eyelash between the whole family. But you should have heard her bitching."

"Some people!"

"Don't tell Teo!"

I agreed. Todd was concentrating on the road anyway. We raced through the winding streets, empty and flagging on another triple-digit day.

"That's weird," I said as we rattled along the road towards the house. The firework gates were standing open. Todd took the drive on three wheels and pulled up at the front steps with a squeal of his brakes.

The door opened as we piled out and we saw Sparky Dolshikov standing there with a swollen nose and bug-eyes from crying.

"We heard about Vi's bail getting lifted," I said. "I just wanted to come and say —"

"You're too late," Sparky said, sniffing. "She's gone. You missed her."

"Oh, Serpentina!" I said. "I am so, so sorry!"

I went to hug her but she put a hand up and stopped me. "Do you have some kind of disgusting disease?"

"No, but good point. Is there anyone else here who could hug you? Are you alone?"

"I had no idea how alone," she said and started weeping again. "My marriage is over. All my plans for Boomshik-a! are in tatters, and now Auntie's gone."

"I'm sorry for your loss," said Todd, coming round the car and hugging her hard, risking all kinds of disaster to his golden perfection. She laid her head on his shoulder and wept. Then she sniffed and straightened up.

"Well, it's probably a net gain," she said. "But just a lot to take in at once."

"Net gain," I repeated.

"My husband wasn't a keeper, as it turned out," she said. "As soon as he heard the terms of Auntie's bequest, I couldn't see him for the dust. The whole marriage was just a way for him to get his hands on Uncle Boom-Boom's empire. Can you believe that?"

"Shocking," I said, deciding that this wasn't the moment for honesty.

"So I've got a company to run," said Sparky, "and a staff to placate after the whispering campaign that tanked my light-show plans. I've got a marriage to end, and I need to go house-hunting. And somehow

I need to get into Auntie's safe to see if there's any information in there that might help me."

"And," I said, unable to help it (occupational hazard), "you need to grieve."

"For that turd?" said Serpentina. "He's lucky I didn't cut up his pants into little pieces."

"I've seen his pants," said Todd. "You'd be doing him a favor."

"I meant for Visalia," I said. "You can't avoid mourning, Sparky. It only gets harder if you do."

She stared at me a minute before she spoke. "Why would I mourn Auntie Fizz?" she said. "She's not dead. She's just gone."

I was surprised at the waves that passed over me then. I really had failed completely at that professional distance thing. All the time she'd been talking I'd been telling myself that my client-counsellor agreement with Visalia had ended and her suicide wasn't on me. But still there was a double wash of relief — a hot flood then a cold one, followed by a short bout of vertigo and finally a warm glow.

"Gone to Sicily?" I said. "Are the plane tickets gone?"

"No idea," said Sparky. "I just know she signed over the business to me on condition of my divorce, gave the house to someone called Barbara Truman" — Todd squeaked — "and left. Where were the plane tickets?"

"She gave *Barb* the house?" I said.

"In recognition of all the unpleasant tasks Barb took off her hands over the years," said Sparky. "Whatever that means. I've no idea. Do you?"

"Not a clue," I lied. "But listen, the tickets were in the safe and I know the code."

Inside, Casa Bombaro had changed. I had always thought of Boom as the spark in the marriage and Vi as the rock, but there was no denying it. This house, without the little woman who reigned over it, was a husk. I wondered what Barb would make of it, but not for long. Anyone who wore peach and black hibiscus-print hot pants in her fifties would take to a house full of gold and mirrors like a duck to water. And, a side benefit, Dorabelle would *hate* her.

Of course, I didn't know the code and Todd could hardly start cracking with Sparky right there in Vi and Clovis's bedroom, but it was easy to get rid of her. I looked around at the stripped bed, the empty nightstands and the bare hangers inside the open wardrobe and gulped. I wasn't entirely acting.

"C-c-c-ould I have a glass of water?" I

asked. Sparky headed towards the en suite bathroom. "Oh. Could I have a bottle?" I said.

"Let me get it," Todd said. He was great at this. Serpentina immediately said she would go, but it took away any lingering notion that we were trying to get rid of her.

I sat on the edge of the bed bracing myself against the slide of the mattress cover and watched him go to work. The door was hanging open by the time we heard Sparky coming back up the stairs. When she entered the bedroom, he was sitting beside me pretending to pat my back, but not actually touching my boil scars.

"Sorry," I said. "I opened it before I thought, but I haven't looked."

Todd *had* looked. There were a few compliment slips and covering letters in the back where they'd washed up and one item only under the light in the middle of the shelf.

Sparky drew it out and frowned at it. "Who's Lay Ga S —" she said.

"It's for me?" I said, managing to sound surprised. She handed it over and I undid the flap.

My dear Lexy, the note said. *I know you only intended to counsel me and yet you ended up doing so much more. I could not have got through the last week without your help and support. Please accept a small token of my friendship and gratitude. It will be delivered in a day or two. Always, Visalia.*

"That's nice but it's no help to *you,* is it?" I said. Sparky was reading the little scraps of paper left over in the back of the safe.

"Neither are these," she said.

"Well then," said Todd. "Looks like that's that. Maybe we should make tracks, Lexy. I was thinking of dropping in on my mom. See how she's doing." I nodded with a smile. I wanted to be there to see what Barb made of this too.

As I gathered myself to stand, the phone at the bedside rang. Without thinking I picked it up.

"Mrs. Bombaro?" said a voice. Probably a cold call.

"Um," I said.

"This is Leila from FA Plus Club at Alitalia." A cold call.

"I'm n—" I said, but she rolled on.

"I'm calling to let you know that there's been a delay in your flight this afternoon. The SFO to Roma leg has been put back to five thirty, I'm afraid, which means your Palermo connection is unlikely. As one of our valued Plus Club members we will, of

388

course, provide you with hotel accommodation."

But I was gone.

"She's flying to Rome and the plane leaves in two hours," I said. "Let's go! We can say goodbye! We can say *bon voyage*! We can say thank you!"

"Tell her to call me," Sparky shouted after us.

I stopped dead, making Todd run into my back. "You're not coming?"

"Uh, no," she said. "If I come I'll be arrested for elder abuse. She's left me a factory and no house to live in while I run it."

I spun, resumed my run, and jumped into the passenger seat, then drummed my fingers while Todd walked sedately to the driver's side and climbed in.

"One of my boils burst on your back when you stopped dead," he said. "If I get a scar on my pec, it's your doing."

"Fair enough," I said. "Come on, Todd! San Francisco! Go, go, go!"

"I'm not driving to San Francisco so you can say goodbye to a client," he said. "I've got two of the little suckers on each buttock and if I drive for three hours, I'll have them forever."

"You're kidding!" I said. "I can't drive to the airport on my own. I'll wrap the car round a lamppost or take it off a bridge."

"Better hope Kathi or Nolly's not busy, then," he said. And there was no shifting him.

Noleen's t-shirt told me everything I needed to know. The front said DON'T and the back said EVEN. I ran over to the Skweeky Kleen, wincing with every chafing step, and prepared to beg Kathi.

"I'm in if we take Roger's road rocket," she said. "He had it detailed yesterday. I'd like to meet this woman who stands up to the Poggios and goes back for more."

I marched into Todd's room, ignored him standing naked in front of his mirror inspecting two miniscule pimples on one buttock, grabbed his keys, and marched out again.

"Way-hay!" said Kathi, sliding into the car like Starsky (or was it Hutch?) through the window. It was a Duke of Hazzard. "San Francisco, here we come!"

"Open up your Golden Gate!" I sang.

"Bay Bridge," said Kathi. "We'll pick up 101 South in the city. The causeway over to the Golden Gate's a parking lot. Let's go, go, go!"

We went, went, went about a hundred yards before we heard the chirp of a police car behind us and pulled over. I looked in the side mirror and saw Mills of God, the slow cop, ambling up to us. I didn't think anything of the fact that he came to the right side of the car. I hadn't been here long enough to really accept that everything was back-to-front. Toll booths to drive throughs, it always seemed lucky that they were on the wrong side too as well as the steering wheel of the car I was driving.

"Jesus," said Kathi, watching him, "he's coming for you, Lexy."

He drew up and twirled his hand to tell me to wind down the window. "Ms. Campbell?" he said. "I saw you passing. Just a word, won't take a minute."

"Right," I said. "Got it. Kathi, bring me some clean knickers if I'm still there on Sunday, will you?" I undid my seatbelt.

"No need to get out," said Soft Cop. "I just reckoned Molly wouldn't have told you how it went down. She's got a real hard-on for you and she's as stubborn as hell."

"Who's Molly?" I said.

"Detective Rankinson," he said.

I blinked. "You mean Mike?"

"I don't like that name," said Mills of God. "I mean, yeah. Mike the Dyke. That's her station nickname and she never says a word about it."

"Oh. My. God," I said.

"I don't like it, though. It's not nice to talk to a lady that way, or put all that crap all over her desk every day."

"Kids' toys and kitchen equipment?"

"They're good guys, but they've got a sick sense of humour."

"Oh God," I said. "And . . . when you say she's got a hard-on for me?"

Mills blushed from his over-tight collar to the roots of his pale ginger hair. "I didn't mean anything dirty," he said. "I mean, she won't tell you to stop and won't show she cares, but you are getting to her."

"And that stopped her from telling me something?"

"Oh! Yeah. We found a Marco Poggio, flew in Saturday, hired a car from the Hertz at the airport, stayed at the Great Northern, and tried to leave yesterday. We picked him up. He said it was a free trip from an anonymous benefactor. To Cuento. Not L.A., not even Yosemite. Cuento. So the DA charged him and dropped the case against Mrs. Bombaro. Couldn't have done it without you."

"Thank you," I said. "Officer, do you think you could maybe give me a parking ticket or something so I've got an excuse to come in and say 'Molly' about ten thousand times?"

"Don't worry 'bout that," he said, with a laugh. "You been lying low but now that you're back on the streets you'll get plenty of chances. Now I'm gonna go. It's too damn hot to be out here."

We said our goodbyes and drove away. Kathi said nothing for a while and then: "Molly. I prefer 'Mike.'"

"I am absolutely mortified," I said.

Kathi was looking in her rearview mirror. "There he goes," she said. "Okay, let's see what this baby can do!"

It could do lots. We shot like a rocket through the endless I-80 strip malls, up and over the hills into the Bay, all the way down through the Berkeley bottleneck and the bridge chaos, skirting the skyscrapers and spaghetti flyovers, and arrived at the airport turnoff in just over an hour.

"International," said Kathi, sliding across four lanes while the anxious tourists pottering along in their rental cars braked and swerved to get out of her way. She parked outside the terminal in the no parking zone, slapped a DOCTOR ON EMERGENCY CALL sign on the dashboard, and jumped out. "I looove borrowing the docs' cars," she said. "Come on, Lexy."

We ran into the terminal, dodged the check-in queues, and pelted to the security line that was snaking along so sluggishly, taking Visalia away. I prayed we weren't too late.

But that's prayers for you. After all we had gone through, we didn't make it. We were indeed far too late to say goodbye.

TWENTY-FIVE

But we saw her.

And we saw her travelling companion too.

"Father *Adam*?" I said. And I'm glad they were so far away, because I said it really quite loud.

They were shuffling forward, just at the slipping off their shoes and emptying their pockets stage. At least, Visalia didn't take her shoes off. Little old ladies of eighty-six who're too old to be any danger to anyone don't have to. Father Adam put his flip-flops and all his rubber concern bracelets in a basin and then waited his turn in the scanner with one of his elegant, gentle, priestly hands firmly cupping Visalia's octogenarian butt.

"What?" said Kathi. "That's not Father Adam. Father Adam is seventy. That's Father Adam's gardener."

"But, but, but," I said.

"Need a kick start there, pal?" said Kathi.

"The heart wants what the heart wants, Lexy."

I stood staring at them and then at the place where they'd been and then at Kathi.

"What the . . ."

"No big mystery," Kathi said. "He dropped off some of Father Adam's clothes just the other day and he said the old guy would be picking it up himself because *he* was headed off on a vacation."

"But," I said, "why did he pretend he was a priest?"

"To get in and see his honey without causing a scandal, I guess," Kathi said. "I pretended I was Nolly's sister for ten years when we went on trips."

"But." The tannoy announced that the Alitalia flight was boarding.

Kathi took my arm. "Come and grab a cup of coffee," she said. "And of course when I say coffee, I mean tea. Or have a bite to eat. You look kinda waxy. Come on. All the good joints are at the gates in this place, but there's a Red Raccoon off the next exit."

"Alitalia," I said. "Dead raccoon."

"*Red* Raccoon," Kathi said.

I didn't argue. I let her lead me back to the car, put me in it, drive me to the diner, and order me meatloaf. By the end of all that, I had marshalled my thoughts and I laid it out for her.

"Visalia killed Clovis," I said. "And the gardener took the cable ties off him and removed the switch. I was handpicked, Kathi. But not as a therapist, for my wisdom and training. I was handpicked because I was wet behind the ears and didn't know anything. I was handpicked as a . . ."

"Stooge?" said Kathi. "Are you sure?"

"Yes!" I said. Again, quite loud. A few customers looked round and I stuffed my mouth with a big chunk of meatloaf and chewed until I had calmed down. "She was rattled when Bilbo screwed up and made it sound like two different people were involved. She got right back to him and told him to abandon the handcuff story. And she was *really* rattled when she thought I had started watching crime drama and knew about investigation. And she guessed that the dead raccoon was there as a host for flies. Who would guess that?"

"Uh, no one," said Kathi. "How *did* she guess that?"

"Because she knew it was a Poggio. That must be how they sent messages in the old days when the Bombaros were their neighbours and *ha*!" Another few looks and another mouthful of meatloaf. "She was supposed to believe a Poggio killed Clovis, right? But it was when she heard about the pranks at the Last Ditch that she got really angry. She said they were stupid feelios of putta-something."

"Sons of bitches."

"Exactly! Do you see? *Stupid* sons of bitches. Not evil — stupid. Because she was an anonymous benefactor who sent a mysterious ticket to Marco Poggio. He was supposed to come here, do nothing, and leave. And who would believe him when he said that? Two things went wrong. One: the only reason he came was to mess with *your* head while he was here. And two: I didn't tell the cops about him because I thought it sounded crazy. *She* nearly went crazy waiting for me to say something."

Kathi chuckled. "You messed with her worse than Marco messed with me."

"*And!*" Meatloaf. "Visalia made two mistakes."

"Killing her husband and killing him with a firework?"

"No."

"Let me guess. The raccoon and . . . what else?"

"Okay, three. Guessing about the raccoon, naming an airline she shouldn't have been thinking about. Wait, four! She shouldn't have agreed to go to the morgue. Hang on! It's five. She looked forward, out loud, to living on the same island as the guy who was supposed to have murdered her husband. She shouldn't be going to Sicily at all, should she?"

Kathi let out a massive breath. I had finally convinced her. "Nope," she said. "No indeedy. So what do we do?"

I clapped my hands. "I go and tell *Molly*!" I said.

"And Marco Poggio walks?" said Kathi. "Or he goes down for a newsworthy series of nasty tricks that'll close the Last Ditch down. And Barb doesn't get the house."

"But Visalia can't get away with a murder!" I said. "I saw his face, Kathi. I saw the look on his face and I saw the marks on his wrists and ankles."

Kathi nodded and pushed her plate of fish tacos away. I looked down at the thick gravy congealing on my meatloaf and pushed it away too.

We were quiet on the way back, sitting in silence in the epic San Francisco rush hour, chugging along at twenty, watching the heat shimmer off the roofs of the snake of cars ahead.

It was dusk when we got to the Last Ditch and a groan escaped Kathi's lips when we turned in and saw the cop car parked outside the office.

"Molly!" I said, when we got inside. "Or do you prefer Detective Rankinson?"

"Sticks and stones," Molly said. "I came to talk to Mrs. and Mrs. Muntz, Ms. Campbell. In confidence."

"She's family," said Noleen.

Molly turned to me. "The postmortem came back."

"Postmortem?" I said

"Clovis Bombaro died of a heart attack," Molly said. "He fell on his left side and cracked a rib. The restraints were applied immediately after death and the firework too."

"He was already dead?" I said. "Why the hell did they go through with it then?"

"They?" Molly said. "They who?"

Kathi had gone very still.

"The Poggio guy," I said. "Oh right. You don't say 'they' like that here, do you? Strunk and White, right? Yeah, I feel like a right old Charlie when I make an arse of trying to say something that should be a skoosh." Kathi pressed her hand down, telling me to cool it.

"As to why he went ahead," said Mike. *Molly!* "That's for him to know. He still denies the whole thing. He won't admit to any of it. Not even the plagues of Egypt."

"So . . . you want Kathi and Noleen to testify?" I said. That would sink the Last Ditch.

"No," said Molly. "We've got him on desecration of a corpse, B&E, breaking the terms of his tourist visa, and resisting arrest. I'd love to get him for the ten thousand felonies it took to give you guys those boils, but with such a shortage of credible witnesses . . ."

"What?" I said. "What shortage of credible witnesses?"

"His wife, his wife's wife, two former gangbangers, and you?" said Molly. "No jury in the land . . . as they say."

"What did *I* do?" I said.

"I'm not saying I agree," said Molly.

"You're not exactly breaking the system from the inside either though, are you? *Mike,*" I said.

"That mouth of yours," she said and was gone.

We were standing like three pillars of salt when Todd came in.

"Have you forgiven me?" he said. "Because I want you to come and help me get Diego's fishes."

"I've forgiven you," I told him. "Mostly because I want to tell you something and it'll kill me if I don't."

I regaled him on the way to the pet shop and I discovered that Teodor "Todd" Mendez-Kroger was hands down the most rewarding tellee of juicy scandal I have ever met in my life. He shrieked, he gasped, he gagged, and then he went kind of crazy. I did too.

Long story short, we bought Diego three clownfish, three angelfish, and a seahorse. And a bunny. And two white kittens.

"I'll square it with Noleen," Todd said, on the way back.

"You'll have to," I said. "I'm leaving." My heart sank to my feet, then down through the floor of the Jeep to lie on the road behind us where it got flattened by a Peterbilt.

"You could stay," Todd said.

"I can't afford to stay," I told him. "I know you're coping with life in a motel room, but it's driving me a bit nuts already. And I need an office to see clients in, if I'm going to afford the rent on a flat. Even a tiny one. And I can't afford the rent on the office. I can't even afford the Last Ditch. I'm still using Branston's credit card and he'll cancel it sometime."

"Right," said Todd. "Well, you can visit."

"Yeah," I said. We took a corner and the

kittens woke up and started crying. Making three of us in all.

Even the quality of deliverymen had dropped to match my mood. That pool guy from the other day was going to feature in my quiet moments for some time to come, but the man who was standing in the darkening forecourt with a clipboard and a logo on his cap was your garden variety . . .

"Is *redneck* a rude word?" I asked Todd.

"What do you think?"

"I honestly don't know," I said. "I haven't been here long enough to learn your ways."

"So stay," said Todd, which wasn't helpful.

The man with the named shade of neck pushed his cap back and shouted over. "Are you" — he looked down at his clipboard — "Lee . . . ?"

"Yes," I said.

"Sign," he said. He handed over the slab of board and I caught the pen swinging at the end of a length of grubby string.

"What am I signing for?" I said.

"Present from a Mrs. V. Bombaro," he said. "Either she's a nice lady or you're a good friend."

"What did she give me?" I said.

"Title deeds and keys are in the office there," the guy said. He licked a finger and

403

ripped off a pink copy from under the white top sheet I'd signed. "And I am out. Got a cold beer waiting for me somewhere. There must be a bar in this town."

"Title deeds to what?" I said. Todd was aquiver. He took the pink slip from me and studied it.

"Property, name of Creek House," said the delivery man. "And that information was me being a good guy. My job ended when you took the customer copy of my delivery note."

"A house?" I said. "She's given me a house?"

"Heh heh heh," he said, a little puzzlingly.

"Where is it?" I said. "Are there directions with the title deeds?"

"It's *here*," he said. "It's just out back." Shaking his head and laughing, he waddled off. I looked after him for a while and then I heard the *ding* of the office bell as Noleen and Kathi came out, turning the sign to closed.

"We can't miss this," Noleen said. "Here's the paperwork." She held out a fat envelope, but Todd took it before I had a chance to.

"I'll just crack a window in the Jeep," he said. "Wait up."

"Crack a window?" Noleen said. "For a fish?"

I was already following Kathi as she made her way, her phone turned to flashlight mode, round the side of the motel. There was a narrow access strip of concrete, but the branches of the scrubby bushes plucked at us.

"Careful of those shrubs," Noleen called ahead to Kathi. "Oleander. You thought the boils were bad."

As we turned the back corner, we heard the slough gurgling and chuckling. Kathi held her phone high as we gathered at a gap in the trees.

"Creek House," Noleen said as Kathi played the beam of light around.

I stared. It wasn't a villa, or a flat, or an ex-council semi. Or a cottage or, God knows, a motel room. It wasn't a ranch, or a McMansion, or a condo, or a duplex.

"It's a boat," I said. I took Kathi's phone, picked my way through the undergrowth, and hopped onto the bottom of six shallow steps. They led up to a deep porch, stretching right along the short end that faced the bank of the slough. It rocked. Like a cradle. I peered in at the open door and stepped inside. The living room had a dark wood floor and wood-panel walls. It had two bowed windows facing the porch and a woodstove in one corner. In a daze, I walked on and entered the corridor. On one side was a little bedroom with a built-in cabin bed. And on the other side, another one, for guests. Beyond them was a kitchen, tiny. Just a stove and a fridge and a sink and about a foot square of worktop, as well as a midget table. Behind the kitchen was a bathroom. Kind of. I'd have to dry the toilet after I showered, but I'd never have to dust the cistern. And finally at the back corner there was a . . . . Well, probably a dining room, but I could already see the comfortable chairs and the soft lighting and the troubled souls who would feel better as soon as they stepped aboard. There was even a back door for them to come in and out of. I stepped through it onto the deck.

As I did so, I heard a click and felt something give under my foot. I looked down and saw a pad with a wire leading from it. Before I had time to wonder what it was, the first of the rockets went off.

Seven of them fired high into the air and then fell, fizzing, into the slough. A rig of sparklers spelling L-E-X-Y crackled into life on the back banisters and three silver chrysanthemums burst open just over my head.

I stood with my back pressed against the wall of the boat, breathing high and fast, trying to stop my legs from buckling. When the sparklers were no more than smoking husks and I was sure there was nothing more to come, I peeled myself free and tottered along the side to where my friends were squawking my name.

Roger had arrived and joined the others.

"What the hell was that?" he said.

"There's quite a mysterious note here, Lexy," said Todd. He had opened the envelope. Of course he had. *"Creek House is a thank you for all your help,"* he read. *"My little display is in payment for all your other contributions."*

It wasn't mysterious to me. Those bloody fireworks were payback for failing to tell the cops about the Poggios like I was meant to.

"What's Creek House?" said Roger.

"This is," I said, finding my voice at last.

"It's a boat," he said.

"A houseboat," said Kathi.

"Awaiting permits," said Noleen. "Good luck with that."

"And it's in need of a complete make-over!" said Todd.

"No," I said, as the sound of a siren told me Mike had heard the rockets and was on her way. "Sorry, Todd. I've got this one. It's my boat. Houseboat." I took a breath and tried it out for the first time: "Home."

FACTS AND FICTIONS

I have lived in northern California for eight happy years, and the town I've grown to love is not Cuento. None of the places, businesses, services, or people of Beteo County are based on real locations, institutions, or individuals, except that the wholly imaginary Professor Cindy Slagle is called after the real Cindy Slagle, who won a character name with a generous donation to support the good work of Sacramento Crisis Nurseries. None of the goings-on in *Scot Free* are based on any real event. And I loved *The Goldfinch*.

ABOUT THE AUTHOR

Catriona McPherson was born in Edinburgh, Scotland, and is the author of multi-award-winning standalones for Midnight Ink, including the Edgar-shortlisted, Anthony-winning *The Day She Died* and the Mary Higgins Clark finalist *Quiet Neighbours.* She also writes the Agatha-winning Dandy Gilver historical mystery series (Minotaur/Thomas Dunne Books). McPherson is the past president of Sisters in Crime and a member of Mystery Writers of America. You can visit her online at CatrionaMcPherson.com.